Nobody's Sorry
He Got Killed

Nobody's Sorry
He Got Killed

Arthur D. Goldstein

Random House: New York

Copyright © 1976 by Arthur D. Goldstein

All rights reserved under International and Pan-American Copyright Conventions. Published in the United States by Random House, Inc., New York, and simultaneously in Canada by Random House of Canada Limited, Toronto.

Library of Congress Cataloging in Publication Data

Goldstein, Arthur D.
Nobody's Sorry He Got Killed
I. Title.
PZ4.G64137No [PS3557.0388] 813′.5′4 75-33162
ISBN 0-394-40028-3

Manufactured in the United States of America
9 8 7 6 5 4 3 2

First Edition

To My Friends at the Amex

Nobody's Sorry
He Got Killed

One

Guttman stood near the entrance to the lounge, watching the five of them at the table, and he sighed. They had something else they were worrying about. Mrs. Kaplan had a new mystery. Maybe somebody working at the Center she was sure was on the FBI's most wanted list, he thought. Like the orderly whose picture she said she'd seen in the newspaper. Or somebody cheating the Center, the electric company was charging too much, or even they weren't putting the right drugs in the prescriptions. Guttman chewed his cigar for a moment, hesitated, and then turned to go outside. He didn't really want to know. Besides, he told himself, I'll find out soon enough, anyway. Better to go outside and play some bocce with Mr. Bowsenior. The court had been completed only a week before, and there was much he had to learn about the game, even after watching it played for years in New York, before he came here.

Dora Kaplan cleared her throat and waited for silence. Obediently, Agnes O'Rourke closed her movie magazine. Miss Brady and Mr. Carstairs spoke another few words before turning to look at her, but Jacob Mishkin merely glanced up, and then turned over another card in his game of solitaire.

"Aren't we going to wait for Mr. Guttman?" Miss Brady asked.

"He's probably busy with his bocce," Mishkin said. Since the court had been completed, Mishkin spent less time playing pinochle and gin with Guttman and more time playing solitaire.

"I think it best that we discuss this matter among ourselves," Mrs. Kaplan said formally. "Before we talk to Mr. Guttman."

Margaret Brady exchanged a quick glance with Mr. Carstairs, but said nothing. There was no point, she thought, in arguing with Mrs. Kaplan before she knew what she was arguing about.

"Mr. Guttman's attitude toward our . . . investigations has not been completely benevolent," Mrs. Kaplan went on, pleased that she'd been able to use one of her new words from *Reader's Digest*. "You remember how he didn't want us to become involved in the investigation of the food kickbacks? It wasn't our business, he said."

"And why isn't it our business?" Mrs. O'Rourke asked. "We're the ones what had to eat the food, aren't we?"

"Precisely," Mrs. Kaplan said. "And what happened when we looked into it? How much did we save? Mr. Carstairs?"

Harold Carstairs took a small notebook from his inside jacket pocket, turned several pages, and announced, "An average of four hundred and seventy-two dollars and sixteen cents per month."

"Exactly," Mrs. Kaplan said. "None of our business, according to Mr. Guttman."

"You have to admit he was right, though, when you thought Jimmy was wanted by the FBI," Miss Brady said.

"No one, Miss Brady, is perfect," Dora Kaplan replied, emphasizing the "Miss."

"I think it would be very dull if a body was perfect," Mrs. O'Rourke suggested.

"But if it hadn't been for Mr. Guttman discouraging us, and insisting that we check first, we probably would have called the FBI and had Jimmy arrested. And that would have landed us in a load of trouble," Miss Brady said.

"Miss Brady," Mrs. Kaplan said quietly, "I was not suggesting that Mr. Guttman's views aren't . . . Well, the point is that no matter what we suggest, he acts as though it's none of our business, that we shouldn't get involved."

"You have a point," Miss Brady conceded.

"And there's a matter, a very serious matter, that I think we should look into," Mrs. Kaplan went on. "I'm only suggesting that we talk about it and agree before we talk to Mr. Guttman, that's all."

"How serious a matter?" Miss Brady asked.

"Very." Dora Kaplan clasped her hands on the table and waited until all of them, even Mishkin, were looking at her. "This afternoon," she said, "I would like to bring before the group a most serious case." She paused for effect, then added, "It's a murder case."

"Who got killed?" Mishkin asked.

"In due time, Mr. Mishkin. In due time. First, I think we should all be agreed that it is our duty to investigate."

"We can't very well do that unless we know what it's all about," Miss Brady suggested. She smiled comfortingly at Mr. Carstairs, who had blanched at the word "murder."

"Naturally," Mrs. Kaplan said. "I wasn't asking anybody to vote already, I was just saying that when we do, it should be unanimous."

"So tell us already," Mishkin suggested, folding up his hand of solitaire.

Guttman balanced the metal ball on his fingertips, studying the long dirt path, the other balls lined up protecting the center at the far end. Finally he stepped forward, leaned over, and rolled the ball slowly along the side of the alley. Still too slow. The dirt along the side of the bocce court was banked, but the ball went too slowly to hold, and curved to a stop well in front of the target area. Practice, Guttman thought. For years you watch and it looks so easy. And now . . . Nu, so you learn something you should've known, he told himself. Just because a thing looks easy, that don't mean it is.

"You'll get the hang of it, Mr. Guttman," Mr. Bowsenior said cheerfully as he walked to the far end to begin measuring the position of the balls and count the points. He'd won handily, again.

"You're being hustled," Mrs. Bowsenior said from her lawn chair.

"I'm always being hustled with something," Guttman told her. "With Mishkin it's pinochle, and he always wins. Almost always. And chess . . . even my grandson beats me all the time. With this, at least there's fresh air. And some exercise."

"I make it twenty-five cents," Mr. Bowsenior said.

Guttman handed him a quarter.

"Another game?"

Guttman looked at his watch, then shrugged. "Sure. Why not? I lost two, I could lose a third. What's another quarter?"

"Watch out for him, Mr. Bowsenior," Margaret Brady said, surprising Guttman. He hadn't seen her approach. "He complains about losing, but don't buy that song and dance. Two months ago he was telling me he hadn't played chess in years, hardly knew what he was doing. Now I've got to fight tooth and nail for every game."

"But still you win," Guttman reminded her.

"I think you're just setting me up," she replied.

Guttman had to smile. He was flattered, even though he knew she was the better chess player. But his game was improving.

"Am I interrupting you?" Miss Brady asked.

"We were just going to start another game," Mr. Bowsenior said.

"I wonder if I might talk to you for a moment," she asked Guttman.

He glanced at Mr. Bowsenior and shrugged. "Okay," he said. "So I'll talk now and I'll lose my money later." Guttman didn't really want to talk. He was pretty sure that Miss Brady had come because of whatever the group had been scheming about. But if she's the one coming to ask, he thought, then maybe whatever it is ain't so bad.

"Mrs. Kaplan's been at it again," Miss Brady began as they walked slowly away from the bocce court.

"So what's new?"

"She's lined up another case for you to work on."

"Another case, like the FBI picture in the papers?"

"No, not exactly."

"I'm not so sure I want to hear about it," Guttman said. "I keep telling everybody I'm not a detective, but nobody believes me." Then he added, "So what's it about?"

"Maybe I'd better let Mrs. Kaplan tell you, since she's the one who talked to Mrs. Stone."

"You don't know what it is?"

"All I know is what Mrs. Kaplan told us, which isn't very much," Miss Brady said.

"This Mrs. Stone, she's the one lives in a cabin, like you?"

"Uh-huh. One down from the Ohlbaums'."

"She's a nice lady?"

"She's okay. She moved in while I was still on the staff, but . . . well, she's not exactly the easiest person in the world to get along with," Miss Brady said. "She's kind of demanding, and she doesn't mix too much with the other residents. Some of them think she's a snob, but I figure she's entitled to live the way she likes, you know? And she doesn't get around very well. She's pretty much confined to a wheelchair."

"Is she very rich? I think I heard something like that, once," Guttman said, almost apologizing for having listened to gossip.

"Rich enough."

Guttman stopped in front of the doors to the main lounge. "Mrs. Kaplan wants I should make like a detective. That I could expect. But what do you say?"

Miss Brady hesitated, and Guttman nodded. "So never mind. I already know what you say, otherwise you wouldn't've come to get me. So let's find out what it's about, already."

They waited silently as Guttman settled himself into the chair at the head of the table, after declining Agnes O'Rourke's offer to get him a cup of tea. As he looked at them, they seemed nervous. Guttman didn't feel very comfortable himself.

"Okay, so now there's another big investigation, huh?" he

said. "And Miss Brady says Mrs. Kaplan should tell me about it. So tell," he said to Dora Kaplan.

"It's a terrible thing," she said quickly. "I don't know whether you know Mrs. Stone, but her granddaughter . . ."

"I don't think I ever met the lady," Guttman said.

"She's a lovely person," Mrs. Kaplan assured him. "And her granddaughter, Susan, is in jail for murder. It's tragic, what it's doing to poor Jessica."

"Jessica, that's Mrs. Stone?" Guttman asked. "And this is the thing you want we should get involved in? A real murder?" He looked across at Miss Brady, but she seemed to be looking elsewhere.

"Of course it's a real murder, Mr. Guttman," Mrs. O'Rourke said.

"There's such a thing as an imitation murder?" Mishkin asked.

"I mean, with the police arresting her already," Guttman explained.

"But she didn't do it," Mrs. Kaplan said.

"You know this?"

"Jessica . . . Mrs. Stone knows it. And I believe her."

"So how does she know?" Guttman asked. "The police don't arrest a person just for fun."

"How does she know?" Mrs. Kaplan repeated. "It's her granddaughter, that's how she knows. If it was your grandson, Joseph, wouldn't you know if he was innocent?"

Reluctantly, Guttman admitted that she had a point. "Okay," he said. "So tell me the details."

"The girl is accused of killing her . . . boyfriend. He was shot. But she didn't do it," Mrs. O'Rourke volunteered.

"That's details?" Guttman asked.

"Mrs. Stone said she'd give you all the details," Mrs. Kaplan told him. "She's waiting for us."

"She's waiting? You mean you . . ." Guttman shook his head, then allowed himself to smile. They all seemed relieved. "All right. So we'll talk to her."

"Agnes, would you tell her?" Mrs. Kaplan asked Mrs. O'Rourke, who got up immediately.

"One thing," Guttman said, watching Mrs. O'Rourke's broad back moving away. "If this Mrs. Stone is rich, like I been told, how come she's asking us to help her? How come she don't hire detectives, real ones?"

"Well, she's not exactly asking us," Mrs. Kaplan said. "But she did hire detectives. And they were no help."

"And we're supposed to be?" Guttman asked. He shook his head slowly. "Oy." He looked at them again and wondered what he was doing. I got involved one time, he told himself—no, two times—and now it's a regular thing. Max Guttman, detective. Only how do I say no? How? You open your mouth and talk. So admit it, Guttman, you're curious.

"Before we go," Guttman said, "I want to know. Everybody here thinks we should do this?" No one answered. "Mishkin, you want to start playing detective?"

"Who's playing? Mrs. Kaplan says the woman got a problem, so what harm is there if we go talk to her?" Mishkin asked, avoiding looking directly at Guttman by playing another card in his solitaire game.

"Mr. Carstairs?"

"I . . . I must agree with Mr. Mishkin. After all, we are somewhat like a family here . . ."

Guttman looked at Miss Brady, but didn't ask for her opinion. She had come to get him in the first place. And there was no need to ask Dora Kaplan what she thought, either.

Jessica Stone was waiting for them in her cabin. Dora Kaplan led the way, Mrs. O'Rourke at her heels. Guttman vied with Mishkin and Mr. Carstairs to be the last to enter. Mrs. Stone sat in a wing-back chair, a small woman, her hair completely gray, thin and fragile-looking. They stood awkwardly for Mrs. Kaplan's introductions, which Guttman didn't think were necessary. She probably knew the others, at least by sight. He was the stranger.

When Mrs. Stone, in a surprisingly strong voice, asked them to sit, it was as though the music had stopped in a game of musical chairs. Guttman found himself in front of a chair that, he thought, was probably an antique. He wasn't as tall or as heavy as he had once been, but still he was nervous about putting his full weight on the chair's spidery legs.

"Thank you. All of you," Jessica Stone said. "I assume you are all part of . . . What was it you called yourselves, Dora, the 'Irregulars'?"

"It's a joke," Miss Brady said. "The name, that is."

"Nevertheless, I thank you for your offer of help. I don't know what you expect to accomplish, but anything that will help my granddaughter will be appreciated. Where do you propose to begin?" she asked, looking directly at Guttman.

He looked at Mrs. Kaplan for a moment, then sighed to himself. "Maybe the best thing would be if you told us about it. What happened, I mean."

"Of course." Jessica Stone looked at him for a moment longer, then glanced at the others. "It's a bit, well, personal . . . All of a sudden I feel as though I'm making a speech . . ." She looked again at Guttman.

"Perhaps it would be easier if there weren't so many of us," Margaret Brady suggested.

"I think . . . I think that might help. It's silly, I know, but . . ." Mrs. Stone smiled at them.

Miss Brady got to her feet and started for the door. Reluctantly, the others followed. Dora Kaplan was the last to leave. "We'll see you in the lounge," she told Guttman. He nodded, and thought that he wasn't really happy that they were going. He wasn't comfortable in this room, with its antique furniture, the absence of sunlight, and the old woman in the large chair.

"Dora had the best chair," Mrs. Stone said. "You might as well be comfortable."

"Thank you," Guttman said, moving to the armchair Dora Kaplan had vacated.

"How old are you?" Mrs. Stone asked.

"Seventy-two," he told her, surprised.

"You're young yet. I'm eighty-seven. You don't look much like a detective."

"I don't feel much like one, either. And you don't sound like you'd be embarrassed talking in front of a couple of people," Guttman said.

"No point in it. Obviously you're the leader, although I don't know why. There's no point in having them all here. You're the one who's supposed to perform miracles."

"Miracles? Who told you that?"

"I'm exaggerating a little. Mrs. Kaplan told me about you."

"Mrs. Kaplan exaggerates too. Only not always a little."

"I'm more impressed by Maggie Brady's opinion of you," Mrs. Stone said.

"You talked to her about me?"

"Didn't have to. I could tell. I've seen you two, now and then. Maggie wouldn't waste her time on you if you weren't all right."

"Thank you very much," Guttman said, because he didn't know what else to say.

"Don't thank me. I haven't done anything. Now, what's this about you being a detective. You've solved two murders, I'm told."

"I was lucky," Guttman said.

"That's what I thought when I heard about it. Well, what do you think you're going to be able to do for me?" Mrs. Stone asked.

"I don't know if I could do anything for you," Guttman told her, growing annoyed. "And I'll tell you, you sound like I came here for you to hire me or something, but Mrs. Kaplan told me it was like a big favor." He stopped suddenly, aware that he'd been too brusque. "I'm sorry," he said. "But the thing is, we both know a real detective I'm not. And besides, I don't even know what the problem is all about, except that the police got your granddaughter in jail. So maybe you could tell me about it."

"That's reasonable," Mrs. Stone said. Guttman thought she was smiling, but he couldn't be sure. "And you don't have to apologize for being rude. At my age I can't be bothered with that sort of thing. It's a waste of time, and I don't have any to waste."

Jessica Stone picked up a manila envelope from the table beside her chair, put it in her lap, crossed her hands over it, and studied Guttman for a moment longer. "I may as well tell you, Mr. Guttman, that I suspect this is a waste of time. I've had professionals looking into this matter—"

"Mrs. Kaplan mentioned it."

"And they were unable to come up with anything useful. However, despite what I said about wasting time, I cannot afford to overlook any possibilities." She fiddled with the envelope for a moment, then went on. "If you don't mind, I'd like to tell it all at once. If you have any questions, save them until I'm through."

Guttman nodded and wished that he saw an ashtray nearby so that he could light a cigar.

"My granddaughter, Susan, is all I have left in the world. My only relative. Only close one, anyway. There may be a few stray cousins somewhere. Her parents, my daughter and her husband, are both dead. An automobile accident, eight years ago. Susan was nineteen at the time. Still in college. Her father didn't leave very much. He was a good man . . . I was fond of him . . . and I suppose, a good provider in his way. But they lived on what he earned. He hadn't saved very much. Still, my daughter was happy with him, and that's what really matters. There was some insurance—"

Jessica Stone stopped and leaned forward slightly to hold the envelope out to Guttman. He took it, but before he could open it she was talking again.

"I helped financially, of course. My husband was already gone, then, and I was alone. Money was no problem. And Susan and I grew close. She went to school here, and although she preferred to live on the campus, she spent her vacations with me. After she graduated she continued to live alone, did some traveling, and eventually married."

Mrs. Stone took a glass of water from the small table, sipped at it, put it back on its tray, then closed her eyes. Guttman waited.

"When she and her husband separated, Susan came to me. I was living here, and I wanted her to stay with me. There's a spare bedroom. She did, but only for a little while. She was too young to live with all of us old people. She moved out about a year ago. Wanted to be independent, too. Insisted on getting a job. Like most of her generation, however, she wasn't really qualified for anything. She could have taught, I suppose, but she wasn't interested—"

"Would you mind if I smoked?" Guttman asked suddenly.

"No, go ahead," she told him, looking at his cigar case as he took it from his shirt pocket. "It will remind me of what I don't have to put up with any longer. My husband, Harry, used to smoke cigars."

"Is there an ashtray?"

"Look around. Anything you find that will do, go ahead and use."

Guttman found a small dish on the coffee table and brought it back to the chair with him. Then, while Mrs. Stone watched him, he unwrapped a cigar, bit the end, and lit it, blowing a cloud of smoke between them.

"Harry never smoked anything so vile," Mrs. Stone said. "At least I don't think he did. Do you really enjoy that?"

"If I didn't enjoy it, I wouldn't smoke it," Guttman told her.

"I'm sure. If, by some miracle, you manage to help me, Mr. Guttman, I'll see to it that you get some decent cigars to smoke."

"If it bothers you so much, I wouldn't smoke it," Guttman said.

"No, go ahead. I can have my nurse spray the air later."

"Thank you," Guttman said, trying to sound sarcastic. He didn't think he succeeded.

"As I was saying, Susan wanted to be independent, to work for a living. At the time I thought it was a sign of maturity, actually. But she wasn't qualified for anything, as I said. I arranged for her to work at Armstrong Industries, an executive trainee position. Glorified secretary, actually. Philip Armstrong is an old friend. Harry and I owned a considerable interest in the company. I still do."

"Mrs. Stone, I—"

"I'll tell it my way or not at all," she said. "I don't like having to backtrack. If I leave anything out, you can ask about it later."

Guttman nodded.

"It was at Armstrong Industries that she met Harry Vincent. She knew he was married, of course. But she fell in love with him anyway, to hear her tell it. Love," Mrs. Stone snorted. "I don't think young people nowadays know what it is. They're too busy talking about it to know what it is. Free love," she snorted again. "If there's one thing in this world that isn't free, it's love. Trouble is, damned few of them are willing to pay the price. For anything."

Guttman wasn't entirely sure that he understood her, but he suspected that he agreed.

"Anyway, she and this Vincent had an affair."

Mrs. Stone took another sip of water, and Guttman relit his cigar. She waited until some of the smoke had dissipated before going on.

"According to the police, and what Susan's attorneys have told me, the day before Vincent was murdered . . . They were living together, at least some of the time. Susan had her own place, and Vincent was still living with his wife, but they had an apartment, he did anyway, and that's where she stayed, usually. At any rate, the day before Vincent was murdered, he and Susan had an argument. The police say that Susan wanted him to marry her. She says she was going to leave him. I believe her. She wouldn't have married him. Either way, Vincent hit her. Beat her, actually. Not that she didn't deserve it. But not from him. What she deserved was a spanking, not a beating." Mrs. Stone paused for breath. "That afternoon, the day after he beat her, Susan went to the apartment to get her things. She found Vincent there. Dead. The police claim that she shot him."

Guttman waited for more, but Mrs. Stone seemed to think the story was finished.

"If you don't mind my asking," Guttman said after a moment, "a minute ago, first you said that she was going to leave him, and then you called her a . . . fool."

"So?"

"If she was going to leave him, why was she a fool?"

"She began that affair months ago."

"So?"

"It certainly took her long enough to end it, didn't it?" Mrs. Stone asked.

"I guess," Guttman said. "To be honest, there's so much with the young people now I don't understand."

"It isn't hard to understand. It's what the sociologists and psychologists call instant gratification. They're not willing to work for things, not willing to make sacrifices. 'If it feels good, do it.' Nonsense."

"I suppose . . ." Guttman puffed on his cigar, shifted his position in the chair, and went over her story in his mind.

"That envelope I gave you. It's the report of the private investigators I hired. They found nothing that would help Susan. Bunch of damned idiots."

"I'll read it. Mrs. Stone, say your granddaughter went into the apartment, like you say, and she saw this man, this Vincent, and he was already shot. What happened then? Did she call the police, or what?"

"She called the police, yes."

"And they arrested her? I mean, aside from him beating her up, why did they arrest her?"

"Because the ninny picked up a gun she found on the floor and her fingerprints were all over it."

"But she called the police herself?"

"Yes. I told you that."

"And because she picked up the gun, they figure she killed him?"

"According to her attorneys, Susan had both motive and opportunity. The police claim that after she killed him she called in an effort to make herself look innocent."

"If I was on a jury, I don't think I'd send somebody to jail just for picking up a gun," Guttman said. "Not if that's all they could prove."

"You are not on the jury, Mr. Guttman. But even if she is found innocent, it may be too late."

"Too late for what?"

"For me, dammit. I'm eighty-seven. I don't know how much longer I have to live."

"You look healthy," Guttman said.

"Let's not kid each other, Mr. Guttman. Neither of us is a child." She stared at him until he nodded. "Besides," Mrs. Stone said, "even if she is acquitted, it would be . . . it would make things difficult for her the rest of her life. She'd be hiding; she'd probably have to change her name. These things always come up. Someone remembers . . . And being found innocent doesn't make you innocent in the minds of many people. Most people. It merely means that the police weren't able to prove what you did, or some smart lawyer got you off. I don't want Susan to have to live with that hanging over her the rest of her life."

"But if she's acquitted, the police would go out and find out who really killed this man, no?"

"No. The police are the first to believe that a guilty party got off. It's the mentality, I suppose. But they had to think she was guilty to arrest her, didn't they?"

"I suppose," Guttman agreed. "So what you want is to find out who really killed this Vincent, if your granddaughter didn't."

"She didn't."

Guttman hefted the envelope in his lap. "There's no clues in this—what the private detectives gave you?"

"Nothing substantial."

"What does that mean?"

"It means they did some checking into this Vincent person's life, but there doesn't seem to be anything pointing at anyone else. In fact, they built their strongest case against Susan."

"Well," Guttman sighed, "I guess the first thing is to read this. Only I got to tell you, if private detectives couldn't do nothing, I don't know what I'm supposed to do."

16

"Probably nothing, Mr. Guttman," Jessica Stone said. "I fully expect that the only result of this is that you, and your friends, will have something to occupy you for a few days. And that will be the end of it."

"That could be," Guttman admitted. "But I got the feeling also there's something you ain't saying."

"If there is, then I'm keeping it to myself with reason. I don't want your pity, Mr. Guttman."

"If you don't want it, I wouldn't give it," Guttman said, trying to smile. "But if it's facts, maybe it would help."

"I don't see how, but . . . All right. I know how long I have to live, Mr. Guttman. A few months at most. That's why this is so urgent. The trial . . . Susan wouldn't be free for months, and I don't think I have that long . . ." She turned her head away from him, and Guttman felt acutely embarrassed, sure that she was crying. "I want to live to see her free, and her name cleared," Mrs. Stone said, still not looking at him.

Guttman stood up slowly, the envelope in one hand, his cigar in the other, wondering what to say. It was difficult. "Mrs. Stone, what you said about being occupied by all this . . . Maybe it's true. I don't know. Also, what I told you about not being a real detective and all, that's true. But if I could help, it won't be just for fun. Whatever I could do, I'll do." She didn't answer, but Guttman hadn't expected her to. "It would help, I think, if I could talk to your granddaughter, your Susan. Would it be possible for that?" he asked.

"I . . . I'll call the attorneys," Mrs. Stone said. "I'll tell them. Tomorrow morning you'll see them. If it's convenient, of course."

"It would be fine. But maybe in the afternoon is better," Guttman said. "It would give me more time to read this, and think a little."

"After lunch, then. I'll arrange for a car to drive you."

"It ain't necessary. I could take a bus—"

"This way will be easier. And, Mr. Guttman, I know you're not a detective, as you say. And I don't want you to feel that I'm

. . . depending on you. It's just that . . ." She turned her head again, and Guttman left quietly. He couldn't see her smile as he closed the door behind him.

Two

They were waiting for him, as Guttman knew they would be, the five of them sitting in the shade of the portico, watching as he crossed the lawn from Jessica Stone's cottage. Guttman knew he couldn't avoid them, although he wanted very much just to sit and try to sort things out in his mind. All of a sudden I'm in the middle of something, again, and I'm not even sure how I got here, he thought. At least I could figure out something to do, I could look at the reports she gave me. He sighed inwardly and joined his little band of Irregulars. They'd left a chair for him.

"We're taking the case. I'm sure," Dora Kaplan said immediately.

"Taking the case. I feel like I'm in the middle, only I don't know where I am," Guttman said.

"I could tell because you have that envelope," Mrs. Kaplan went on. "What's the story?"

"The story is we don't know yet," Guttman told her. "It's like you said. Mrs. Stone figures her granddaughter didn't kill this person—his name is Harry Vincent. But what we don't know, not really, is what the police got on her. Mrs. Stone says the girl found this Vincent dead and called the cops, only she touched the gun what killed him first, so there's fingerprints. And he beat her up the day before, so that's a motive."

"How well did they know each other?" Miss Brady asked.

Guttman hesitated before answering. It was silly to feel embarrassed, but he did. "They was living together, sort of," he said.

"Sort of?" Mishkin repeated.

"A love-nest murder," Agnes O'Rourke sighed.

"How could people be living together sort of?" Mishkin asked.

"The way Mrs. Stone says it," Guttman explained, "they had an apartment, that's where this Vincent was killed, but they didn't live there all the time. The girl had her own apartment and Vincent lived with his wife."

"He was married?" Mr. Carstairs asked, shocked.

"Now you know what I know."

"That's all we have to work on?" Mrs. Kaplan asked.

"Except they both worked at the same place."

"That must be where they met," Mrs. O'Rourke noted.

"Well, where do we begin?" Mrs. Kaplan asked after a moment.

"I don't know for sure," Guttman admitted. "Mrs. Stone says these reports from the private detectives don't tell much, but I figure I should read them anyway."

"Naturally," Mrs. Kaplan said.

"And then, tomorrow, she's going to arrange to talk to the lawyers what's representing her granddaughter," Guttman said. "So maybe we could find out something from them. We should also talk to the girl, probably."

They thought about that for a moment, but no one had any more questions for him.

"It's almost time to go home," Guttman said. "So I guess the best thing is for us to just think about what we could do, at least until tomorrow."

"What do you mean, think about what we can do?" Mrs. O'Rourke wanted to know.

"Well, the thing is, how're we supposed to solve a mystery like this? If detectives was working on it, and they couldn't help, then we got to figure a different way maybe," Guttman told her.

"Maybe," Miss Brady said slowly. "Maybe the detectives were only trying to prove that Susan didn't do it."

"Of course they were trying to prove she's innocent. What else could they do?" Mrs. Kaplan demanded.

"They could—and maybe we'll have to—prove that someone else killed him. Maybe that's the only way to clear her."

"Forgive me," Mr. Carstairs said hesitantly. "But all of this is beginning to sound like a television show."

"Art imitates life," Mrs. Kaplan said.

"You sure it ain't the other way around?" Mishkin asked.

"What's your question, Mr. Carstairs?" Guttman asked.

"Well, the point is, I suppose, that in fiction we always assume that the detective's client is innocent."

"I saw a TV show where they was using the detective to try to frame somebody else," Mrs. O'Rourke corrected him.

"Still, we seem to be making the assumption that she's innocent," Mr. Carstairs went on. "And what do we really know about it? We know that the police arrested her, that they think she's guilty. And they don't really make very many mistakes, you know. I mean, well . . ."

"I know what you mean," Miss Brady said. "But I don't quite agree with you. The police do make mistakes, at least if you can believe juries. Lots of people tried for crimes are acquitted. And there are lots of crimes that simply remain unsolved, Harold."

"And we owe it to Mrs. Stone to try," Dora Kaplan said. "Or don't you agree, Mr. Carstairs?"

"Oh, of course I agree," he answered quickly. "I was merely cautioning—"

"It's enough already," Guttman said. "We could talk about it some more tomorrow. And figure something out maybe. Meanwhile, it's time to go home."

"Is Lois coming to pick you up, or do you want a lift with me and my Phyllis?" Mrs. Kaplan asked.

"She's coming," Guttman said, hoping that for a change Lois would be early. Normally he didn't mind waiting a few minutes, but tonight was different. The less time he had to spend standing in front of the Golden Valley Senior Citizens' Center with Dora Kaplan, the better he'd like it.

"I'm sorry I was late, Pop, but I got tied up at the last minute. Somehow the phone always rings just as you're leaving, and it's always someone you've been trying to reach for days, and you can't just hang up on them."

"It's okay," Guttman said, chewing his dead cigar. Lois didn't like cigar smoke in the car, and he couldn't really blame her. Not with the windows closed and the air conditioning on.

"Anyway, I've been trying to reach these people in the Parks Department for days, because if we can't get things straightened out with them before the hearings next week, it'll just be a mess."

Lois and Michael had agreed that until the children were a little older, a full-time job for both of them wouldn't be a good idea. But there were social and community projects that needed good people, and Lois had become what she called a "professional volunteer." For the past three months she had been involved in a program to increase the Parks Department budget. Ordinarily, Guttman listened to his daughter with pride. It would be a shame, he thought, if she went out and took an ordinary job when she was doing so much good this way. But tonight his mind was elsewhere.

After dinner I'll tell her about it, he thought. There's no point in fighting and ruining dinner. There's time enough to fight later. Unless Dora Kaplan tells her Phyllis and she calls up Lois right away and tells her. Then it would be worse. Lois would think I'm trying to keep it a secret. Guttman decided to gamble and wait until after dinner anyway.

Lois carried much of the conversation during dinner, although, as usual, she had to compete with the children. Joseph was entering a chess tournament, and David's science project had received an "A" and he was thinking about entering it in a contest, and little Sara simply wanted attention, as she always did. Guttman approved of Lois' idea to feed the baby with the rest of the family. The child might make a bit of a mess, but it was nice having her there at the table. And it saved Lois from having to clean up twice. After dinner the boys went off to do their homework, and Michael volunteered to give Sara her bath, leaving Guttman alone in the kitchen with his daughter.

He cleared the dishes while she scraped them and rinsed off those that needed it before putting them in the dishwasher. When they were through it was time for their second cup of coffee, which had almost become a ritual.

"So, Pop? You've been very quiet tonight," Lois said.

"I didn't realize I had to make a lot of noise."

"Come on, Pop. You can't fool me. You've got something on your mind." Guttman didn't answer for a moment. "How are you and Mrs. Kaplan getting along?" Lois asked casually.

"What's to get along? She's a nice lady."

"Uh-huh. That doesn't tell me very much."

"There's nothing to tell," Guttman said. "But you're right, there is something I wanted to talk with you about."

"I knew it," Lois said, satisfied. "What's up?"

"The way you're looking at me, Lois, I don't think what's up is what you're thinking about," Guttman said.

"I don't know what you mean."

"Dolling, I ain't gonna fight with you about this, but you might as well decide, between me and Mrs. Kaplan, there's nothing. And there ain't gonna be, either."

"Now, Pop. Dora Kaplan is a lovely lady, and—"

"I didn't say she wasn't nice. I said there was nothing between. But that's not what I was going to talk to you about anyway," he went on quickly.

"Okay. So tell me," Lois said, clearly a little disappointed.

Well, Guttman thought, the boys are still too young for her to make matches, so she practices on me. Like I need it. Still, he smiled. "I was going to tell you . . . at the Center today, something . . . funny happened."

"Trouble?"

"Not exactly. But your 'lovely lady' Mrs. Kaplan, she's the one what started it."

"Did you two have a fight?"

"What's to fight about? No. Listen, sweetheart, it's easier if you just let me talk, okay?"

"Okay, Pop."

"Now, the thing is, you know how Mrs. Kaplan likes to . . . find out about things? You know, like everybody else's business?"

"You mean she's a little bit of a yenta, huh?" Lois smiled.

"A little bit? Okay, a little bit."

"I still like her," Lois said.

"I didn't say no. She's a nice lady, like you said. Only she's got this idea that, well, that I'm a detective."

"Oh, no, Pop. Not again. What is it this time? Did she see someone else's picture in the newspaper?"

"Worse," Guttman said. "Now I want you should just listen to me. I don't want you should interrupt."

"Go ahead."

"Well, there's this lady at the Center. Mrs. Stone. And her granddaughter is in trouble, so naturally, Mrs. Kaplan finds out, and right away she decides we got to do something—"

"Who's 'we'?" Lois said warily.

"You said you wouldn't interrupt. We is some people there. But the thing is, I couldn't convince Mrs. Kaplan that it was none of my business," Guttman went on, forgetting that he hadn't tried very hard. "So now we're involved in this thing."

"What kind of trouble is this woman's granddaughter involved in?" Lois asked cautiously.

"The police arrested her."

"For what?"

"Well, there was this person what died, and—"

"This person . . . you mean murder?"

"Well—"

"No," Lois said.

"No what?"

"No, I don't believe it. No, I don't believe my father is really crazy. No, you can't get involved in it. That's final. No arguments, no more talk. That's it!" Lois said, her voice rising.

"That's what?" Guttman demanded.

"That's it! I won't allow it. And wait until I get Phyllis Sobel on the phone. I won't have her mother trying to . . . Pop, don't look at me like that."

"Look at you how?" Guttman asked.

"Oh . . . never mind. But . . . Oh, Pop, don't you remember what happened to you last time? You were almost killed. That crazy doctor . . ."

"He wasn't crazy. He just wasn't such a nice person," Guttman said lamely.

"Oh, my God. I don't believe you, Pop. I really don't. That man killed an old woman and was trying to kill you, and all you can say is he wasn't such a nice man." She shook her head, exasperated.

"Lois, Lois dolling. You're getting all upset."

"You're damned right I'm getting upset. What do you expect me to do?"

"I don't expect you should raise your voice to your father!" Guttman said sharply. "I don't expect you should treat me like a child."

There was silence for a moment, and then Lois spoke, her tone more reasonable. "I'm sorry, Pop, but you have to understand. I worry about you. You don't know what you're getting yourself into. You're not a detective, Pop."

"I figured out about how that Dr. Morton killed poor Miss Walters over the phony insurance, didn't I? And back in New York, I figured out how the police had the wrong person in jail, that time—"

"Look, Pop. I don't want to argue with you about this, but—"

"Okay, so look. Let me finish explaining, and then see if there's still something to argue, okay?" Guttman asked reasonably.

"Okay," Lois said reluctantly. "Explain."

"This Mrs. Stone, she's a rich lady. And her granddaughter is in jail, only Mrs. Stone says her granddaughter didn't kill this person."

"Naturally."

"That's what I said. And Mrs. Kaplan told me if it was

Joseph, I'd know whether he did or didn't, so how could I argue?" Guttman asked, and was relieved when Lois suddenly smiled.

"You're impossible, Pop."

"Nu, so nobody's perfect," he agreed. "But all I'm gonna do is, I'm gonna read this stuff she gave me, and maybe, if I could think of something, we'll see."

"Okay, Pop. No more fooling around. Let's get serious about this." Lois leaned her forearms on the table and looked straight at him. "You are not a detective. You are simply not qualified to investigate a murder. That's the first thing. Now, the second thing. It's dangerous, Pop. I mean, you're talking about killing. It's not like that business where Mrs. Kaplan found out about the overcharging on the food. That was bad enough, but this . . ."

"You know, Lois, I don't know how come you're always yelling on me with these things, when it's Mrs. Kaplan what gets me into it in the first place."

"I'm not yelling on you. Or at you," Lois added, smiling. "But I expect you to have more sense. Besides, Dora Kaplan is Phyllis' problem."

"And I'm your problem?"

"Oh, Pop . . ." Lois shook her head slowly.

"Do you need a referee, or am I free to take sides?" Michael asked from the doorway. "I don't know what it's all about, but I'd love to. So would Joseph and David. And Sara's waiting for her mother to kiss her goodnight, if she isn't asleep already."

"Michael, maybe you can talk some sense into Pop," Lois said.

"Referee," Michael said quickly. "It sounds like I'm going to referee, and not take sides. I think that will be safest."

"It don't need a referee," Guttman said.

"Why don't you go tuck Sara in, and I'll talk to Pop," Michael suggested. Lois hesitated, but he nodded at her and she finally left.

"I could never understand how you do that," Guttman told his son-in-law.

"What?"

"Just say something to her and she does it."

"It doesn't work often," Michael said. He poured himself a cup of coffee, then stood by the sink and lit his pipe. "Okay, so tell me about it before she gets back."

Guttman explained the situation as quickly as he could, wanting Michael to understand as much as possible before Lois returned. Although he'd said he was going to referee, Guttman knew that Michael was more likely to understand. He'd always liked Michael, but since coming to California to live with them, Guttman had learned just how well his daughter had chosen her husband. Of course, he'd known all along how lucky his son-in-law was. When he was through with his story, he waited while Michael fiddled with his pipe.

"It's a tough one, Pop," he said finally. "I don't know what to tell you."

"Tell me about what?"

"About how to handle Lois, naturally."

"You mean you think it's okay if I do this?"

"I didn't say that. As a matter of fact, I have a lot of reservations. But I'm not going to tell you what to do. If you want to get involved in something like this, well, you're old enough to know what you're doing. But let's face it, Lois is right when she worries that it could be dangerous."

"That doesn't worry me," Guttman said.

"That's what makes it dangerous," Michael said. "But okay, suppose you don't get yourself into a position where you're in any real danger. It's still kind of a tricky business."

"Look, Michael, the worst that could happen is it turns out a bunch of old people is sticking their noses in where they don't belong. Except Mrs. Stone asked us, and it's her granddaughter, so who could say we don't belong?"

"What are you going to do, Pop? I mean, specifically."

"Specifically, I'm gonna start by reading the stuff Mrs. Stone gave to me to find out what's going on. And after that, I'll see."

"In other words, you don't know," Michael said.

"You could say that," Guttman admitted.

"Well, what did you two decide?" Lois asked, coming back into the kitchen. "Do we have our own Sherlock Holmes living here, or are we going to be sensible?"

"I don't know what Michael decided," Guttman said, "but I decided that I'm gonna do what I promised Mrs. Stone I'd do. I'm gonna look at what she gave me, and I'm gonna see if there's something I could do to help." Even as he said it, Guttman wondered why he was being so stubborn. Mrs. Stone didn't expect him to solve the problem. Was it because of what she said about having only a few months longer to live?

"I see," Lois said. "Well, I guess that's that." And she turned and left the kitchen.

Guttman looked at his son-in-law for a moment, and then shrugged. Whatever Lois was thinking, she wasn't forgetting it just like that. So he'd have to wait and see. Meanwhile, he'd go to his room and read the reports.

Three

Lois was still cool in the morning. She entered the kitchen after Guttman had finished his cereal, poured a cup of the coffee he'd made, and began getting breakfast ready for the rest of the family. Guttman sipped his coffee and waited.

"I won't be able to drive you in today," Lois said. "Do you want me to call Phyllis and see if she'll take you with her mother?"

"It isn't necessary," Guttman said. "I could take the bus. It's a nice day, and a couple of blocks' walk to the station would be nice."

"Whatever you say," Lois replied, busying herself at the stove.

Guttman finished his coffee quickly, then went to his room, where he collected Mrs. Stone's reports, put several cigars in the leather case Joseph, David and Sara had given him at Chanukah, with, he was sure, some assistance from Lois, and made sure he had enough money in his pocket to cover his expenses. The bus fare was no problem, but he didn't know what he'd run into when he went to see Jessica Stone's granddaughter, and the lawyers. Rather than put a tie on and risk getting Lois started again, he folded it carefully and put it in his pocket. After saying goodbye to the family, now sitting around the breakfast table, he walked the two blocks to the bus stop. Guttman remembered the route from his last trip, several months ago, but still he watched the street signs carefully.

The San Martin police station still didn't look like a police station to him. The two-story building, with its green lawn, wide steps and big double doors, might have been a library, or some kind of office, but the weathered brick front just didn't look severe enough for a police station. Inside, he went to the raised desk and waited until the uniformed officer noticed him.

"Can I help you?"

"I wonder, could I talk to Lieutenant Weiss?"

"I'll see if he's in. Your name?"

"You could tell him it's Max Guttman."

The officer dialed, asked for Lieutenant Weiss, listened for a moment, then hung up. "He's not here right now. Can somebody else help you? Maybe if you tell me what it's about . . ."

"It's okay," Guttman said. "Lieutenant Weiss knows me," he added, wondering if the detective would really remember him. "Do you know maybe when he'll be here?"

"He's on a call now, but I'd guess within half an hour," the officer said.

"Would it be all right if I wait?" Guttman asked, indicating the bench opposite the desk.

"Sure. Help yourself."

"Thank you." Guttman went to the bench, sat down, and after a moment opened the envelope of reports. He didn't expect to get anything new by reading them again, but he had nothing else to do. It was forty-five minutes before Lieutenant Weiss arrived. He looked a little more tired than Guttman remembered him. And, Guttman thought, his hair was even thinner than before, unless he was combing it different. One thing, he didn't gain no weight. He still looks skinny, Guttman decided. He came in the front door quickly, and was almost past the old man before he stopped.

"Mr. . . . Guttman?" he asked.

"How do you do, Lieutenant Weiss. I wasn't sure you'd remember."

30

"Oh, I remember, all right. Uh . . . Are you here for some
. . . reason?"

"I came to talk to you," Guttman said.

"Uh-huh. Okay, uh . . ." Weiss stared at Guttman for a
moment. "The girl," he said, "her grandmother lives out there,
doesn't she?"

"I beg your pardon?"

"Susan Eliot."

"That's the one," Guttman admitted.

"I should have known," Weiss said, and then he smiled.
"Okay, Mr. Guttman. How about a cup of coffee?"

"Thank you very much, I already had. But you go ahead if
you want. I could wait."

"No, I meant can I offer you a cup of coffee. Anyway, why
don't we go into my office, okay?"

"Fine," Guttman said, and then he followed the detective up a
flight of stairs and into a large room with a railing dividing it
almost in half. There were a number of desks, mostly empty, and
in the corner, opposite a row of file cabinets, a wire cage. That,
too, was unoccupied. Weiss held open the door, half wood, half
frosted glass, with the lettering LIEUTENANT, and Guttman went
in.

The furniture—desk, chairs, couch, file cabinets—was old,
and there was a slightly musty smell to the room. Probably,
Guttman thought, because it's hard to open the windows with
the wire in front of it. Weiss motioned Guttman to a chair, then
took off his sport jacket and hung it on a rack, removed his
revolver and holster from his belt and put them in the desk, and
finally sat down behind the desk.

"Okay," he said. "Let's have it."

"Have what?"

"Mr. Guttman, the last time you came here to talk to me I
didn't pay much attention to what you said."

"You were very polite. I didn't think you wasn't nice."

"Thank you, but I didn't listen just the same. And I got my
ass chewed out, but good, for that. So this time I'll listen."

"I'm sorry you got your . . . you got chewed out because of me."

"Forget it. What is it this time?"

"Well . . . Would you mind if I smoked?" Guttman asked. Weiss shook his head and waited while Guttman took a cigar from his case, unwrapped it, and lit it carefully.

"Okay?" the lieutenant asked finally.

"Thank you."

"Then what can I do for you, Mr. Guttman?"

"Well, it's like you said downstairs. It's about Susan Eliot. I didn't know, actually, if it was something you was involved with, but I figured I'd ask for you because I know you."

"I'm involved," Weiss said.

"Okay, that's good. But like you also said, her grandmother lives at the Golden Valley, and yesterday she was asking if I could maybe help her."

"And here you are, right?"

"I guess so," Guttman said. "Right."

"And what do you want to know?"

"Well, to be perfectly honest, what I want to know is what the story is," Guttman said. "I mean, I could understand Mrs. Stone being upset and all, it's her granddaughter, but like I told the others, the police don't just arrest people. They got to have a reason. It's natural Mrs. Stone would figure there's a mistake, but that don't mean she's right."

Lieutenant Weiss studied a letter opener on his desk for a moment, then looked up at Guttman. "The last time you came to see me, Mr. Guttman, about your Mr. Cohen and that Miss Walters, I told you there was nothing to get involved in, nothing to worry about. As it turned out, I was wrong. But the point is, last time, after I told you to forget it, you went right ahead and got yourself involved. You didn't listen to me."

Uncomfortable, Guttman puffed at his cigar, letting the smoke protect him a bit.

"I realize that you turned out to be right the last time," Lieutenant Weiss went on. "But what I'm trying to say is that this time, if I tell you there's nothing you can do, will you believe me?"

Weiss sat back and waited, and Guttman knew he had to answer. But he didn't want to lie. "Lieutenant, it's like this. You're a policeman. All you got to do is arrest people what do wrong, and then they go to court and they get convicted if they're guilty, right?"

"I only wish it was that simple."

"You know what I mean," Guttman said. "But the thing is, here you got an old lady what got a grandchild in jail, and maybe all I could do is . . . What I'm trying to say is if the girl did what you say, maybe all I could do is convince the grandmother. And that's harder than to convince a jury what ain't related to her."

"Uh-huh . . ." Weiss looked at him and shook his head, smiling. "If I understand you, you're saying that you won't take my advice and stay out of it, right?"

"Do I have to answer that?" Guttman asked.

"You just did." Lieutenant Weiss sighed deeply. "I think I need that cup of coffee. Sure you don't want some?"

"Thank you, I'm sure."

Weiss crossed the room and went out of the office, leaving the door open behind him. He returned quickly, a mug of coffee in his hand, and sat on the edge of the desk. "This Mrs. Stone obviously has some pull. Since this thing broke, I've heard from the mayor, the commissioner and the captain," he said.

"They tried to get you to stop?" Guttman asked, surprised.

"No, but they told me to be damned sure I was right."

"And you're sure?"

"We've got a good case against her, Mr. Guttman. I don't know why I'm doing it, but let me explain it to you. The girl was living with this Vincent character. They had a fight, broke up, from what we can gather, because she wanted Vincent to divorce his wife and marry her, and he wasn't about to do that. The girl isn't talking about it now."

"Did this Vincent love his wife?" Guttman asked.

"I wouldn't know. But whatever his reasons, he wasn't going to marry the Eliot girl. Anyway, they fought, and Vincent worked her over pretty good. The girl herself says he's the one who did it, and we have no reason to doubt her. Okay. Now, the day Vincent died, the morning after the beating, the girl called her office and said she wouldn't be in. The switchboard operator who took the message said the Eliot girl sounded funny, whatever that means.

"Okay," Weiss went on. "Now we get to the nitty-gritty. The girl says she went to the apartment to get her things. She had a suitcase with her, so that part holds up, except that the case could have been in the apartment all the time. Still, that's not important. But she says she used the stairs, walked up the one flight, unlocked the door, and went in and just found Vincent. Then she picked up the gun, she saw that he was dead, and she called the police."

"It could've been that way," Guttman suggested.

"There's more. There was a neighbor, next-door neighbor, who was home at the time. She heard the shot, Mr. Guttman, and she called it in. She was sure it was a gunshot, her husband was in the army and she said she knew what gunshots sounded like. We've got a record of when that call came in. We have a record, also, of when Susan Eliot called in. The two calls arrived sixty seconds apart." Lieutenant Weiss stopped to drink some of his coffee.

"Now, just think about that for a moment. Think about the timing. There's no way Susan Eliot could have walked up the stairs, unlocked the door, found Vincent, seen that he was dead, picked up the gun, and then dialed the police in just sixty seconds. Not without hearing something or seeing something. No, she's lying about something, Mr. Guttman. And I make it that she killed him, herself. And there were no signs of a struggle."

"What does that mean, no struggle?"

"It means she probably was waiting for him, or else had the gun with her, found him there when she arrived, and shot him."

"That's probably," Guttman said. "It ain't proof definitely."

"There's the gun, though," Weiss said. "It was Vincent's gun, but the girl herself told us that he kept it hidden in the apartment. It was legal, registered to him, but the point is that she'd have known where it was, since she was living there with him. And nobody else would have." Weiss took another swallow of his coffee.

"I guess," Guttman said after a moment, "it don't look too good for her."

"Not good at all. I'm sorry, Mr. Guttman. Really. I'm sorry you got dragged into this. I'm sorry for your Mrs. Stone. Hell, I'm even sorry for the girl. I kind of hope she makes a deal with the D.A.—he'd probably offer a second degree, or maybe even manslaughter, rather than murder one, but that's not my department."

"What does that mean?" Guttman asked.

"The question of whether it was premeditated or not. You know, she could have gone there, maybe Vincent walked in, threatened her, she picked up the gun and shot. It's a lesser sentence, that's basically what it means. If she agrees to plead guilty, the D.A. may go for the lesser charge."

"I see." Guttman thought for a moment. "Well, I appreciate you talking to me about it."

"Well, you're Mrs. Stone's emissary, in a way, and she seems to swing a lot of weight around here."

"Lieutenant, was there anybody else what would've wanted to kill this Vincent?"

"Mr. Guttman, I told you—" Weiss broke off and smiled ruefully. "You're going to do it, aren't you?"

"Do what?"

"Get involved."

"Well, it was just a question . . ."

"Okay. No, there was nothing in the way of a lead elsewhere. Everything points to the girl. Oh, there were a couple of possibilities we took a look at, but nothing that amounted to anything."

"Like what?" Guttman asked.

"Well, the wife. You know, with Vincent shacking up with this girl, she might have had a motive, except it turns out she wasn't worried about what he was doing because she was too busy with her own social life, if you know what I mean. And then there was some guy in the office who was supposedly mad because Vincent got the job he wanted, but that stuff was just smoke her lawyers were blowing around. There was nothing we could find that could be considered a motive for murder."

"I see," Guttman said, thinking that it sounded as if the lieutenant hadn't tried very hard to find any other suspects, besides Susan. "Well, I want to thank you again, Lieutenant, for spending the time."

"Not at all. Uh . . . Look, Mr. Guttman, I really hope you just forget about this, that you don't start getting involved . . ."

"I understand that, Lieutenant. You don't have to apologize."

"I wasn't going to. What I was going to say is, if I can't keep you out of it, well . . ."

"Yes?"

"Well, considering the people who've been calling me, and all, if you come across anything, would you let me know? I don't know what it would be, but . . . just in case . . ."

"Lieutenant Weiss, if I find out something, I probably wouldn't even know it. But naturally, if it's something to do with this, I'll tell you."

"Thanks. You know, sometime you'll have to tell me how you got involved in this. Playing detective, I mean."

"I'll do better," Guttman said. "I'll introduce you to Mrs. Kaplan personally."

Weiss looked at Guttman strangely, then shrugged. "Would you like a lift? One of our cars will probably be going that way . . ."

"I wouldn't want to put you to any trouble," Guttman said. For a moment he thought it would be best not to accept the offer, but then he remembered that he wasn't keeping secrets from anyone now. And the bus ran only every half-hour, sometimes.

"It's no trouble," Weiss assured him.

"In that case, thank you very much. A ride would be nice. So long as it isn't no trouble."

Guttman found Mrs. Kaplan and Mrs. O'Rourke sitting at their usual table in the snack bar with Mishkin, his worn deck of cards put aside for the moment. Without asking, Guttman knew that Mishkin had just won a game of solitaire. Whenever that happened, he put the cards away for a while before he started a new game. Guttman stopped to get a cup of coffee before joining them.

"Well, look who's here, finally," Mrs. Kaplan said. "We were afraid you decided not to come today."

"Why wouldn't I come?"

"We were thinking it might be you decided not to go ahead with the case," Mrs. O'Rourke explained.

"As a matter of fact," Guttman said, "I been working already this morning, thank you very much."

"Working?" Mrs. Kaplan asked. "On the case?"

"Why not? I guess we should all talk now," Guttman said quickly. "Is Miss Brady and Mr. Carstairs around?"

"They're probably playing chess in the library," Mrs. O'Rourke said. "I'll get them."

"You want to play a little pinochle while we wait?" Mishkin asked. "If they decide to finish the chess game, it could take a while."

Guttman glanced at Mrs. Kaplan and decided that playing pinochle was a good idea. It might keep her from asking too many questions before the others arrived. Mishkin pushed his solitaire deck further away and began shuffling the deck of pinochle cards.

"Would you at least care to tell us where you were when you were working this morning?" Mrs. Kaplan asked.

"I went to the police," Guttman said.

"What for?"

"What for? To find out what they got on Mrs. Stone's granddaughter, that's what for."

"What did they say?" Mrs. Kaplan asked.

"It ain't good," Guttman told her. "But it would be better if we wait until everybody's here, so if somebody's got a question, we'll all hear it. Also, I read the reports last night," he added.

"And?"

"And nothing," Guttman told her. "You could look while we're waiting," he suggested.

Mrs. Kaplan slid the envelope in front of her and opened it. Guttman had time to lose fifteen cents to Mishkin before the group was assembled.

"Okay," Guttman said when they were all settled. "I guess we could get started now." He told them most of what Lieutenant Weiss had told him, omitting only the request that he keep in touch and the references to the last case the Golden Valley Irregulars had been involved in. They didn't really know Lieutenant Weiss, and Guttman didn't want them to think he'd make trouble.

"How about the reports from the private detectives?" Mr. Carstairs asked when Guttman paused in his narrative.

"I was just looking them over," Mrs. Kaplan said quickly. "And I don't think they're going to be of much help."

Guttman knew that it pleased her to know something the others didn't. After all, he thought, she was the one who had started the whole thing. "What Mrs. Kaplan says is so," he told them. "What we got is nothing to point to somebody else what would've wanted to kill this Vincent character. And what makes it even less good is the business with the gun, which Lieutenant Weiss tells me the girl said was always hidden away. That makes it like only somebody who knew where it was could've used it."

"What if this Vincent had the gun, you know, maybe was protecting himself with it, and the killer took it away from him?" Miss Brady suggested.

"That's a good question," Guttman told her. "But the police say there wasn't a fight or anything like that."

"It's still a possibility," Miss Brady said.

"Maybe I could ask the lawyers when I talk with them," Guttman said.

"That reminds me. What time are we supposed to go?" Mrs. Kaplan asked.

"Mrs. Stone just said this afternoon. I guess I better talk to her and get the details. I wonder if she's in her cottage?"

"She isn't likely to be anywhere else," Margaret Brady said. "She can't get around very well."

"So maybe I should go say hello," Guttman said. He took another swallow of his coffee. "But first, maybe somebody's got an idea they want to mention?" He looked at them hopefully, but no one responded.

"Okay. I was thinking about it a little, myself," he told them. "And I think the best thing is to find out as much as we could about this Vincent. We ain't gonna find clues at the apartment, or anything like that, since it's a couple of weeks already, and the police done that anyway. And I wouldn't know what we should look for anyhow."

"I'm curious about something," Mr. Carstairs said. "I wonder whether it wouldn't be a good idea for us to check, ourselves, the matter of the time element you referred to."

"The time element?"

"Yes. Your Lieutenant Weiss indicated that it was impossible for Mrs. Stone's granddaughter to have done what she said she did within the space of one minute. But sixty seconds is really quite a long time. I think it would be worth investigating. The lieutenant may have been exaggerating."

"That sounds like a very good idea, Mr. Carstairs," Guttman said. "Maybe somebody should do that and find out."

"I'd be happy to volunteer," Carstairs replied, then started to add something but changed his mind. Guttman noticed him looking past his shoulder, and he turned. Mrs. Johnson, the Center's secretary, was only a few feet behind him.

"Mr. Guttman? I wonder whether you could stop in and see Dr. Aiken for a moment. He asked if you would."

"Now?"

"Well, I know he's free now."

"Okay," Guttman said, puzzled. He'd met Dr. Aiken, of course, when he had returned to take over the administration of the Center again. But he didn't know what Dr. Aiken wanted him for now. Guttman knew that he felt all right, and he hadn't taken any tests or anything. Maybe that was it, he thought. Maybe I'm supposed to get a checkup.

Mrs. Johnson escorted him to the doctor's office, knocked, announced him, and then closed the door behind Guttman. Dr. Aiken got up from the desk and motioned him to a chair. Again Guttman found it hard to reconcile this man with some of the stories he'd heard from Miss Brady, who had been with the doctor through most of World War II. According to her, Dr. Aiken was "quite a man," and had risked his life to help wounded soldiers, had operated on them in terrible conditions, and had shown very little regard for any kind of regulations. What Guttman saw was a very small man, perhaps only two inches over five feet, with a fringe of white hair around his pink scalp, heavy glasses, and a pipe always drooping out of his mouth. The pipe, Guttman thought, was the only thing Dr. Aiken had in common with his predecessor. Fortunately.

"Sit down, Max. Relax." Dr. Aiken had insisted on calling him by his first name—and asked to be called Frank—from the beginning.

"Thank you," Guttman said.

"And you can light up one of your stinking cigars, if you like. My pipe should be more than a match for it. If not, I'll open the window."

Guttman knew he was being teased, but still he shook his head. "Is something wrong?" he asked.

"That's what I was going to ask you. And the answer is, sort of," Dr. Aiken said, sitting down in his large swivel chair. It made him look even smaller. "I had a call from your daughter this morning. She was kind of upset."

"Oy. I should've known," Guttman said.

"What's it all about?" Dr. Aiken asked. "I mean, she was suggesting that you'd lost your marbles, and that this business with Mrs. Stone is my fault. I figured I'd better ask you about it."

"I'm sorry she called and upset you," Guttman said.

"Don't worry about it. Keeps me on my toes. God, I retired for six months and I must have aged six years. The more problems I have, the more I seem to thrive. I just wish Marsha felt that way. You've met Mrs. Aiken, haven't you?"

"One time, yes. When we had the party after you first came back."

"Yeah. Well, she's always saying I work too hard, but I tell her if I didn't, she wouldn't have anything to worry about, and she'd be bored stiff."

Guttman nodded his head as if he understood. "What did Lois tell you?" he asked.

"You want her exact words?"

"It isn't necessary."

"I didn't think so. Well," the doctor said, striking a wooden match to light his pipe, "she tells me you're back in the detective business, that you have no business being involved with it, and it's my responsibility, so if I don't get you to stop, she'll have the whole place closed down."

"My Lois . . . she said all that?"

"And she mentioned some of the people she knows at City Hall who'd pull the strings to make things difficult for us."

"She can do that?" Guttman asked. "I didn't know . . . I mean, I know she's doing a lot of things, like with getting new parks, but I didn't know she had so much . . . pull."

"She seems to think she does," Dr. Aiken said. "Or she wants me to think she does. That's probably more like it."

"Well, it don't matter, I guess," Guttman said. "I mean, I don't want you to have no trouble . . ."

"But," the doctor went on, "I'm sure of one thing. I'm sure your daughter, who I'm also sure is a lovely person and has your best interests at heart, doesn't have nearly as much influence as Jessica Stone."

"I see," Guttman said after a moment.

"So the threats don't worry me. I spoke to Jessica after your daughter called, and got the story. I hope you don't mind."

"Why should I mind?"

"Anyway, so far as I'm concerned, you're free to do as you

like. But I am a little concerned about things between you and your daughter."

"To tell the truth, I'm a little concerned now, too."

"What's the story?"

"The story," Guttman said, "is that she figures because I'm old, she has to take care of me all the time."

"Uh-huh. Typical. Tell me, how are you going to handle it?"

"Well, I guess I'll have to talk to her. Have another fight, probably, except sooner or later she's got to know that I could take care of myself. While I could still do it," Guttman added. "This is the thing I was worrying about when I said I'd move here and live with her."

"That's not quite what I meant," Dr. Aiken said. "I was asking how you're going to handle this business with Mrs. Stone's granddaughter."

"I'm not so sure about that, either," Guttman admitted.

"For the record, but mostly for my own curiosity, Max, let me ask you something. Do you really think of yourself as a detective?"

"No," Guttman answered quickly. "No, and maybe yes."

"That's a nice, straight answer," the doctor said, smiling.

"Well, the thing is, if you just ask me am I a detective, I got to say no. I'm a retired cutter, that's what I am. Only two times already I got involved in detecting. Now it's three. And . . ." Guttman hesitated, then decided to go ahead. "I don't know if you're gonna laugh, but I'll tell you the truth. I like doing it. It gives me something to do, something to think about."

"You'll notice that I am not laughing," Dr. Aiken said. "Well, if there's anything I can do, let me know. I don't know whether you're really good at detective work, although you did manage to get me out of my retirement, for which I'll always be grateful, incidentally, but I do know that doing something, anything that you can get interested in, is good for you. For you and the people working with you. Hell, I think everybody at the Center knew about this thing as soon as it happened. They were all talking about it last night. It gives them a lift, lets them feel like they're part of something."

"I'm glad it helps," Guttman said. "Doctor, there's a personal thing I want to ask, if you don't mind. I don't know if you could tell me, but when I talked to Mrs. Stone yesterday she was upset, and the thing is . . . How is she? I mean her condition."

"Her condition? I'm happy to say that Jessica Stone is as healthy as a horse. I'd like to be in that kind of shape when I'm eighty-seven. I've got another twenty years before I reach that point, if I do, but I wouldn't be disappointed if I was as well as she is. Granted, she's not mobile, but her mind's sharp, and generally speaking, she's healthy."

"For me it's only fifteen more years," Guttman said. "Well, I'm glad she's okay," he added, wondering why it didn't bother him more that Jessica Stone had lied to him. He could understand why she had—she wanted him to take the case. That was all right. But how come, he wondered, I don't feel mad about it?

"I wonder, Max, if I could make a suggestion?"

"Sure."

"About your daughter. How would it be if I talked to her? I don't want to butt into family matters, though."

"It's okay with me, but what would you talk to her about?"

"What I just told you. The truth. Only I'd sweeten it up a bit, you know, let her think she—and I—would be humoring you. I'd tell her how important it is for people to be involved in things, but make it sound like constructive therapy."

"That would be nice, if she understood," Guttman said. "But are you sure that's not what you're doing now? Humoring me?"

"Could be," Dr. Aiken said. "Except that I'm too close to your age to humor you. And you don't need it, anyway."

"I guess it don't make a difference either way. In the end, it's the same."

"See, I told you you didn't need to be humored," Dr. Aiken said, rising briskly from his chair. "What would be a good time to get your daughter?"

"I don't know. But she's coming to pick me up about five. Maybe I could say you wanted to talk to her . . . if you got the time then."

"I'll make the time. And remember, if there's anything I can do, let me know. You realize, incidentally, that I should be angry with you."

"Angry? Why?"

"Because of Maggie."

"Miss Brady?"

"Uh-huh. When I came back I told her I wanted her on the job again, as head nurse. She said no, and I told her okay, part time. She still said no. My personal opinion, although she didn't exactly say it, is that you, and this detective business of yours, is the reason."

"I . . . I don't know nothing about that," Guttman said, somewhat confused.

"Well, never mind. I'll be here, waiting for your daughter, at five," Dr. Aiken said.

Guttman left, feeling relieved but still a little confused. This business with Miss Brady was something he'd have to think about. Meanwhile he had to talk to Jessica Stone.

When he got to the cottage he was surprised to find a nurse opening the door for him. He recognized her but didn't know her name. The residents of the Center knew the staff much better than the day people, like him.

"Is Mrs. Stone here?" he asked.

"She'll be out in a minute," the nurse said. "I'll tell her you're here."

Guttman waited in the living room, looking at the paintings on the walls, picking up a small china figure, turning it over in his hand and then putting it down carefully. Finally he sat down in the easy chair he'd used the day before and waited. It was a few minutes longer before the nurse wheeled Mrs. Stone in.

"I'd like to talk to Mr. Guttman alone, Barbara," Mrs. Stone said.

"I'll finish getting lunch ready," the nurse said.

"Well, are you ready to go see the lawyers?" she asked Guttman.

"That's mostly what I came about, to check on when the cab would come."

"What cab?" Mrs. Stone asked.

"The cab to go to the lawyers."

"Not a cab, Mr. Guttman. A car. And a driver. It's all arranged."

"Oh. I . . . I didn't know." A car with a driver, he thought. "There was something else I wanted to ask you about. I read the reports, Mrs. Kaplan has them now, and I guess the others will read them also. And I talked to the police."

"Indeed?"

"I figured it would help to know more of the story," he explained.

"I'm not being critical."

"I didn't say you were. But the thing is, I think if I'm going to be helping, it's definite I should talk also to your granddaughter, herself."

"Naturally," Mrs. Stone said. "I assumed that you would. When?"

"Whenever it's okay. Today maybe."

"I'll call Gordon immediately, and have him arrange it."

"Gordon?"

"Gordon Richardson. His firm is representing Susan."

"He's the lawyer?"

"Yes. This sort of case isn't exactly in his line, but it's a good firm and he assures me that one of the young men on his staff is very experienced in criminal matters. And the firm itself is not without influence. Since I've been a client for a number of years, they're obliged to do what I ask. I'm a good client, I might add."

"I'm sure," Guttman said.

"Is there anything else?"

"You didn't say exactly what time the car would be here."

"One-thirty."

"One-thirty," Guttman repeated. "There's one more thing."

"What's that?"

"Well, it looks like the only way to prove your granddaughter didn't kill this Vincent person is to prove somebody else did. That means we got to find out all about him."

"You said you read the reports."

"I did. That part worries me, that they didn't find out anything to talk about," Guttman told her.

"Mr. Guttman, if you feel that this is more than you can handle, please don't feel you have to proceed. I . . . I'll manage." There was a catch in her voice, and Guttman was tempted to mention that he'd talked to Dr. Aiken, but decided not to. Let her think she'd convinced him to help because she was sick. Maybe she felt better that way, he thought.

"Mrs. Stone, I don't know if I could handle it or not. All I said was I'll try. But it would help if we could find out more about Vincent, and you could make it easier, maybe."

"How?"

"Well, there's the place where he worked, him and Susan. Maybe we could talk to some of the people there . . ."

"My detectives did that."

"I know. But I'm not a detective, really, and sometimes when people see an old man, they don't worry so much about what they say." He shrugged his shoulders. "At least we could try."

"You tell me when, and I'll arrange it," Mrs. Stone said.

"I'll tell you later."

"If . . . if you see Susan today," Mrs. Stone said, "would you tell her for me . . . would you tell her I send my love, and that I'm going to try to visit soon. If Dr. Aiken will let me."

"Of course," Guttman promised. He got as far as the door before he remembered something else. "Mrs. Stone, how many people would it be all right to take?"

"I beg your pardon?"

"Well, there's six of us altogether, and I was wondering . . ."

"I don't think you need a whole platoon to talk to Gordon. And I'm sure they won't let all of you in together to see Susan."

"I was just wondering . . ."

"Do you mind if I make a suggestion?"

"Of course not."

"Well, Maggie Brady knows Susan," Mrs. Stone said. "She met her a few times here. And I think Susan liked her. I don't know why. She always struck me as a crusty type . . ." Mrs. Stone smiled. "Like me, in her way. I'd suggest you take her. She's got a good head on her shoulders."

"I know," Guttman said. "And thanks for the suggestion."

Four

The car was a limousine. The driver, a middle-aged man named Clinton, wore a gray uniform with brass buttons. Guttman, in his new sport jacket and old slacks, felt somehow shabby, although he'd put his tie on. He wasn't accustomed to this sort of thing. He had felt awkward when the chauffeur had held the door for them and asked if there were any special instructions, and now, trying to relax on the leather seat, he still felt uncomfortable. There's always new things, he thought. You live your whole life, and still you could be doing things you never done before.

"I hope this isn't going to cause too much trouble," Miss Brady said.

"What's that?"

"Well, Mrs. Kaplan wasn't exactly overjoyed when you announced that you could only take one of us with you, and that it would be me."

"To tell the truth, I made that up, a little. Mrs. Stone said not everybody should go, and she mentioned that you met Susan. Besides," he added, "they had to check on how long it takes to climb the stairs at that apartment."

"I'm flattered," Margaret Brady said.

"Do you know the girl very well?" Guttman asked, not knowing how to respond.

"Not really. I don't even know Jessica that well. She's been at the Center five, six years now. I see her every now and then, and we make the usual small talk."

Guttman nodded and tried to think about what he would ask the lawyer, and what, after that, he could ask Susan herself. Unconsciously, he found himself looking at Miss Brady at his side. She didn't look uncomfortable in the limousine. She sat with her back straight, the way she always did, her hands in her lap, like it was her car and she rode in it all the time. When she caught him staring, Guttman turned his head quickly. "I wonder how long a ride it is," he said.

"Half an hour," she told him. "And if you're wondering about your cigar, go ahead. I'll light a cigarette too, and that way the only one the smoke will bother is the driver. And he's getting paid for this."

Guttman smiled at her and took a cigar from his case. She held her cigarette until he was ready to light his cigar, and then accepted a light from the match he held. Her hand touched his slightly, and Guttman averted his eyes.

"Do you mind if I ask you something?" she asked after a moment.

"No. Why should I mind?"

"It seems to me that I remember you being very reluctant to get involved in this sort of thing before. You don't seem nearly so reluctant now," she said, smiling.

"That's a telling, not an asking," Guttman said.

"Sorry."

"No, it's okay. I was thinking about the same thing," he told her. "I wasn't so sure of the reasons until I was talking to Dr. Aiken before. He was saying that it's a good thing for everybody at the Center, something like this, because they all got an interest in it. Something they could think about. I guess for me it's the same."

"Yes, that's one of the problems with retiring, with getting old," Miss Brady said quietly. "Some of it's great, but every once in a while you wake up in the morning and wonder what you're going to do all day."

"I . . . Dr. Aiken said something else," Guttman said hesitantly. "If you don't mind my asking."

"Why should I mind?" Miss Brady said, smiling.

"Well, he said how he wanted you to work at the Center again. And you said you didn't want to."

"Well, that's about three-quarters right."

"Three-quarters?"

"Uh-huh. Three-quarters I didn't really want to, and one-quarter I didn't think it would be a good idea. Or maybe it's the other way around."

"I don't understand."

"It's a year now that I've been retired," Miss Brady said. "That's a year of living at the Center as a resident, rather than staff. The people on the staff have changed—you know, when Frank first left, some new people came in with that . . . Dr. Morton, and then some left when he did, but mostly," she went on, "mostly it's that I'm part of the resident population now. I guess I'm too close to it. I couldn't get that objectivity, that distance, that you need once in a while. At least I don't think I could. And, well, age has something to do with it too."

"You don't act like you feel your age," Guttman said, knowing right away that it didn't sound the way he had meant it.

"That's not what I mean, but thank you for the compliment. It's that I'm getting—I am—too close in age to everyone else. I'm vulnerable in the same ways. Maybe I just don't want to keep saying 'there but for the grace . . . go I.' Because I could be next. Does that make any sense?"

"It makes sense," Guttman said slowly. "But I don't know it makes good sense. Everybody is different. Everybody is themselves, not somebody else."

"I know," Margaret Brady said. "But it's a matter of perspective. Let me tell you something about the medical profession, Mr. Guttman. When you're dealing with sick people, you begin to feel invulnerable. It can't happen to you, you feel. Oh, you know that isn't true, but you don't really feel it. That's what makes it possible for you to deal with sickness."

She stopped and thought for a moment. "I saw a lot of that

during the war. A man would see his buddy get shot and he'd feel awful, but somehow, most of them had convinced themselves that it was only for the other guy. It wouldn't happen to them. If you asked them about it, of course, they'd say they know that they could be next. But they didn't really feel it. That was their defense, what kept them from breaking. I guess I've just reached an age where I don't feel invulnerable any more," Miss Brady said, managing a quick smile.

"I know the feeling," Guttman said. "Only I don't think about it too much."

"Neither do I, ordinarily. But you asked, and that's why I didn't accept the offer to go back to work. Even part time."

"I guess Dr. Aiken don't feel that way. He ain't so young, himself."

"No, Frank's one of the lucky ones. He just loves what he's doing. Anyway," Miss Brady said, "I think it's more fun playing detective than emptying bedpans."

"On that I got to agree one hundred percent," Guttman said. "Even if I don't empty a bedpan since I was a boy in the old country."

"You didn't miss anything," she assured him.

"That much I remember."

The offices of Richardson, Greenberger and Zimmerman, Attorneys-at-Law, were on the seventh floor of an imposing new building. The chauffeur held the door open for them, asked how long they would be, and said that, naturally, he would wait. Guttman suggested there was time for him to go get a cup of coffee, and the chauffeur thanked him. In the elevator, Guttman had a sudden thought.

"I was just wondering," he told Miss Brady, "is we supposed to give a tip to the driver?"

"Well, we might. But Mrs. Stone is paying for this, so she should really handle it."

"I was just wondering," Guttman said.

They were expected, and the receptionist offered them a seat in the carpeted front office while she announced them. They'd hardly had time to get settled before they were being greeted by Mr. Richardson's secretary, who led them back to his office. Mrs. Stone, Guttman thought, must be as good a customer as she said, with this kind of service.

Gordon Richardson was in his late fifties or early sixties, tall and thin, wearing a pin-striped blue suit with a vest, gray hair neatly brushed, black shoes highly polished. Guttman's practiced eye told him that the suit was expensive and made-to-order. It looked like good-quality material, too, but he couldn't be positive without touching it. Richardson met them at the door, shook hands, escorted them to the two high-backed leather armchairs in front of his large oak desk, and only then sat down himself. The office was impressive. The carpeting was thicker than in the reception area, maybe, Guttman thought, because there's fewer people walking on it; the walls were paneled and decorated with several large paintings, each with its own light. There were curtains across the windows, but Guttman was sure that the view was a good one.

"It's very nice you should take the time to see us," Guttman said.

"Not at all. Jessica Stone is an old friend. Anything I can do to help her in any way, I am only too happy to do."

"That's very nice," Guttman said. "With us it's a little the same, only she ain't such an old friend. But we're trying to help also."

"So I understand. Jessica wasn't very specific when she told me you were coming, however," Richardson said. "She just said it was in connection with Susan."

Guttman glanced at Miss Brady, but she only raised one eyebrow and shrugged slightly. He'd have to explain it himself. And he sensed the reaction he'd get from Mr. Richardson.

"Mrs. Stone asked if maybe we could help prove her granddaughter didn't kill this Vincent person." He hadn't been able to think of any other way to put it.

"Well . . ." Richardson said. "I see." He pursed his lips, clasped his hands, rubbing his thumbs together, and finally looked up at them. "I see," he repeated. "And how do you go about that?"

"It's a good question," Guttman replied. "The only way I could see is to find out who really killed him."

"To find out who really killed him," Richardson repeated quietly.

"We realize, Mr. Richardson," Miss Brady interrupted, "that you will be doing everything possible to gain an acquittal for Susan. But you'll be trying to establish, to a jury, that she did not commit the crime. We wouldn't presume to attempt to suggest how you might go about that. But since Mrs. Stone asked us to help, we felt that the best thing would be to undertake an investigation of the crime itself."

"I see," Richardson said.

Guttman wondered whether he was going to say anything else at all. He did.

"You've certainly taken on quite a task," Richardson told them. "I hope you won't be offended, but how do you expect to accomplish what the police haven't been able to do?"

"The police seem satisfied that Susan did it," Guttman said.

"Well, the problem is . . . you see, if there were evidence pointing to someone else . . ." Richardson said, "well, surely they would have pursued it."

"You make that sound like you don't think somebody else was involved," Guttman said.

"Not at all, not at all. But there doesn't seem to be any evidence, that's the point. They have a fairly strong case against Susan, I'm sorry to say."

"It ain't what they call circumstantial?" Guttman asked.

"I've discussed this with Mrs. Stone, and, well, to answer your question, not really. I'm not sure at this point how we'll conduct her defense. It's going to be difficult."

"I'm sure Mrs. Stone realizes that," Miss Brady said. "That's why she asked us to help."

"By 'us' I presume you mean the two of you?"

"There's others," Guttman said. "But that's not important.

What matters is, if you say it's going to be hard to get her out of jail, then the thing is how we could help."

"Well, certainly we'd appreciate any assistance you provide," Richardson said. "And I have the best man in the firm handling the case."

"You're not working on it?"

"Trial work, criminal trials, that is, is not my specialty," Richardson said, shifting uncomfortably in his chair. "It isn't the specialty of the firm, really. We deal in corporate matters, financial dealings primarily. However," he went on, "a young man joined our firm recently, and he has a great deal of criminal experience. Quite fortuitous, really, otherwise I might have had to arrange for someone outside the firm to handle the case."

"Mrs. Stone said that we'd be able to see Susan," Miss Brady said. "I think we should talk to this new member of your firm as well." She made it sound as though she didn't think Richardson was important any more, and Guttman was both surprised and pleased. He didn't like Richardson.

"Naturally," Richardson said coolly.

"And we appreciate you taking the time and talking to us. I'm sure you're very busy," Guttman said.

"Not at all," Richardson said, hardly mollified. "If Jessica thinks you can help, well, I'm not going to suggest otherwise. In her situation . . ."

"Like you, Mr. Richardson, we're only doing what we can," Guttman said. "And like you said, it ain't an easy thing."

"Uh . . . yes." Richardson looked at Guttman queerly, and he knew that the lawyer was trying to remember whether he'd said just that. If Miss Brady could get a dig in, he could too, Guttman decided. "Could we talk to this other lawyer now?"

Richardson pushed a button on his desk, and when his secretary appeared he told her that Mr. Taylor was expecting them. "If there's anything else I can do, please call on me," he told them. "And give my best to Jessica when you see her. Tell her to try not to worry." Richardson got up to see them to the door.

.   .   .

Paul Taylor's office was considerably smaller than that of Gordon Richardson, but the walls were also paneled, although the pictures didn't have individual lights. The desk wasn't as large, either, and the books on the shelves behind him weren't as richly bound. Paul Taylor looked different too. He stood behind the desk as they entered, a short, intense-looking man in his early thirties, his tie loose and his sleeves rolled halfway up his forearms. There was a coffee cup on his desk, and the piles of papers weren't very neat. Taylor waved them to a seat, ran a hand through his curly hair, and then sat down, pulling out a desk drawer to put his feet up, after the introductions were completed.

"We've got a couple of minutes before we have to leave," he told them. "Gordon tells me you're friends of Mrs. Stone. So what can I do for you?"

"It could be the other way around," Miss Brady said. "We may be able to do something for you."

"Any help will be gratefully accepted. It was cases like this that got me out of the criminal courthouse and into this gray-flannel world."

"It sounds like you're not so happy about the case," Guttman said.

"It's a lousy case. And Mrs. Stone is a good client for the firm, so I'm on the spot. If I blow it, I'm probably out of a job. And just when I was getting used to the good life." The young lawyer grinned. "So I guess I'd better not blow it."

"Just from curiosity, you mean you'd lose your job if Susan goes to jail?" Guttman asked.

"Probably."

"And you're afraid that you might lose?" Miss Brady asked.

"Well, you never know with a jury. But it's a rough one. It all depends on how the jury sees things, though."

"That's natural, I guess," Guttman said.

"Anyway, what kind of help are you two dear souls offering me?"

"Mrs. Stone asked us to see if we could figure out who really killed this Vincent," Guttman said, annoyed.

"She asked you . . ." Taylor shook his head and smiled. "Well, why not? Have you figured out who did it yet?"

"Mr. Taylor," Margaret Brady said icily, "we realize that it may seem amusing to you that we conduct this investigation, but Mrs. Stone did not find it amusing."

"Sorry," Taylor said. "But if you'll forgive me, you two just don't strike me as Sherlock Holmes and Doctor Watson."

"We don't have to strike you any way," Guttman told him. "Maybe you could just tell us some things and not worry about the rest."

"I'm sorry," Taylor said. "Really. I guess this thing is just bothering me more than I like to admit."

"Bothering you in what way?" Miss Brady asked.

"Well, it's a tough case, like I said. And winning means a lot to me."

"It also means a lot to Mrs. Stone. And her granddaughter," Guttman suggested.

"Of course. And I'm not supposed to get involved emotionally. Clouds my judgment. Anyway, please accept my apology. And ask me anything you like. Provided it only takes a couple of minutes. After that, we'll have to talk on the way."

"Okay," Guttman said. "So first, maybe you got an idea of who else could've killed this Vincent?"

"Not a one. I've talked to Susan about it, but she hasn't given me anything concrete. I could point to a few people, but there's nothing substantial."

"Even pointing is more than the detectives Mrs. Stone hired were able to do," Miss Brady said.

"Not really. They checked things out pretty well, but when they wrote up that report—I saw it—they only included facts. For example, there's Susan's husband . . ."

"She's still married?" Guttman asked.

"Separated, but married. Now, he knew she was having this thing with Vincent, and he might have known about Vincent beating her, although I don't see how. Even so, from what Susan says, he was still in love with her. So you've got a motive. Jealousy. But that's all you've got."

"Nevertheless . . ." Miss Brady said.

"No good," Taylor interrupted what she was going to say. "How would he have known where the gun was? Remember, Vincent kept it hidden away."

"And also, if Vincent had the gun, the husband would've had to fight with him, and there was no struggle, and the neighbor didn't hear nothing," Guttman said.

"Well . . ." Taylor said. "You've done a little research, haven't you?"

"I talked to Lieutenant Weiss this morning."

"Is he a friend of yours?"

"I know him."

"Well, then you probably know as much as I do about what they have on Susan."

"How about somebody else?" Guttman asked. "Did Susan tell you maybe about somebody with a grudge against Vincent?"

"She mentioned the wife, but I don't think there's anything there."

"Why not?" Miss Brady asked.

"She had nothing to gain."

"She might have been angry that he was having an affair with Susan."

"Could have been. But remember," Taylor said, "it was nothing new. And Susan says that Vincent told her he wanted a divorce but his wife wouldn't give it to him, not without taking him for everything he had, anyway. The way it looks, from what the detectives were able to turn up, Mrs. Vincent was satisfied to let her husband go his way while she went hers."

"It sounds a little strange to me," Guttman said.

"Well, people are funny. You know, whatever turns you on . . ."

"You mean she didn't mind that he was . . . having an affair with someone else?"

"It wasn't the first," Taylor said. "And he was supporting her pretty well, and she was free to do as she pleased. Which she did. You might call it a marriage of convenience."

"Still," Guttman said hopefully, "with something like that, you never know."

"I think we'd better get started," Taylor said, rising. "I've got my car in the lot, so if you want to meet me out front . . ."

"We got a car," Guttman said. "Mrs. Stone arranged it. If you want to come with us, you're welcome."

"I guess we'd better use both cars, then. I've got to come back here afterward—unless you'll be heading back this way?"

"We don't know," Miss Brady said. "You see, we don't know where Susan is being held."

"In San Martin. The apartment where Vincent was killed is just inside the town limits, so it's their jurisdiction. Kind of a pain driving out there all the time," Taylor added.

"I didn't know that," Guttman said.

"I guess your friend Lieutenant Weiss just forgot to mention it."

"We won't be coming back this way, then," Miss Brady said quickly.

"Okay. I'll be in a blue Mustang. Kind of beat up. You can follow me out there."

Five

The San Martin House of Detention was a two-story concrete building with heavy frosted glass windows, set back from the street, with a freshly sodded lawn and newly planted trees in front of it. The limousine followed Paul Taylor's car into the adjacent parking lot. As they got out of the car Guttman realized that they were only a block from the police station where he'd talked to Lieutenant Weiss just that morning.

"This is where she is?" he asked Taylor.

"This is the place. It's co-ed. Men in one wing, women in the other."

"The police station is only a block away," Guttman said.

"Makes it convenient, doesn't it?" Taylor led them up the six steps to the door. Just inside was an area that looked, to Guttman, like a bank teller's window, with doors on either side. One was marked "Men," the other "Women." They waited while Taylor spoke to the policeman behind the barred window.

"Miss Brady, if you'll go in that way . . ." He pointed at the door marked "Women." "They want to check for weapons," he explained. "We'll meet you inside." She hesitated for just a moment, then nodded and walked briskly to the door. Guttman followed Taylor to the left.

There was another policeman inside, sitting behind a desk. Taylor spoke to him for a moment, then emptied his pockets and opened the briefcase he was carrying. The policeman glanced through it, then nodded. Guttman, in turn, emptied his pockets as well. The policeman opened the cigar case, nodded, and Guttman retrieved his belongings. Through another door and they were in a corridor. After a moment Miss Brady joined them. Again they followed Taylor until they reached still another desk with another police officer, this time a woman. Taylor spoke to her, she pointed at one of the rooms off the corridor, and the three of them went inside.

It was a small room, without windows, furnished only with a metal table bolted to the floor. There were four chairs, two on each side, all bolted to the floor. Even the metal ashtray was screwed into the center of the table. Guttman noticed that the lights were recessed in the ceiling and protected by wire mesh. Taylor sat down, and after a moment Guttman and Miss Brady sat across from him.

The door opposite them opened and a matron entered, then stepped back. Guttman was a little surprised when he first saw the girl. He didn't know what he had been expecting. Maybe, he thought, anything would've surprised me. Susan Eliot looked younger than he'd expected, though. Her light-brown hair was neatly brushed, she wore lipstick and a little eye make-up, he noticed, and except for the dress, which was a dull gray, she could have been anywhere besides a prison. And, he thought, she didn't look like she was very worried.

"Mr. Taylor," she said. "How nice of you to come."

"How are you, Susan?"

"I'm fine, thank you. And how are you?" She smiled at him and then sat down across from Guttman and Miss Brady. "Margaret Brady, isn't it?"

"That's right. I'm . . . I'm sorry about all of this, Susan."

"No need," Susan Eliot said. "And you are . . . ?"

"Max Guttman," he told her. "And I'm sorry, too."

"Paul told me someone would be coming," the girl explained. "For some reason I have to put you on my list, so to speak, before you're allowed to visit. Did you know that?"

"I didn't," Guttman said.

"Before I just let Mr. Guttman and Miss Brady go ahead," Taylor said, "I might as well ask if there's anything you want to tell me, since yesterday?"

"Not unless you'd like to know that the other girls feel mine is a case of justifiable homicide," Susan Eliot said. "They didn't exactly vote, but that seems to be the consensus."

"They think you're guilty?" Guttman asked, surprised.

"We think that everyone here is guilty. Since we all claim to be innocent, we can either spend our time talking about what a lousy deal we're getting, or show support by claiming that we were entitled to do what we're accused of doing."

"Interesting," Miss Brady said. "It must be a great comfort."

"It is," the girl answered. "And it's a lot easier than trying to convince everyone that you're innocent."

"We think you're innocent," Guttman said.

"Why?"

Guttman hesitated, and then said, "For no good reason. But it's a place to start."

"To start what?"

"Your grandmother, Susan, has asked us to help," Miss Brady said.

"How?"

"By trying to prove your innocence," she explained.

The girl looked across the table at them, turned to look at Taylor, who carefully averted his gaze, and finally she shrugged her shoulders. "Good luck," she said.

"We was wondering," Guttman said quickly, "maybe there's something you could tell us that would help."

"I can't imagine what," Susan Eliot said. "I've told Paul what I know, which is nothing. The only way I could help would be to tell you who really killed Harry, and even if I knew, I'm not sure I'd say anything."

"Why not?" Miss Brady asked.

"Why punish someone who's just done you a favor?" the girl asked.

"Maybe it's not my business," Guttman said, "but if you felt that way, I mean, since you and him was . . ."

"We were lovers," Susan Eliot said for him. "That's the polite terminology." She paused for a moment. "I suppose I didn't feel that way always. At least not until the son of a bitch beat me up. It served me right, though. I deserved to get my tail kicked for being so dumb."

"But you don't deserve to be in jail for killing him," Guttman suggested.

"It's temporary. After all, Paul's going to get me off, aren't you, Paul?"

"I'm going to try," Taylor said.

"You see?" the girl asked Guttman.

"I see he said he'd try. That ain't the same thing as doing it. No offense," he added, looking at the lawyer.

"None taken."

"I have confidence in Paul," the girl said. "He's a fine lawyer. The best that money can buy, right, Paul?"

"That money could hire," Taylor said evenly.

"He's touchy about that," Susan Eliot told them. "But to get back to your question, I don't know who killed Harry. Or why. Sorry."

"That's all you got to say about it?" Guttman asked.

"That's all I know," she replied.

"Susan, you realize that this is a serious situation," Miss Brady said.

"Oh yes, I realize."

"Was there anybody else who could've had a reason for killing him?" Guttman asked.

"Half the population of Los Angeles and surrounding counties," the girl said. "That is, if they got to know him the way I did."

"Miss Eliot, all this may not worry you, but it worries your grandmother," Guttman said.

"I'm sorry about that."

"Let me ask you something, then. You was . . . lovers with this man. Then all of a sudden he hits you, and you hate him. That, if you'll forgive me, don't make a lot of sense."

"Stupidity rarely does. And that's what I was. Stupid. Dumb."
A note of bitterness entered her voice.

"You was so dumb you didn't know what he was like?"
Guttman asked. Then, before she could reply, "Okay. So was
you also so dumb you don't have no idea of who he could've
been like that with?"

"You mean other women?"

"I mean anybody. A person what beats up a woman, that's
not such a nice person. So maybe he did wrong things to other
people too."

"I never saw it," Susan Eliot said, her voice flat. "I never saw
it."

"Miss Eliot, the day it happened, is there something else you
could remember you didn't tell the police?"

"Nothing."

"Maybe somebody else knew you was going to the apartment
to pack?"

"I didn't tell anyone."

"Did you talk to somebody at the office maybe?" Guttman
suggested.

"I told the police about it already. I called in sick, in the
morning, but I didn't tell them where I was going. I couldn't
show up looking the way I did."

"Did you think Vincent would show up, when you went to get
your stuff?" Guttman asked.

"He was supposed to be at work. I don't know what he was
doing at the apartment in the first place."

"Are you sure, Susan?" Miss Brady asked.

"I'm sure. Oh, I know what you're thinking. Did I go back
there hoping to see him, hoping he'd apologize and then we
could forget it? No, I did not." She said it easily, but Guttman
wasn't sure he believed her.

"Are you a hundred percent sure you don't know somebody
else what might have a grudge against him, might've wanted to
kill him?" Guttman asked.

"No one. That is, no one that I know of."

"Was Vincent upset, or did he do anything different, lately?"

"He beat me," the girl said wryly.

"I mean besides that."

"No . . . not really."

"What do you mean, not really?" Miss Brady asked.

"Well, he was uptight about money, for a change. But it wasn't the first time."

"Was he worried about his job, or something?" Guttman asked.

"No. Harry gambled a bit. He was just a little short, he said. It happened before. Anyway, it was a week or two before . . . I remember he said it was just a matter of a little time . . ."

Guttman digested that and wished that it was more than it seemed to be to the girl. "We're trying to help you," he said after a moment.

"And it's very nice of you," Susan answered. "I'm sure Grandmother means well . . ."

"It can't do any harm for us to try," Margaret Brady said.

"Well, as I said, good luck."

"I'll be back day after tomorrow," Taylor told her. "We've got a hearing coming up, and I want to go over some things with you."

"Be sure you call first, so I don't make other plans," Susan Eliot told him.

They sat and watched while she got up and knocked on the door. The matron opened it and then closed it behind the girl. It wasn't until they were out on the street again that Guttman spoke.

"I don't understand it," he said.

"What's that, Mr. Guttman?" Taylor asked.

"The way she was. The way she acted. I didn't know her from before, but it was like she was mad at us."

"It happens," Taylor said. "People on the inside, for whatever reason, they resent those of us who are out."

"But it was almost as though she didn't want us to help," Miss Brady said.

"It's not unusual."

"But why?" Guttman asked.

"I can only give you kind of a half-baked analysis," Taylor said. "But when people are thrown in jail, they lose something. They don't want to think about it being permanent, but they're afraid to let their hopes build up too much. So they start to accept. And they try not to think. They develop a kind of armor, a kind of disillusionment . . ."

"Do you think she's innocent, Mr. Taylor?" Miss Brady asked.

"Uh-huh."

"Why?"

"Instinct. I pride myself on having had enough clients, guilty and innocent, so I can tell the difference. Maybe I'm kidding myself, but lots of times that's all I've had to go on. My instincts."

"She didn't seem to care very much what we think," Guttman said.

"That's another story," Taylor told him. "It's hard to know why. Maybe she's kind of enjoying being punished for something else, maybe she feels guilty about something . . ."

"For what does she feel guilty?"

"Maybe for being dumb enough to fall in love with Vincent," Taylor said. "I don't know. It could just be that she's afraid they have enough evidence to get a conviction, and she just doesn't want to think about it, so she acts as if it doesn't matter."

"It's sad," Margaret Brady said in the car.

"It's very sad," Guttman agreed. "And it's confusing for me, too."

"How so?"

"Well, the way they was together. 'Lovers,' she called it."

"Don't tell me that shocks you, Mr. Guttman," Miss Brady said teasingly.

"I admit I ain't used to it. I mean, people did it when I was young, too. But not so much."

"It's a convenience, that's all. Living together without marriage offers them companionship and sex, but it doesn't entail any real responsibility. No ties, is the way they put it."

"If you ain't got ties, then you ain't got love," Guttman said.

"Responsibility isn't easy for a lot of people, Max."

"It ain't easy for anybody."

"Well, they avoid it by telling themselves that they're free," Miss Brady said.

"I could understand that," Guttman said. "But to me, if you're free, it means you're free to do something. Not just to . . . to do nothing."

"Well, there are some who make their commitments anyway, but who just don't want a piece of paper telling them what they have to do."

"That kind I wouldn't worry about," Guttman said. "But a girl what's living with a man and he's the kind beats her up . . . even that I could understand. Beating up women ain't something that was just invented. But that she wouldn't care if he was dead, she wouldn't care who killed him . . ." Guttman shook his head.

"I think she cares," Miss Brady said after a moment. "She just didn't want to admit it."

"It could be. But anyway, what matters now is what we're going to do next."

Guttman slowly stirred sugar into his tea, which he didn't really want, and wished that he could be alone somewhere, to do some thinking. But as he had expected, the others were waiting for them when they returned to the Center, and with just a little while left before he and Mrs. Kaplan would be going home, he knew he had to bring the others up to date.

"What we found out," he told them, "isn't so much. We seen the girl, and she says she got no idea who would've wanted to kill Vincent. The police, likewise, this morning said they didn't have nobody else for a suspect. And the lawyers said there was nothing special either."

"Then we don't have anything to work with?" Mr. Carstairs asked.

"Maybe, maybe not. One thing the girl finally said is this Vincent was worrying about money . . . a little."

"Everybody worries about money," Mishkin said.

"It isn't much to go on," Mrs. Kaplan agreed.

"Well, it's all we got for now, except she said he gambled also. And we got to begin somewheres," Guttman said.

"But how?" Mrs. O'Rourke wanted to know.

"That I'm not so sure of."

"Perhaps . . ." Harold Carstairs said softly.

"Perhaps what?" Guttman asked.

"Perhaps we could get a credit rating on the late Mr. Vincent."

"A credit rating?" Guttman asked.

"Yes. We could find out perhaps if he was in debt, and how heavily."

"That sounds okay," Guttman said. "But how would you do this?"

"There are ways. If we were a bank," Mr. Carstairs said, "it would be no problem at all."

"Mrs. Stone might be able to help," Miss Brady said. "From what she says, I mean, with her money, that is, maybe she has a contact at a bank."

"That's a possibility," Guttman agreed.

"Let's go ask her, then," Mrs. Kaplan said.

"In a minute," Guttman told her. "There's other things we should think about first. Maybe we got something else to ask her at the same time."

"Like what?" Mrs. O'Rourke asked.

"Like at the scene of the crime," Guttman said. "Mr. Carstairs, you said you was going to see about how long it took to climb up the stairs."

"We went with him," Agnes O'Rourke said. "And it wasn't easy getting in. We had to wait outside till someone with a key came along."

"The sixty-second estimate is in keeping with our client's story, I think," Mr. Carstairs interrupted.

Our client, Guttman thought. So even Mr. Carstairs is thinking like he's a regular detective.

"As Mr. Carstairs pointed out," Dora Kaplan said, "sixty seconds is a long time. Let's demonstrate, Agnes. We practiced before, so we know it's right," she added.

And then, as Guttman watched with his mouth half open, Dora Kaplan and Agnes O'Rourke re-enacted their version of the death of Harry Vincent. Standing a few feet apart, Mrs. Kaplan pointed her finger at Mrs. O'Rourke and shot her, saying "Bang," and nodding at Mr. Carstairs, who was staring at his watch. Mrs. Kaplan mimed throwing the gun down next to Mrs. O'Rourke, who had seated herself in a chair rather than falling on the floor dead, to Guttman's relief. Then Mrs. Kaplan walked a few feet away, pretended to open a door and close it behind her, and walked on until she pushed a button, and after a brief pause, took another step and turned around.

"How long?" she asked.

"Twenty-two seconds," Mr. Carstairs announced.

Mrs. Kaplan waited, moved a few feet away, then "unlocked" the door, stepped inside, threw her hands up in surprise, bent over the imaginary body, picked up the gun, and finally walked a few feet away to call the police.

"How long all together?" Mrs. Kaplan asked.

"Fifty-eight seconds," Mr. Carstairs replied. "And each of us climbed the steps separately. The mean time elapsed to go from the front door to the second floor, that's one flight up, was eighteen seconds. Actually," he continued, "we estimate that no more than fifty-five seconds was needed between the time Susan Eliot entered the building to the time she contacted the police."

"I'm impressed," Guttman said sincerely.

"So am I," Margaret Brady added.

"I didn't think the acting was so hot," Jacob Mishkin said, just quietly enough so that Mrs. Kaplan didn't hear him.

"It's close, but Susan's story could be the truth," Mrs. Kaplan said, settling herself at the table.

"We'll have to tell the lawyer about it," Guttman said. "It could help him."

"Shall we go see Jessica now?" Mrs. Kaplan asked.

"In a minute," Guttman told her. "Coming back in the car, I was thinking about something. The thing is, we got to find out more about this Vincent."

"What do you have in mind?" Miss Brady asked.

"Well, we got two places to start. First, there's the wife. And second, there's the office where he worked, and also Susan."

"Didn't the detectives check that?" Mrs. Kaplan asked.

"Not so good," Guttman said. "But anyway, maybe we could do it different."

"Differently?" Miss Brady asked.

"Different," Guttman repeated. "They just walked in and talked to some people that was there."

"And what are you suggesting that we could do?" Mrs. O'Rourke asked.

"Supposing somebody from here was to go to work at this place," Guttman said.

"An undercover agent!" Mrs. O'Rourke exclaimed.

"Something like that. Somebody who could just talk to the other people around there, maybe find out something about Vincent. Like the girl said he was worrying about money, only nobody else said nothing about it. So there could be things nobody found out yet, besides that."

"That's all well and good, Mr. Guttman," Margaret Brady said. "But there's a little problem. None of us is exactly at an age where it's normal for us to go out looking for a job. Assuming that there's a job available." She sounded as though she was sorry to be critical of his idea.

"I know that," Guttman said. "That's the other thing I was going to talk to Mrs. Stone about. She said how she owned a part of the company, so maybe we could work something out."

"Wouldn't they be suspicious?" Mrs. Kaplan asked.

"It would depend on how it was done," Guttman said. "Suppose she calls the big boss, and he takes care of it. Then not everybody would know about it. And I remember, when I was working, there was always stories around about people. Not facts maybe, but at least stories, ideas for us to think about."

"Who did you have in mind for this undercover work?" Mrs. Kaplan asked.

"You, and maybe Mrs. O'Rourke, you could get some kind of job there . . ."

"What's wrong with me?" Mishkin asked, surprising Guttman. He hadn't expected Mishkin to volunteer, and it took him a moment to find an answer.

"What's wrong with you is the same thing what's wrong with me," Guttman said. "I was a cutter, you was a plumber. So we could work in the shop maybe. If they got a shop. But this Vincent was working in the office part, so probably nobody in the shop would have stories to tell about him. They might not even have known him personally."

"But what could we be doing, Mr. Guttman?" Mrs. O'Rourke asked. "What kind of work would there be for us?"

"I don't know. But that's what I want to talk to Mrs. Stone about. Maybe she could have an idea."

"If they need help in their accounting department . . ." Mr. Carstairs suggested.

"That could also be a possibility," Guttman said. "But first you was going to see about the credit check." Besides, Guttman thought, Mr. Carstairs would probably spend all of his time actually working. With Mrs. Kaplan, he was sure, if there were stories to be heard, she would hear them.

"What will you be doing while we're out working?" Mrs. Kaplan asked.

"Well, I figure I might as well talk to people anyway. Maybe they'll say something to me, you know how it is, an old man, nobody worries very much what they say."

"Well," Miss Brady said after a moment, "if you're going to talk to Mrs. Stone, you'd better get started before you have to leave."

"Okay," Guttman said. He took a step or two away from the table, then stopped. "I tell you what. I think this time maybe it would be better if everybody was there. Even if Mrs. Stone don't like making speeches."

Eagerly they rose to follow him through the lounge, while the other residents and members of the Golden Valley Senior Citizens' Center watched.

Jessica Stone was sitting in the large wing-back chair she'd occupied when the group had first come to visit her. Feeling a little like the head of an invading party, Guttman led the others inside and quickly took the armchair opposite Mrs. Stone. This time, he thought, let Mrs. Kaplan sit on the spindly chair. She was so small she couldn't possibly break it.

"I see you've brought everyone with you, Mr. Guttman," Mrs. Stone said. "Tell me, how was Susan?"

"She seemed okay. She didn't seem upset or anything."

"I wish she were," Mrs. Stone replied. "It worries me, the way she's so withdrawn."

"Mr. Taylor seemed to think it was understandable," Miss Brady said.

"I'm glad he understands it. But I don't like it," Mrs. Stone told her. "Well?" She looked at each of them in turn, finally settling her gaze on Guttman.

"Well, we talked about some ideas, and we was thinking maybe you could help," he said.

"You don't expect me to hinder you, do you?"

"What we want is help," Guttman repeated. "We was wondering, maybe you know a bank?"

"Maybe I know a bank?"

"Mrs. Stone, we were hoping to look into the deceased's financial condition," Mr. Carstairs explained. "Although I have some connections at several financial institutions, under the circumstances it might be better if you could provide us with an entrée."

"What did you have in mind?"

"Mr. Guttman says he thinks the victim was in some financial difficulty," Mr. Carstairs said. "It would be helpful to learn the extent of his difficulties."

Mrs. Stone nodded, looked at her wristwatch, and said, "First thing in the morning. The bankers I know leave their offices early. I've learned that it's fruitless to try to reach them after four. What else?"

"Well, this is a little bit tricky," Guttman said. "But you told me how you own some of the company where Vincent was working, and also your granddaughter."

"More than just some, Mr. Guttman."

"Okay, so that makes it better. What I was thinking was maybe we could get somebody working in the company, and that way we could learn something."

"Like what?"

"Like if I knew, we wouldn't have to get somebody working there," Guttman told her, irritated. He didn't like her questioning, and he was very tired. It had been a full day. And he still had Lois to deal with.

"What did you have in mind?" Mrs. Stone asked. "I mean, what sort of work?"

"Something in the office. Maybe a secretary."

"Who would be doing this work?"

"I was thinking Mrs. Kaplan. And Mrs. O'Rourke."

"Mr. Guttman, the last job I had I was a girl," Mrs. Kaplan said. "I was a salesgirl."

"Okay, so not a secretary. So something else," Guttman said wearily.

"I suppose there must be some sort of filing position, or perhaps a telephone receptionist . . ." Mrs. Stone said.

"Whatever," Guttman told her. "The only thing is, nobody should know why they was working there, except maybe the boss."

"That makes it a bit more difficult."

"But you could do it?"

"I'll call first thing in the morning," Mrs. Stone promised.

"It would be a big help," Guttman said.

"And what will you be doing, if I may ask, while you have everyone out working?" Mrs. Stone asked.

"I'll also be working. I want to talk to your granddaughter's husband, and also, maybe I could talk to the people at the company, if it wouldn't be a trouble arranging it."

"It seems to me I'm doing all of the arranging," Mrs. Stone said.

"You'll pardon me if I don't apologize," Guttman said. "But it's your granddaughter, and besides, we're not getting no pay for this, you know." He was sorry as soon as he'd said it, but he felt that Mrs. Stone had pushed him too far.

"Quite right," she said after a moment of silence. "I have an unfortunate habit of forgetting things like that."

"And I'm sorry I was so cranky."

"Not at all. You were right. Is there anything else?"

"I think that's everything for now," Guttman told her. "But I guess you want Mr. Carstairs to be here when you call the bank tomorrow."

"Certainly. Nine o'clock, Mr. Carstairs. And, Dora, you might as well stop in here as soon as you arrive. We may be able to get you started right away," Mrs. Stone told Mrs. Kaplan.

"Oh, and one more thing," Guttman said after they'd all stood up and started for the door. "When I go talk to these people, you should tell them Miss Brady would be with me, if she wants to go, and"—he hesitated for an instant—"Mr. Mishkin too." That way, he thought, everybody would be doing something.

"Certainly," Mrs. Stone said. "You'll need transportation as well."

"I have my car," Miss Brady said.

"I'll have the car, and the driver, available whenever you need it. That way you won't have to worry about parking or expenses."

"That's very thoughtful," Guttman told her. And then he remembered that if he was going to talk to Susan's husband, he'd need the address and phone number. Mrs. Stone directed him to the desk, where he looked it up in her address book and copied it on a piece of notepaper.

Crossing the back lawn, Guttman stopped and let the others go ahead while he watched Mr. Bowsenior practicing on the bocce court. If I wasn't feeling so tired, he thought, and if it wasn't so late, I'd go and play a game. It could help me relax. But Lois might even be waiting already. He found Mishkin standing at the front door.

"Guttman, I appreciate you want to include me, but what am I supposed to be doing while all this is going on?" Mishkin asked. "I mean, you and Miss Brady, maybe you could ask questions pretty good, but me . . . I'm just a plumber."

"So I'm just a cutter," Guttman said. "You don't want to go?"

"I don't want to go if I'm not gonna help."

"How could you know unless you try?" Guttman asked.

Mishkin hesitated, then shrugged his shoulders. "Okay, so it would be nice to go for a ride anyway. It was a nice car you was in this afternoon."

"With air conditioning," Guttman said. "And real leather seats."

When he found the car out front, Guttman was surprised that Lois wasn't sitting there waiting impatiently. She was always in a hurry so she could get home and start dinner. Then he remembered his conversation with Dr. Aiken that morning. Such a day, he thought. Something like that and I'm forgetting it already. He got into the car, rolled the window down to let the smoke out, and lit a cigar. At least he'd have a few minutes alone to relax and think.

"Hi, Pop. Sorry it took so long," Lois said, opening the door.

"It gave me a chance to relax. You talked to Dr. Aiken?"

"I talked to him," she said, sliding behind the wheel. "And now we're late. As usual." She managed a small, only slightly concerned smile.

Guttman waited until they had driven a few blocks before he said anything else. "Dr. Aiken told you all that stuff?" he said.

"All what stuff, Pop?"

"About how it would be a good thing for me to play detective? He called it therapy, I think."

"More or less," Lois said. "I'm not sure I buy all of it, though."

"I don't agree with everything either. He makes it sound like an old person's got to be humored, like a baby."

"No, Pop—"

"And don't you start," Guttman told her. "You don't think this detective business is a good thing, okay. You're entitled to your opinion. I don't like when you're upset, or if we argue, but I like it better than if you pretend." He'd been thinking about this conversation while he waited for her.

"Okay. So I don't like it."

"Fine. Only I'm a grown-up person, and I got to make my own choices," he said. "If I don't like something you and Michael was doing, I'd tell you. But it's still your choice to make, what you do."

"What don't you like that we're doing?" Lois asked.

"Nothing. It was an example. But if something should be, then I'd tell you. You wouldn't want I should pretend, would you?"

"I guess not," Lois said. "Listen, did you and Dr. Aiken rehearse this?"

"No. Rehearse what?"

"Well, you sound just like he did," Lois said. "And I guess you're right, the two of you. But I can't help worrying, that's all. I can't help wishing you'd never gotten yourself into this detective stuff."

"I appreciate you worrying," Guttman said. "And I'm sorry it causes you upset. And I'll tell you also, sometimes I wish I didn't get involved too."

"What do you mean? Are you changing your mind?" Lois asked hopefully.

"I'm not changing my mind. But sometimes there's things to think about, and I ain't sure I could do it so good. Maybe after dinner we could talk about it a little."

"Great," Lois said, unable to suppress a smile. "Now you're going to have us playing detective too."

"Why not?" Guttman asked. "It could be fun, in a way."

Six

There was no discussion of the case that night. Lois and Michael left shortly after dinner to attend a P.T.A. meeting, and Guttman helped Joseph put the baby to bed and then sat with the boys while they watched television. He was never quite sure whether he was the baby-sitter, or if Lois relied on Joseph to make sure that everything was all right. Probably both, he decided. Joseph to make sure everything for the baby is done right, and me just in case Joseph gets worried being alone in the house at night. At twelve, Joseph was responsible, but, Guttman thought, this way Lois knows he goes to sleep when he's supposed to.

In the morning she drove him to the Center without mentioning the detective business, although Guttman expected some comment, since he'd again dressed up to look right for his visit to Armstrong Industries. He wasn't quite sure whether or not Lois was still a little upset with him.

He found Mishkin sitting alone in the lounge. It was a little past nine, and although he'd hoped that Lois would drop him off first, he hadn't said anything when she explained she had to pick up one of David's classmates, which meant they'd have to go there first, then to the school so the boys wouldn't be late, and then to the nursery school to leave Sara before going to the Center.

"Nu, so where is everybody?" he asked Mishkin.

"Everybody is busy," Mishkin said. "Mrs. Stone is getting jobs for Mrs. Kaplan and Mrs. O'Rourke, they're supposed to go to the personnel office at the company right away, and Mrs. Stone is getting a car for us, too, I guess."

"We could go in the same car and save a trip," Guttman said.

"I don't know about it. You said you wanted I should go, so I'm ready." For the first time Guttman noticed that Mishkin wasn't wearing his usual sport shirt. Today he had a white shirt on, and a sport jacket that looked just a little too big for him. Maybe, Guttman thought, what he was saying about losing weight is true, even though he still looks big.

"I got a tie in the pocket," Mishkin said. "I didn't want to put it on until I was sure, but since you're wearing one . . ."

"I figured it would look better," Guttman said. "I guess I should go over and find out what's what."

"Carstairs was there too. Everybody was running around right after breakfast. Mrs. Kaplan came early today."

Mrs. Kaplan, Guttman thought, probably told her Phyllis that she had to be there early, and that was that. With him and Lois, it was different. "Okay, so I better go find out what's happening," he said again.

Mishkin shrugged and began shuffling a deck of cards. He had a game of solitaire laid out in front of him when Guttman returned a little later.

"So what happened?" Mishkin asked.

"Nothing. This Armstrong we're supposed to talk to, the boss, he ain't gonna be in the office today. Mrs. Stone made the arrangements for Mrs. Kaplan and Mrs. O'Rourke, they left already, but we can't talk to anybody, at least until tomorrow."

"It's only a Wednesday," Mishkin said. "How come he ain't in his office?"

"He's got to go to a meeting or something."

"So we'll see him tomorrow."

"Mrs. Stone's gonna call again. Carstairs already went to the bank for the credit-checking stuff. He went in the car with the women."

"You want to play some pinochle?" Mishkin asked.

"Maybe in a while. Since we're not going any place, maybe I'll read the papers first."

Guttman settled himself in a comfortable chair in the library and began looking through the morning paper. He found it difficult to concentrate, though, and after a few minutes decided to go outside and see if Mr. Bowsenior wanted to play some bocce. He stood in the sun for a moment, watching the usual quartet of croquet players, once again wondering what there was to the game that kept them playing almost every day. Guttman had never really understood what people liked about golf, either, except that there was lots of walking, which was good exercise. When he reached the bocce court no one was there, and he decided that a little practice might help anyway.

Half an hour later he went back inside. Something was still bothering him, and he wasn't sure what it was. It was time to light a cigar, to sit quietly and to think. The library was still empty.

Okay, he told himself after he had his cigar burning properly, so now it's time to think already. It's the mystery business again. There's something about it what bothers, and you might as well figure out what it is so you don't walk around just feeling funny, he told himself. Even if you don't get an answer, maybe you'll know what the question is.

You're scared, he thought. And then he said it out loud. "You're scared, Guttman." Okay. So now, what is there to be scared about? You worried somebody's gonna come with a gun and shoot you, like Vincent? No, it's not that. It could happen, I suppose, but it don't worry me. Not now, anyway. Maybe later, if I ever find out anything. He chewed on his cigar and then took it from his mouth to remove a piece of tobacco from his tongue.

If I ever find out anything, he repeated to himself. That's the thing. All of a sudden you get this big idea that you don't know what you're doing. Congratulations, Guttman. Some smart guy. You wait until you're in the middle of something, telling people to do things, sending Mrs. Kaplan and Mrs. O'Rourke to work even, and now you start to worry you don't know what you're doing. Oy, such thinking.

Nu, so what are you scared of? You're scared you're gonna look stupid, right? You solved one mystery, you was involved in figuring out another, so you went ahead now and you're in the middle of a new one. Only you don't know if you could figure it out. And you're scared you're gonna look stupid. So why didn't you think about that before you got started?

Now you got Mrs. Stone, she's counting on you to get her granddaughter out of jail, except she don't really believe you could do it. And she was trying to trick you, saying how she's dying and only got a couple months to live. And the girl, she ain't exactly the nicest person you ever met, either, he reminded himself. So it's not them what bothers you so much. It's the others. You got Lois at home thinking her father's so old he don't think good any more, and now you ain't so sure she's wrong. And even worse, you got Mishkin, all dressed up, and Mrs. Kaplan and Mrs. O'Rourke, out working on jobs to be detectives, and . . . and you got Miss Brady too. They all come to you and say, 'Here, Guttman, solve the mystery.' And you, you like an idiot, you say sure. Why not? What's so hard about solving a murder? Oy . . .

Guttman crushed the half-smoked cigar in an ashtray and got up from his chair. He walked to the windows and looked out across the lawn to the row of trees that shielded the private cottages from the main house. If I don't solve the mystery, I'm afraid everybody's gonna think I'm dumb. No, he admitted, that ain't it. It's worse. It's my . . . my self-respect. My ego, the way Lois calls it. I like it the way everybody says Guttman will take care of it. Guttman will solve the mystery. I like it the way people look up to me with something like this. I like it, and I'm afraid they wouldn't do it no more if I can't find the answers. Okay, he sighed. So now you know what's bothering you, he thought. Only it don't help.

He jammed his hands into his pockets and started to walk from the library, only to stop at the door. Walking around ain't gonna solve anything, he told himself. You're in the middle of something you put yourself into, and now you got to get yourself out. Or else maybe you just live with it.

The worst thing that could happen, he told himself, is you don't find out who killed Vincent. So then the lawyers could still get Susan out in the trial, and what really bothers you, anyway, is everybody would say Guttman's dumb. Lois makes fun about it, and . . . and that's about it, he realized. Mishkin wouldn't think I'm any different, and Mrs. Kaplan it don't matter so much what she thinks. She's a nice lady, but she makes too big a fuss anyway. And Mrs. O'Rourke only thinks what Mrs. Kaplan thinks. Carstairs wasn't so hot to do this in the first place, and besides, he ain't the kind to make fun. So I'd feel bad about Susan, especially if she didn't get free after the trial. And, he reminded himself, there was still Miss Brady. It did make a difference to him what she thought. That was something, he decided, that he'd have to think about a little more.

Mishkin was still in the lounge, playing solitaire, when Guttman suggested a game of pinochle—but only if they could play outside. "It's too nice a day to be inside all the time." Mishkin agreed.

After lunch Guttman said he didn't feel like playing cards any more for a while, and he went outside, strolling aimlessly, until he had crossed the lawn and reached the trees on the far side. Then he realized where he was going. He hesitated for a moment before knocking on the door, and then, when there was no answer immediately, wondered whether to knock again. Now that he was there, he wasn't so sure he wanted to be. But he knocked anyway, louder.

Margaret Brady came to the door carrying a cup in one hand and a book in the other. "Like some coffee?" she asked. "It's instant."

"No, thank you. I just had, with my lunch," Guttman told her.

She sat down on the couch, putting her book on the coffee table in front of her, and began fishing in the pocket of her sweater for a cigarette. After a moment Guttman sat down in one of the wicker armchairs.

"There's another ashtray on the table next to you," she said, dropping a match into a nearly full ashtray on the table. "Sure you don't want some coffee?"

"I'm sure," Guttman said, unwrapping a cigar.

"I saw Jessica this morning, so I knew our trip downtown was off," Miss Brady said. "Figured I'd catch up on some correspondence. I'm terrible. I've got letters a month old that I haven't answered."

"A month don't seem like such a long time," Guttman said. He had rarely written to anyone since his son, Joseph, had died during the war. With Lois they had used the telephone, but still, a month didn't seem like too long to him.

"Well, I don't like to let things pile up," Miss Brady said. "So when I was through I figured I might as well have my cottage cheese and salad here, as in the dining room, and then I thought I'd read for a while. It just felt like a lazy day."

"It's quiet," Guttman agreed. Margaret Brady looked at him for a moment, and then she smiled. Guttman thought she looked surprisingly young when she smiled.

"If you want to talk, fine," she said. "Or if you'd rather read, you can take anything that interests you from the shelf . . ."

"I guess it's talk," Guttman said. "Only I'm not a hundred percent positive. I guess I'm upset about this . . . case."

"How so?"

"I'm not so sure we could solve it," Guttman admitted.

"I see." She seemed to be thinking for a moment. "Did you worry about that the last time, you know, with Miss Walters?"

"Not exactly. But then it was different. Then nobody else was doing anything, and also, nobody was expecting us to do anything either. All we had to do then was try at least."

"That's all you have to do now," Margaret Brady said quietly. "Just try. That's all anyone can do."

Guttman looked at her for a moment, then shook his head and smiled. "So simple," he said. She smiled back at him.

"Maybe a cup of tea, instead of coffee, would be nice. If it's not trouble," he said.

"Coming up."

Of course it was simple, he thought. Simple to say and simple to understand. But feeling it, that was a little harder. Still, it made sense. It's always nice to do something, what you was trying to do. But nobody could do everything, he told himself. And you could never be sure, no matter what, how something's gonna turn out when you start. Even cutting to a pattern, after all those years, sometimes you could make a mistake, he reminded himself. By the time Miss Brady returned with a mug of tea for him, Guttman felt better.

"There was something else I was thinking about," he said after she was settled again on the couch. "I'm not so sure of it, though, so talking out loud could help."

"Shoot."

"Well, that's what it's about, really."

"What?"

"Shooting," Guttman said with a smile. "The thing is, Susan said the gun was kept hidden."

"Uh-huh."

"So that means, according to the police, only somebody what knew where it was could've killed Vincent."

"Right," Miss Brady said.

"Well, that makes it sound to me like whoever killed Vincent might not have gone there to kill him."

"I'm not sure I follow you."

"Well, let's say it wasn't somebody what knew where the gun was, okay? Because the only person who knew, according to the police, is Susan, and we're figuring she didn't kill Vincent."

"Okay."

"So, also let's say it's possible, without the struggle and all, that Vincent could've had the gun out himself and the killer took it away. It still means the killer probably didn't go there to shoot him. Because the thing is, if you go to kill somebody, would you figure you could borrow a gun when you got there?"

"I see . . ." Miss Brady said. "That makes a lot of sense.

Except . . . What if Vincent had the gun, and the killer had his own gun and got the drop on Vincent, and then—"

"I don't think this is like the movies," Guttman said. "Let's say you got a gun and you're gonna kill somebody. And then that person all of a sudden also has a gun. So what do you do?"

"Shoot," Miss Brady said. "Of course. Psychologically they'd be set to kill him anyway, so they wouldn't hesitate."

"That's the way I figured it," Guttman said. Of course, he hadn't figured it in exactly those words, but . . .

"Well, where does that leave us?"

"I'm not positive," Guttman said. "But now, instead of thinking just who wanted to kill Vincent, we could think about who could've been at the apartment, maybe found the gun by accident, and then could've gotten mad enough to shoot all of a sudden. But not that it had to be planned."

"Spur of the moment," Miss Brady said. "But there's still the question of how they got the gun. Of course, it could have been that someone was looking for something else."

"Or maybe, also, Susan wasn't the only one what knew where it was," Guttman suggested. "Everybody says how Vincent and his wife lived their separate ways. He had girl friends before Susan. If she knew about the gun, probably they did too."

"I'll bet they did," Miss Brady said. "If Vincent showed off to her, he probably did to every woman he met. It's phallic, you know."

"No," Guttman said. "I didn't."

"Well, *cherchez la femme.*"

"I beg your pardon?"

"Find the woman," Miss Brady explained.

"Do you think Susan would know about it?"

"Maybe, but somehow I don't think so. She might have said something about it if she did."

"Well, maybe Mrs. Kaplan and Mrs. O'Rourke could learn something about it."

"It's only their first day on the job," Miss Brady reminded him.

"I know, but with Mrs. Kaplan usually it don't take long for her to learn things about people," Guttman said. "She's got a knack."

"True. But even if she doesn't come up with anything right away, we have the other angle to work on."

"What angle?"

"That we could be looking for someone who had any kind of grudge against Vincent, not just someone who'd plan a murder. Just enough of a grudge to fly off the handle and pull the trigger."

"So now we could wait," Guttman said. "At least until tomorrow."

"I guess so. Feel like a game of chess?" Miss Brady asked.

At four o'clock Guttman left the cottage and walked to Mrs. Stone's similar, but larger, cottage. The nurse answered the door and then went into the other room, leaving him with Mrs. Stone. She was sitting in her wheelchair this time.

"I just come to check on what's happening tomorrow," Guttman told her.

"The car will be here at nine tomorrow morning. Philip Armstrong is expecting you at nine-thirty."

"Thank you," Guttman said. "But could you make it maybe an hour later?"

"Why?"

"Because I don't know if Mr. Carstairs will come back before I got to go home today, and that way I could talk to him in the morning, for sure."

"All right. The car will be here at ten. I'll tell Philip to expect you at ten-thirty."

"Thank you." He started to leave, then decided to tell her about their research at the apartment where Harry Vincent had been killed. It might make her feel better, he thought, if it seemed as if they'd accomplished something. When he was through he suggested that she could tell the lawyer about it, if he hadn't worked it out himself already. Mrs. Stone said she would, but she didn't seem very impressed.

He found Mishkin in the lounge, as usual, and sat down with

him. "Tomorrow at ten o'clock we'll take the car and go see the man Vincent worked for," Guttman told him.

"I got to get dressed up again?" Mishkin asked.

"I don't think you got to wear the tie."

"Are you gonna wear one?"

"I don't know. Maybe."

"I'll see too. I could always keep it in my pocket," Mishkin said.

"You ain't seen Carstairs, did you?"

"No."

"When he comes back tonight, tell him we should have a meeting tomorrow morning. At nine o'clock," Guttman instructed.

"How about Mrs. O'Rourke? Mrs. Kaplan would probably go home, but Mrs. O'Rourke lives here," Mishkin said.

"I know. If she learned anything with Mrs. Kaplan today, she should tell you. But they'll probably have to go back to work a couple more days anyway. The first day on the job you wouldn't expect they'd get too many secrets."

"With Mrs. Kaplan you can't be sure," Mishkin said.

"I know. So we'll find out tomorrow."

Seven

Mishkin, Mr. Carstairs and Miss Brady were waiting for him when Guttman arrived at the Golden Valley Senior Citizens' Center a little after nine the next morning. Guttman got a cup of coffee and joined them at the table.

"So, how did it go yesterday?" Guttman asked Mr. Carstairs.

"Quite well, really. But I am glad that we knew of Mr. Vincent's gambling before I began."

"Why's that?" Guttman asked.

"Well, if not for that, I wouldn't have been able to find any reason for him to be concerned about finances," Mr. Carstairs explained.

"You mean there was nothing on the credit check?"

"Only that his credit was good." Mr. Carstairs opened his small notebook and adjusted his glasses. "There was no unusual activity in Mr. Vincent's accounts, which were joint, by the way, with Mrs. Vincent, and—"

"You mean you were able to see his bank accounts?" Miss Brady asked. "I thought they were confidential."

"Naturally," Mr. Carstairs explained. "That's why Mrs. Stone's assistance was important. Without that, no one would have allowed me to do my research. It is somewhat irregular."

"Go ahead, Mr. Carstairs," Guttman suggested.

"The checking account had a reasonable balance, and although the Vincents' savings account was small, there weren't any withdrawals for the past several months, and nothing substantial prior to that. What money they had was invested, mostly in bonds, with some stock holdings as well. According to the records I was able to check—fortunately, the bank people knew the Vincents' broker as well—everything was held jointly by Mr. and Mrs. Vincent. They lived well, but not, it would seem, excessively. But if Mr. Vincent needed money, then it wasn't reflected by his holdings, if you see what I mean."

"I think so," Guttman said. "But you mentioned everything was joint. That could mean that maybe if he lost money gambling, his wife wouldn't let him take from the accounts to pay it."

"Her permission would be necessary for them to sell the stocks and bonds," Carstairs said, "but it wouldn't be required for him to have made bank withdrawals."

"So maybe he didn't want his wife to know," Mishkin said. "Lots of people, when they're gambling, don't want their wives to know."

"I guess we'll have to have a talk with Mrs. Vincent, before long," Miss Brady said.

"She might not've known about the gambling, like Mishkin says," Guttman said. "But now we're talking about it, I'm just thinking, Vincent had this apartment, where everything happened, and he and his wife also had to live someplace . . ."

"They owned a fairly expensive house," Mr. Carstairs said. "There's a mortgage, but only a first mortgage. Still, the upkeep, according to the figures, was sizable."

"How sizable?" Miss Brady asked.

"Sufficient to make me inquire, through Mrs. Stone, last evening about Mr. Vincent's salary at Armstrong Industries. It would have been very difficult for him to support both residences on the basis of what he earned," Mr. Carstairs noted.

"So you thought of the same thing," Guttman said.

"I try to be thorough."

"And you are," Guttman told him. "This is good information to have."

"Is there anything else you'd like me to look into?" Mr. Carstairs asked.

"I couldn't think of anything at the moment. But maybe when we talk to these people today we could come up with something. Meanwhile, the car's going to be here in a little while, and I got to make a phone call first."

He left them at the table and went into the main lounge, to the pay phone, where he dialed the number for Donald Eliot that Mrs. Stone had given him. There was no answer.

They ran into what the driver said was unusually heavy traffic, and it was just ten-thirty when they arrived at Armstrong Industries, a two-story building on the edge of the city, in an area that was commercial but not run-down. The driver pulled the limousine into the short oval driveway and stopped at the front entrance. Guttman had the door open before the driver could get there to assist him. A chauffeur, he had decided, was one thing. A servant was another. He wasn't so helpless he couldn't get out of a car by himself.

He could see several trucks at the far end of the parking lot, near a loading dock, but he had no idea of whether that indicated activity for the company or not. Producing electronic components was a business that Guttman knew nothing about. In the garment business there were always trucks making deliveries and picking things up, even when a firm was about to go out of business. A little store, he thought, you could tell how they was doing by watching if people came in a lot. But in the garment business, it was different. And with electronics . . . He shrugged mentally.

"I'll wait here," Mishkin announced from the back seat of the car.

"What do you mean?" Guttman asked.

"I mean I'll stay here while you go inside."

"What kind of thing is this? We got to see Mr. Armstrong. We're late already," Guttman told him.

"So go see. You don't need me for that."

"Mishkin, what is this?"

"Go, Guttman, or you'll be late."

Guttman looked at Miss Brady, then back at Mishkin. "You like it in the car so much, with the radio and everything, you don't want to come out?"

"You don't need me for this," Mishkin repeated.

"You could help," Guttman told him.

"I could also sit here."

"Mishkin, we ain't got time to argue. Already we're gonna be late, and Mr. Armstrong runs the whole company, he don't have time probably to sit around and wait for us."

"So stop arguing and go. I'll stay here."

Guttman looked helplessly at Miss Brady, but she could only shrug her shoulders. Oy, he thought. Temperaments I need. He shook his head and looked into the car again, but Mishkin was looking the other way.

"We'll see you later," Guttman told him, unable to think of anything else to say. "I don't understand," he told Miss Brady as they walked to the front door of the building.

"Maybe he just felt out of place."

"This ain't exactly my kind of place either."

"Well, Mr. Mishkin has been at the Center for a few years now. Living there we tend to, well, lose some of our confidence. We become reluctant to get out, to involve ourselves in new things."

"If he felt that way, why did he come in the first place?" Guttman asked, still annoyed.

"Maybe he just got cold feet," Miss Brady suggested, allowing him to open the door for her.

Philip Armstrong's office wasn't as impressive as Guttman expected a company president's to be. Unlike Gordon Richardson, Armstrong worked at an ordinary-sized desk, in a room without wood paneling and soft lighting. Fluorescent bulbs were built into the ceiling, and instead of oil paintings, Armstrong decorated his walls with pictures of his company's products, large color photographs of transistors against clear backgrounds, or against a black that made them look as if they were floating in space. Armstrong himself would have looked out of place in Gordon Richardson's office, Guttman thought.

He was in his mid-fifties, short and heavy-set, balding and with a somewhat harried look about him, as if he wasn't quite sure what might happen to him next. Guttman and Miss Brady sat on a small couch in one corner of the office, while Armstrong leaned forward in a chair placed at right angles to them. The coffee table in front of them was glass, with chrome legs.

"I'm sorry if we're late," Guttman said after they had shaken hands, "but there was some traffic. The driver said there must have been an accident."

"You're not late," Armstrong said. "Besides, I've got enough paper work here to keep me busy the rest of the week, let alone the morning." He looked over at his desk and shook his head. "Every now and then I wonder why I ever put myself behind a desk."

"Oh?" Guttman wasn't sure what he meant.

"Life was simpler when all I had to do was boss a production line. But I had to get ambitious, decide to go into business for myself. Now I worry. Every day I worry. Been like that for fifteen years. You ever hear of Murphy's law?"

"No," Guttman said, wondering whether it was a new television show.

"Is that the one that says if something can go wrong, it will?" Miss Brady asked.

"That's the one. Except they ought to call it Armstrong's law."

"The business got problems?" Guttman asked.

"No. No, things are going fine, as a matter of fact," Armstrong said, smiling. "But I worry anyway. Sooner or later, something will go wrong. That's the thing, you see. A boss has to worry about these things." He glanced over at his desk again. "Well, anyway, what can I do for you?"

"I don't know how much Mrs. Stone told you," Guttman began.

"That you two were helping her with . . . Susan's situation."

"Well, we're trying. The thing is, we're trying to find out now whatever we can about Harry Vincent," Guttman explained.

"Why?"

"Well, for Mrs. Stone . . . That is, if Susan didn't kill him, then somebody else must've."

"Makes sense," Armstrong said.

"And the only way to figure out who it was is for us to learn as much as we can about Vincent," Guttman continued.

"Uh-huh. And that's why you have your spies here in the office, right?" Armstrong said. "Jessica didn't exactly say that, but I figured it had to be something besides a couple of old women who needed part-time work. Okay, so what can I tell you?" And then, without waiting for an answer, he went on. "Harry came to work here about a year and a half ago. He'd worked for another firm in the area, not exactly a competitor but more or less the same kind of business."

"Why did he quit?" Miss Brady asked. "Or did he?"

"He quit. And he came over here for the best of reasons. Money. Harry figured he could earn more working for me. And he did," Armstrong added. "As I said, that was about a year and a half ago. Six months ago he was promoted to assistant sales manager. He was a good salesman, Harry."

"You must be upset about . . . losing him," Guttman said.

"Armstrong's law. I told you." He rubbed his hand across his forehead. "It hurts, of course. But fortunately, we've got plenty of business to keep us going for a while . . ."

"I guess you'll have to hire somebody else," Guttman said.

"Yeah. We're looking now. But we're not likely to get someone as good as Harry. Not unless we get very lucky."

"It could hurt the business eventually, huh?"

Armstrong looked at him for a moment, then smiled. "You know, Jessica said you were coming down here about Susan, but it sounds like you're checking up for her, trying to find out what shape we're in."

"Mr. Armstrong, I don't think you understand—"

"It's okay," Armstrong said, interrupting Miss Brady. "Jessica owns a chunk of the operation, she's entitled to know."

"Mr. Armstrong, Mr. Guttman and I are simply trying to find out whatever we can about Mr. Vincent. Believe me, we're not reporting back to Mrs. Stone on your situation. I'm sure there are accountants and auditors to see to that," Miss Brady said.

"Listen, if Jessica wants you two to ask around, it's okay with me. I don't mind. I'm not hiding anything from her."

Guttman looked at Miss Brady, and she raised her eyebrows but didn't say anything. He couldn't help wondering why Armstrong was so sensitive about things, but it probably wasn't any of his business. He decided to change the subject.

"Mr. Armstrong, was you and Vincent friendly?" he asked.

"We got along."

"Well, I mean, like was you friends outside of work?"

"No, not really."

"You must have gotten together socially once in a while," Miss Brady said.

"Why?"

"Pardon?"

"Why must we have gotten together?" Armstrong asked. "Never mind. Yeah, a couple of times. But it was mostly business. You know, maybe a client was in town and Harry and I took him to dinner. My wife and I had him and his wife over to dinner . . . twice, I think. Once when he first started here. But I don't socialize much with the people who work for me. Kind of a general policy, you might say."

"You knew his wife?" Guttman asked.

"I know her, sure. Well, I've met her. Vivian's been to the house."

"Did they get along okay?"

"How would I know?" Armstrong asked.

"Well, I thought maybe you could tell by seeing them together . . ."

"They got along okay, I guess."

"Mr. Armstrong, you said you wanted to cooperate, for Mrs. Stone's sake," Miss Brady said. "We know that Mr. Vincent and his wife weren't very close."

"Okay," Armstrong said. "I guess I just don't like talking about things that really aren't any of my business, that's all. But it was common knowledge. I mean, like Harry and Susan. I find out that just about everyone in the place knew about it except me."

"You didn't know they was having . . . a relationship?" Guttman asked.

"No. I told you, I don't like to get involved with my employees' private affairs. But if I had known, I'd have put a stop to it. I would have tried, anyway."

"Why, if you don't like to get involved in their personal affairs?" Miss Brady asked.

"Because of Jessica. If she found out, she wouldn't have been very happy with me."

"She knows about it now, though," Miss Brady told him.

"Yeah, and I don't imagine she's very pleased, either."

"You was saying, about Vincent and his wife . . ." Guttman prompted.

"Yeah. Well, I mean, I knew Harry played around, you know, but like I said, I didn't know about him and Susan. But you know how it is, people talk, so I knew that Harry and Vivian weren't exactly close, but I figured what the hell, so long as he did his job, the rest was none of my business, you know."

"Naturally. But do you know if maybe they had fights?" Guttman asked.

"What married couple don't? But, well, the thing is, Harry didn't try to hide what he was doing, you know? Like if a customer showed up and I had to take him to dinner, I'd always have to go through this song and dance with my wife. But not Harry. He just came and went as he pleased."

"Did she like that arrangement?" Miss Brady asked.

"I don't know. I guess she accepted it," Armstrong said.

"Mr. Armstrong, how many salespeople do you have?" Guttman asked.

"Well, there's five, really. That is, five here. But I've got some regional representatives too. They don't actually work for me, that is, they're not on salary, but they represent us on a commission basis. Most of our business is here on the West Coast, you see."

"Was Vincent the newest one?" Guttman asked.

"As a matter of fact, no. We've got one kid, hired him a couple of months ago, fresh out of school . . ."

"Mr. Vincent was promoted rather quickly, wasn't he?" Miss Brady asked.

"Like I said, Harry was a good man."

"Could there have been some resentment on the part of one of your other salespeople, perhaps someone with seniority?"

"You'd have to talk to Nick Forester about that. Nick's my sales manager. If there was any, well, friction, he'd have taken care of it. He's the one who actually promoted Harry, a little while after he took over the manager spot, when my last man left. Retired." Armstrong waited, looking at them. "Anything else?"

"I don't think so," Guttman said. "Not now, anyways. Except, we should talk to this Mr. Forester, then."

"Sure. Uh . . . Look, Jessica's convinced that Susan didn't kill Harry, and I want you to know I hope she's right. Jessica can be a pain sometimes, but, well, she and her husband, I don't know whether you ever knew him . . ."

Guttman shook his head, as did Miss Brady.

"Well, they helped me out a couple of times, helped me get started, saw me through some rocky times, and anyway, well, I hope you come up with something that helps. That's all."

"Thank you," Guttman said. "We already got some ideas, so you never know."

"Oh yeah? What kind of ideas?" Armstrong asked.

"It's too soon to talk about them," Guttman told him. "It could be nothing. You can't tell until later."

"Okay. I didn't mean to pry. But if I can help, just ask."

Armstrong took them to the door and told his secretary that Mr. Forester was expecting them, and then shook hands with each of them again. Guttman wished that he could have had a few minutes to think about their interview, but it would have to wait.

Nick Forester was vice-president and sales manager of Armstrong Industries, according to the lettering on his office door. And he was on the telephone when Guttman and Miss

Brady were ushered into his office. He waved them to seats and continued to talk quietly for five minutes, by Guttman's estimate. Forester was in his early forties, wearing a plaid suit that Guttman's eye told him was expensive but not made to order. The pale-blue shirt and darker tie also looked expensive, although tasteful. The longer Forester stayed on the phone, the more restless Guttman became. Finally, after watching Miss Brady light a cigarette and pull an ashtray over to her side of the desk, Guttman decided that he could smoke too. The smell of his cigar might have encouraged Forester to end his phone call.

"Sorry about that," he told them as he adjusted himself in his chair and leaned forward slightly, hands folded on the desk. "Business," he added unnecessarily. They'd been able to get that much from what they could hear of the conversation.

"We're sorry to be bothering you when you're busy," Guttman apologized.

"Well, it won't take too long, will it?" Forester said it as if he was telling them, rather than asking.

"Not too long," Miss Brady said. "As I'm sure you know, Mr. Armstrong arranged that we speak to you, as a favor to Mrs. Stone."

"Yes, I know. But I don't think I'm going to be able to tell you anything about Harry that will help Susan. I wish I could, but . . ." He shrugged.

"I guess, with Vincent dead, it means a lot of extra work for you," Guttman said.

"Not too much, really." Forester took a cigarette from a silver box on his desk, tapped it lightly, and then used a matching lighter.

"We understood that Mr. Vincent was your assistant. Surely that would mean some additional work for you, things which you used to delegate to him," Miss Brady suggested.

"Oh, a little. But the title was more or less for show. Kind of a reward."

"A reward?"

"A step up the corporate ladder," Forester said. "I know. I was assistant sales manager myself for a while. It helped me handle this job, but so far as Harry is concerned, well, I have someone else doing most of the administrative things he handled."

"Who would that be?" Guttman asked.

"Dave Hiller. He's pretty familiar with the operation."

"You don't seem very upset about Vincent dying," Guttman said.

"Professionally, I'm not, if that's what you're asking."

"I was thinking personally, too."

"Well, hell, nobody likes to see anyone die, really. But I wasn't close to Harry, so it isn't really a personal loss. That makes me sound cold-blooded, doesn't it?" Forester looked at Guttman for a moment. "I'm not, really, but I don't like to pretend about these things."

That, Guttman thought, was an interesting thing for a salesman to say. The salesmen he'd known were always pretending about one thing or another. He remembered someone saying once that salesmen would be good actors, or maybe it was the other way around.

"Since you don't like pretending," Guttman said, "maybe I could ask if you liked Vincent?"

"Not particularly," Forester said easily.

"How come?"

"Call it personality differences. Oh, I didn't actually dislike Harry, but we weren't close. We got along on a business level."

"That must have been hard sometimes," Guttman suggested.

"Why?"

"Well, if you had a customer and you had to entertain him, or something, and you was with Vincent at the same time, well . . ."

"As I said, Mr. . . ."

"Guttman."

"As I said, Mr. Guttman, I didn't feel an active dislike for Harry. We just weren't close, that's all."

"Mr. Forester, you said something about the assistant sales manager position being a stepping stone, I believe . . ." Miss Brady said.

"More or less."

"And was it, that is, would it have been a stepping stone to your job?" she asked.

"Eventually," Forester said, smiling. "But by the time Harry was ready for my job, if he ever was, I would have been promoted myself. Harry wasn't a threat to me, if that's what you're suggesting. And since you two are here because of this business with Susan, I might as well tell you that I didn't kill Harry. No reason to."

"But you wouldn't have killed him, even with a reason, would you?" Guttman asked.

"No, I wouldn't," Forester said.

"Since you and Vincent weren't close," Miss Brady said, "I don't suppose you'd know much about his personal life, would you?"

"Not much, no."

"But a little?" Guttman asked.

"A little," Forester conceded.

"Do you know how he and his wife got along? I mean, do you know for sure if she knew he was . . . about Susan, for example?"

"She knew he was playing around, but I don't know whether she knew about Susan specifically. I don't think it mattered very much, though."

"It didn't matter?"

"Harry always had some girl on the string. And if he was between regulars, he had some girls he could just call up and see when he felt like it. I'm sure Vivian knew that much. I know she did."

"How do you know?" Miss Brady asked.

"Harry told me."

"He talked to you about this?" Guttman asked.

"Bragged, is more like it. Harry was always trying to impress people. Every now and then he'd even offer to fix me up," Forester added.

"But you didn't accept," Guttman said.

"No, I didn't. There are enough problems making a marriage

work in my kind of business, without inviting trouble. Traveling, weird hours, having to take visiting firemen out at night . . ."

"Did Vincent want your job?" Guttman asked.

"Sure."

"And it didn't bother you?"

"If it bothered me, I wouldn't have made him my assistant," Forester said.

"Mr. Forest, maybe you—"

"Forester."

"Mr. Forester, I'm sorry, but maybe you could tell us, did you know if Vincent had any special problems, like money?"

"No . . . not that I know of. Oh, once in a while he'd borrow a couple of bucks, but he always paid it back. You know, it's easy to run short in this business. You use credit cards mostly, but maybe you're at a place where they want cash, so you have to lay it out, and then you're a little short for a couple of days."

"How about woman problems?" Miss Brady asked. "If Mr. Vincent was a womanizer, as you indicate, perhaps he had some difficulties?"

"Beating them off with a stick was his only problem," Forester said. "That is, if you believed Harry. Womanizer," he repeated. "I'm trying to remember the last time I heard anyone use that phrase."

"About a minute ago," Guttman told him, coming to Miss Brady's defense. "But you didn't answer, was there any special problems?"

"No . . . Well, there was . . ." Forester shook his head.

"Go ahead, please," Miss Brady asked.

"Well, before he started seeing Susan Eliot, Harry was going out with one of the other girls here. She worked for him at the time."

"What happened?"

"Harry got tired of her, I guess."

"Did he fire her?" Guttman asked.

"No . . . No, as I recall, about the time Harry dropped her she moved into another department. Carole Edwards, that's her name. But if you're thinking she had anything to do with Harry's death, you're barking up the wrong tree."

"We wasn't barking at anything, yet," Guttman told him. "But why do you think it would be wrong?"

"Well, Carole and Dave Hiller kind of have a thing going now. Matter of fact, my secretary told me they're engaged. I haven't talked to Dave about it, this was just a little while ago, maybe two weeks, and she said it was supposed to be a secret . . ."

"Hiller's the one you made the new assistant sales manager?" Guttman asked.

"Uh-huh."

"I was just thinking," Guttman said, "you made Vincent the assistant I guess when you got your job, is that right?" Forester nodded. "But he wasn't here for such a long time, then. And maybe there was somebody else what wanted the job, that could've been jealous . . ."

"Mr. Guttman," Forester said patiently, "if you're seriously looking for someone who had a motive to kill Harry, I don't think that's where you're going to find it. I mean, you're talking about murder. That's a pretty strong reaction to someone beating you out of a job, especially six months after it happens."

"Mr. Forester, when you start with nothing, you look into everything," Margaret Brady said. "Would it be that this Mr. Hiller was in line for the job originally?"

"It would be," Forester sighed. "And I suppose you want to talk to him?"

"It could help if we could," Guttman said. "Also the girl you mentioned, his intended."

"I'll check." Forester picked up the phone and spoke quietly, then waited, looking at them and drumming his fingers on the desk until it buzzed for him. He listened for a moment, then hung up.

"Carole Edwards isn't in today. She called in sick. And Dave's out of the office, although his secretary expects him back about one-thirty."

"Could we make an appointment to see him then?" Miss Brady asked.

Forester sighed and picked up the phone again. "Okay," he told them when he had hung up. "Dave's secretary says he's clear, and she wrote you in for one-thirty. But he might be a little late. And if he's made another appointment without letting her know . . ."

"We appreciate your help, Mr. Forester," Miss Brady said. "As you can imagine, Mrs. Stone is terribly concerned about Susan being in jail. It isn't pleasant."

"Oh?" Forester said. "Have you been in jail?"

"As a matter of fact, I have. Nothing quite so nice as what Susan is going through. Mine was more of a prison camp." She rose quickly and Guttman followed her.

Margaret Brady didn't stop until she was standing outside the front door of the building. "It would have pleased me to hit that smug, lying little . . ." She shook her head. "I have a terrible temper," she said.

"I didn't like him so much, either," Guttman said. He smiled at her until she managed to smile back.

"It was silly of me to blow up like that," she said.

"It's even more silly, sometimes, to put up with somebody like that. Like when he plays games as if he can't think of who this girl is, and then knows she's engaged to this Hiller person . . ." Guttman loosened his tie and looked at his watch. "Well, we got plenty of time for lunch, anyway," he said. "And by now Mishkin must be starving, if he didn't fall asleep in the car."

Eight

Mishkin was missing. It took them a moment to locate the limousine in the parking lot, but finally Miss Brady recognized the chauffeur leaning against the fender, reading a newspaper. She started to get into the car as he held the back door for her, then stopped halfway in and slowly backed out.

"Where's Mr. Mishkin?" she asked.

"The gentleman said he had some business," the driver told them.

"He had some business?" Guttman repeated. "What kind of business? Where?"

"I don't know, sir."

"You don't know? But where did he go? He just walked away?" Guttman asked, incredulous.

"No, sir. I drove him to the bus stop. I offered to drive him wherever he was going, but he said he just wanted the bus stop."

"The bus stop?"

"Which bus?" Miss Brady asked.

"The bus to the city, ma'am," the driver replied politely.

"What time? When?" Guttman asked.

"A few minutes after you went inside. Maybe a quarter of an hour."

"Tell us exactly what happened, please," Miss Brady said.

"The gentleman just sat in the back for a few minutes, and

then he asked me if I knew where he could get a bus to the city. So I drove him there and he got out, and then I came back here."

"Did he say anything, any message?"

"Yes, sir. He said to tell you he'd return to the Center later."

Guttman looked at Miss Brady and shook his head. "It's my fault," he said. "I shouldn't've insisted he come along. He didn't want to, and I said he should."

"Well, it's certainly nothing to get so upset about," Miss Brady said. "Mr. Mishkin's quite capable of taking a bus back to the Center whenever he's through with whatever he had to do."

"I know, but I can't help feeling responsible."

"I'm only surprised he didn't mention it to us before. I suppose he didn't think of it until after we went inside."

"I guess so," Guttman said, unconvinced. Then, after a moment, "I guess we better get some lunch anyway."

The driver was able to recommend a diner only a few minutes away. Guttman invited him to join them, but he said he'd eaten earlier and preferred to wait in the car. After they'd been seated in a booth alongside the window, and had given their orders to the waitress, Guttman forced his mind off Mishkin's strange disappearance and onto what they had learned that morning. Miss Brady smoked a cigarette and watched him. Guttman tried not to notice.

Armstrong, he thought, seemed like he was okay. The other one, Forester, he just didn't like. Neither did Miss Brady. And Guttman didn't believe that Forester just didn't care much one way or the other about Vincent. He had disliked him, Guttman thought, otherwise he wouldn't've made such a big fuss about how he didn't care.

"This Hiller we're supposed to see may be able to give us something," Miss Brady said, interrupting his thoughts.

"I hope so."

"At least he may be able to fill in a couple of the gaps. We both know, I'm sure, that Forester was lying, or at least stretching the truth, when he acted so casual about Vincent."

"I was just thinking that," Guttman admitted. "But also, I

couldn't help wondering about Mishkin. What kind of business does he have in the city?"

"Maybe he wanted to go to the bank, or perhaps do some shopping. He probably decided that he might as well go, rather than just sit in the car and wait for us."

"I guess," Guttman said, resolving not to think about it any more. He'd find out from Mishkin, himself, what it was about later on. Miss Brady was halfway through her cottage cheese and pineapple salad, and Guttman had finished almost all of a disappointing corned-beef sandwich before he finally brought up the other question that was on his mind.

"Miss Brady—"

"Max," she said, "if you're going to persist in calling me Miss Brady, I'm going to be insulted. I know," she went on before he could protest, "I call you Mr. Guttman sometimes, but that's over too. I like my friends to call me Maggie, or Margaret if they have to, and I like to call them by their first names. And that's all there is to it."

Guttman looked at her for a moment, just a bit embarrassed, and then nodded and smiled. He wondered whether he was blushing. It felt like it, and that made him feel even sillier. I'm seventy-two years old, so how come all of a sudden I'm blushing?

"Okay," he said. "But I think Margaret would be easier for me."

"Fine. Now, what were you going to say?"

"I forgot. Oh, well, it's just curiosity, but, well, since we're first-name friends, I guess I could ask. You said you was in a prison, before. I didn't know that."

"It isn't really a secret, but it's not the sort of thing that just crops up in conversation very often, either." She took another bite of cottage cheese, and Guttman waited. He wanted to light a cigar, but he was worried that the smoke would bother her while she was eating.

"Not a criminal prison," Miss Brady went on. "It was during the war. Near the end, fortunately. Only a few months before we were released. Some of us were cut off in a Japanese counter-attack. We stayed with the wounded, and were captured. Fortunately, the Japanese didn't have time to get us off the island, otherwise we'd have been shipped God knows where."

"I . . . I heard some bad things about that . . . about what happened in the prison camps," Guttman said hesitantly.

"It wasn't pleasant," Margaret Brady said. "But we were lucky, I suppose. No atrocities. Just hunger, disease . . . and fear." She looked up from her plate and smiled at him. "It was a long time ago."

"I didn't know the nurses in the navy was that close to the fighting," Guttman said.

"Why not?"

"I don't know. I thought the navy, you know, they'd be on ships."

"We had hospitals ashore. Navy medical units took care of the marines in the Pacific. The marines were part of the navy, you know."

"I never realized," Guttman said.

She had finished her lunch, and he could finally light his cigar. It was still early, and so they ordered a second cup of coffee and began talking about what they could ask of David Hiller that afternoon. Before they finally left, Guttman went to the row of phone booths at the rear of the diner and tried again to reach Donald Eliot.

At one-thirty they announced themselves to David Hiller's secretary and were ushered into his office immediately. The assistant sales manager for Armstrong Industries occupied a very small office. It seemed to Guttman that if they'd put in another piece of furniture, besides the desk, swivel chair, file cabinet and the two chairs which he and Miss Brady occupied, there wouldn't be room to turn around. But, he thought, David Hiller didn't seem like the type to really need a large office. He might, Guttman thought, get lost in it. He knew it wasn't fair, but an impression is an impression, he told himself. He wondered how a man like Harry Vincent had felt about such a small office.

"I'm glad I didn't make other plans for this afternoon," Hiller said pleasantly as he seated them.

Guttman smiled and wished that this wasn't the third interview of the day. Someday, he thought, when I'm playing detective, I'm only going to talk to one person at a time, maybe a different one every day. And I'm also going to know what I'm doing. That's good, Guttman. Now all of a sudden you're worrying about a next case? Oy.

"Mr. Hiller," he said, "before we talk about anything, I want to say that if we talk about things what might be personal, I don't want you should take offense."

"You've heard about me and Carole, then," Hiller said, looking annoyed. "Well, I won't take offense. But right now, all I know is that Nick said you wanted to talk about Harry Vincent."

Guttman was a little surprised at the reaction. Hiller was an average-looking young man, probably thirty or thirty-five, Guttman thought, and already going bald. He wore a gray suit that made him look pale, and Guttman hadn't expected him to be aggressive.

"We're here on behalf of Mrs. Stone," Miss Brady said. "As I'm sure you know, she owns a substantial interest in Armstrong Industries, and Susan Eliot is her granddaughter."

"On Mrs. Stone's behalf to do what?" Hiller asked.

"We're trying to find out if somebody else killed Vincent, not Susan," Guttman told him.

"And your first question is about me and Carole. I think I'm getting your message."

"It wasn't a question," Guttman reminded him. "It was a telling, that we're sorry if it seems like we're butting into personal business."

"All right," Hiller said. "So you want to split hairs. I suppose Mr. Armstrong knows all about this?"

"We talked to him first, this morning."

"So I don't really have much choice, do I? Not when your Mrs. Stone owns a . . . how did you put it, a substantial interest in the company?"

"Okay," Guttman said. "So if you don't want to like us, you don't have to. You wouldn't be the first person in my life didn't like me so good. But meanwhile, could we talk to you, or no?"

"Talk," Hiller said.

"Okay. So, since you already brought it up, maybe you could tell us about you and your fiancée?" Guttman said.

"Carole and I are engaged. What you're really asking is did I know that she had an affair with Harry Vincent."

"I wasn't going to ask exactly that way," Guttman told him.

"Why not? Never mind. The answer is yes, I knew. And before you ask your other questions, let me answer them for you. It bothered me, sure. And no, I didn't like Harry Vincent. Hated him, actually. But . . ." Hiller shook his head and took a deep breath. "I told you I was glad I hadn't made any other appointments this afternoon. The reason is, I wanted to say all this right up front. Everybody in the office knew why you were here, almost as soon as you arrived, I guess. Look, Carole's twenty-seven years old. You can't expect a grown woman to have lived in a convent, for God's sake. Nobody does. If it hadn't been Harry, that is . . ."

Hiller stood up suddenly, and then, as if he realized that there wasn't any room to walk around, he sat down again. "Why the hell am I talking to you two about this? Look, if you have any more questions, ask them and get it over with."

"We're sorry if this is upsetting you, Mr. Hiller," Miss Brady said.

"Forget it. It's been a bad day. And I was afraid that something like this would start."

"Afraid?"

"Afraid, worried, whatever you want to call it. Look, just ask your questions, okay?"

"Okay. How about you and Mr. Vincent?" Guttman asked. "You said you hated him. It must have been hard, then, working with him."

"Maybe hate is a little too strong. But anyway, we managed," Hiller said. "We didn't fight. I don't know, maybe it's like you said. It wasn't the first time in my life I didn't like someone and they didn't like me."

"Vincent didn't like you, either?"

"I don't think Harry really liked anyone. But some people he treated better than others."

"Mr. Forester left us with the impression that you would have been in line for . . . your present position if Mr. Vincent hadn't been here," Miss Brady said.

"It isn't my present position," Hiller told her. "I'm only acting assistant sales manager. I don't have the job or the extra pay. Not yet, anyway."

"Is there a lot of extra work, though?" Guttman asked.

"Some. Anyway, your question. Yes, I thought I was in line for the job when Nick was promoted. Harry got it instead."

"Did it bother you?"

"No, I loved being passed over. Of course it bothered me. But what the hell was I supposed to do, cry?"

"Mr. Hiller, since you and Vincent didn't like each other, I don't guess you knew much about things like if he needed money, did you?" Guttman asked.

"He never discussed it with me."

"Well," Guttman said after a moment, "I don't know what else there is to ask. If you wasn't friendly, Vincent wouldn't've told you if he was having trouble with his wife, maybe she was mad at him or something . . . ?"

"No, he wouldn't have told me."

"So I guess that's it," Guttman said. "Except, I suppose I could ask if you know anybody what had a reason to kill Vincent."

"Susan Eliot," Hiller said. "I mean, if he beat her that way. But I don't know . . . To kill someone. Maybe at the moment," he said quietly. "But to come back the next day and kill someone in cold blood. It doesn't make sense."

"Why not?" Miss Brady asked.

"Look where she is now," David Hiller said.

· · ·

When they got back to the car Guttman handed the driver the slip of paper with Donald Eliot's address and phone number. "Do you know where that is?" he asked.

"Sure."

"Is it on the way back to the Center, or the other way?"

"Other way."

"Okay."

Guttman left Miss Brady at the car and walked back to the reception room of Armstrong Industries, where he asked if he could use the phone. The receptionist remembered that Mr. Armstrong himself had been expecting this old man that morning, and she helped him get a line. There was still no answer at Donald Eliot's number. When he got back to the car he explained to Miss Brady, and then told the driver to take them back to the Center. Maybe, he thought, Mishkin would be there. It was Friday, and he didn't want to spend the weekend worrying about Jacob Mishkin's whereabouts.

Mishkin hadn't returned, but to Guttman's surprise, Dora Kaplan and Agnes O'Rourke were waiting for them in the small lounge.

"So, the wanderers are finally back," Mrs. Kaplan said. "We was afraid you got lost."

"What happened, you got fired already?" Guttman asked.

"What kind of a question is that?" Mrs. O'Rourke wanted to know.

"So what are you doing here, it's only three o'clock in the afternoon? You was supposed to be working today, no?"

"We only work half a day," Mrs. Kaplan explained. "Mornings only."

"I didn't know. You wasn't here yesterday all day, so I just assumed it was a regular job."

"It's regular, but it isn't full time," Mrs. O'Rourke told him.

"Some job," Mrs. Kaplan said. "Half a day is enough. You take papers and you make them alphabetical. Any idiot could do it."

"But still, it's nice to have something to keep you busy," Mrs. O'Rourke said.

It was as close as Guttman had heard her come to disagreeing with her friend. "So how is the other stuff going?" he asked. "You know, we was at the company today."

"So we heard."

"Who told you? Mishkin?"

"Mr. Carstairs. He was around a little while ago and told us the two of you were over there, interviewing people. It's a good thing we didn't run into you," Mrs. Kaplan said. "You might have forgotten and said hello and blown our cover."

Blown their cover? Guttman decided to let it pass. "So how's it going?" he asked.

"It's only our second day there, Mr. Guttman. After all, you can't expect us to solve the case in two days," Mrs. O'Rourke said.

"I only said how's it going, not who's the killer."

"There's no need to be nasty," Mrs. Kaplan said.

"I wasn't being nasty, I—"

"Never mind. Do you want to hear what we've learned, or not?"

"Of course I want to hear, but—"

"All right, then. We'll give you our report," Dora Kaplan said. "But wouldn't it be better if we were all together before we begin?"

"Okay," Guttman agreed. "So where did Carstairs go?"

"I think he's outside on the lawn," Mrs. O'Rourke said. "I'll get him."

"And Mr. Mishkin?" Mrs. Kaplan asked.

"If he didn't come back, I don't know where he is," Guttman said.

"Mr. Carstairs said he went with you," Mrs. Kaplan said. "What do you mean you don't know where he is?"

"Mr. Mishkin left us," Miss Brady explained.

"Left you?"

"He didn't want to go inside with us, and when we returned, he was gone."

"He disappeared?"

"The driver said he took the bus into the city. That's all we know."

"Just like that?" Mrs. Kaplan demanded. "He didn't ask Mishkin any questions?"

"What could he ask? It ain't like he's one of us," Guttman said. "He's only the car driver."

"But where did he go?" Mrs. Kaplan asked. "Where in the city, and why?"

"That's what we've been wondering all afternoon," Miss Brady said.

"It ain't like Mishkin," Guttman noted.

"We'll have to find out about it as soon as he comes back," Mrs. Kaplan decided.

Mrs. O'Rourke returned with Mr. Carstairs, and immediately Mrs. Kaplan explained about Mishkin's absence. "We got another mystery now," she said when she was through.

"I hope he's all right," Mrs. O'Rourke said.

"Why wouldn't he be all right?" Guttman demanded. "All he done was take a bus to the city. So when he's finished with whatever, he'll take a bus back. There's nothing to worry about. I thought he'd be back already."

"But he isn't," Mrs. O'Rourke said, still worried.

"So we'll go ahead anyway," Guttman announced. "Mrs. Kaplan, you was gonna give a report. After that, we'll tell what happened with us. And then, Mr. Carstairs could go over again what he told me this morning, since you wasn't here."

"We couldn't very well have been here when we were on an undercover assignment," Mrs. Kaplan reminded him.

"Nobody said different, I was just . . ." Guttman gave up. "Go ahead with the report, please."

"Well," Mrs. Kaplan began. "We haven't been able to learn very much, yet. We don't want to make anyone suspicious by just going around and seeming too nosy. But naturally we asked if this was where that man who was murdered worked, and naturally everyone was only too anxious to tell us about it."

"So what did they tell?" Guttman asked.

Mrs. Kaplan adjusted herself on the chair and continued. "Without seeming too inquisitive, we were able to ask a few questions, but all the women there wanted to talk about at first was how Mr. Vincent was having an affair with Susan Eliot, and how they hadn't liked her too much, and they weren't really surprised when things happened the way they did."

"You know," Mrs. O'Rourke interrupted, "I think some of them, especially that Ethel woman, were a little jealous."

"She wasn't the only one, though," Mrs. Kaplan agreed. "Netta what's-her-name, she's no better. You'd think they had nothing to do but poke around in other people's business."

"I didn't think she was so bad," Mrs. O'Rourke said. "But that Ethel, the tall one . . ."

Guttman raised his eyes toward the ceiling and sighed. He didn't want to interrupt, but he had to. "Since it's getting a little late, maybe you could just go over what looks most important," he said. "And the rest you could tell us later, if there's time."

"Harry Vincent had an affair with one of the other girls there," Mrs. Kaplan announced. "Before Susan Eliot."

"That would be Carole Edwards," Miss Brady said.

"How did you know?"

"Somebody we talked to also mentioned it," Guttman said quickly.

"Well, did your somebody also tell you that he jilted her?"

"Dropped her like a hot potato," Mrs. O'Rourke added.

"I don't imagine she cared for that very much," Miss Brady suggested.

"There was a fight between her and Mrs. Stone's granddaughter," Mrs. Kaplan reported.

"Surely not a . . . a fist fight," Mr. Carstairs said.

"Just a yelling fight," Mrs. Kaplan assured him. "But everybody knew they didn't like each other."

"I guess she didn't like Vincent too much after that, either," Guttman said. "Except now she's engaged to somebody else, so it might not be so likely she still had a grudge against Vincent."

"You heard about that, too?" Mrs. Kaplan asked.

"Somebody mentioned it," Guttman admitted.

"Well, that still doesn't eliminate her as a suspect," Mrs. Kaplan continued. "There could have been something else."

"Like what?" Miss Brady asked.

"Like maybe telling her fiancé what went on," Mrs. Kaplan offered.

"He knows," Guttman said. "He told us so himself."

"Oh. Well, he may know that they had an affair, this girl and Vincent," Mrs. Kaplan said, "but he may not know everything."

"What does that mean?"

"There's nothing definite, but there are rumors," Mrs. Kaplan said.

"I'll say," Mrs. O'Rourke agreed.

"So tell us anyway," Guttman said.

"I'd rather wait until we're sure," Mrs. Kaplan said. "It might not pan out."

"So we'll worry about panning out later." Guttman knew that she was really anxious to talk, even if it was just a rumor—at least he thought she was.

"I think we should tell, Dora," Mrs. O'Rourke said quietly.

"Oh, all right. Our man Vincent," Mrs. Kaplan began, "was well known for . . . that is, he had a reputation. The girls in the office all knew about him . . ."

"What about him?" Guttman asked.

"Well, did you know that he used to give parties at his little love nest?" Mrs. Kaplan asked.

"What kind of parties?"

"Wild parties," Mrs. O'Rourke said.

"This Vincent would entertain customers by throwing parties at that apartment. And he'd have girls there," Mrs. Kaplan said.

"What kind of girls?" Guttman asked.

"Party girls," Agnes O'Rourke said very quietly.

"Party girls? You mean, like . . ."

"Exactly," Mrs. Kaplan said.

"And . . . what you said about this Carole Edwards, you think maybe she . . . ?"

"We don't know yet. But it stands to reason that if she was

Vincent's girl friend, living with him, and he was having these parties . . ."

No one spoke for a moment, and Mrs. Kaplan savored their silence. She had, indeed, come up with something. And it seemed to impress the others as much as it had impressed her. But finally she had to speak.

"We may not be able to prove she was involved," she said. "No one else from the company was ever at the apartment, at least none of the girls, so—"

"Except, perhaps, Susan Eliot," Margaret Brady said.

And then they were quiet again, until Mr. Carstairs said, "Mrs. Kaplan, a moment ago you said 'at least none of the girls' attended one of Mr. Vincent's parties."

"Well, you don't expect them to—"

"I see what Mr. Carstairs means," Guttman said. "If none of the girls, how about somebody else, some of the men maybe?"

"Like the other people in the sales area," Miss Brady said. "If Vincent was entertaining customers this way, the other salesmen might have been there too. They said they used to entertain customers sometimes."

"It would be nice to know," Guttman said.

"I don't know who . . ." Mrs. Kaplan stopped to think for a moment. "Yes I do. I didn't talk to her much, but I met her. She'll—"

"Who?" Mrs. O'Rourke asked.

"Mr. Forester's secretary. Since he's the sales manager, she should know about the parties, at least who went to them."

"Would she tell you?" Guttman asked.

"Mr. Guttman, working undercover you don't just go up to people and ask them questions," Mrs. Kaplan said in the tone usually reserved for children and incompetents. "You gain their confidence, and then you maneuver the conversation around so that you find out what you want to know without them ever knowing what you're doing. And you have to be a good listener too."

That, Guttman thought, was probably Mrs. Kaplan's explanation for how she always seemed to know more about other people's affairs than anyone else. She operated undercover, and she was a good listener. Oy.

"Okay," he said finally. "So anyway, it's something for you to work on for Monday. Finding out who went to these parties. I'm just thinking, maybe it wouldn't be a good thing for you to talk to the girl, Carole Edwards."

"Why not?"

"Well, we talked today to her fiancé, Hiller, so he'll probably see her and tell her about it, and if you ask questions on Monday, she'd be suspicious of you. It could . . . blow your cover," he said. "Anyway, we'll probably have to talk with her direct."

"Well . . ."

"If it looks like a good idea for you to talk to her, you could always do it a day later," Guttman said. "Maybe we could even suggest what special things to find out."

"Time to sum up?" Miss Brady asked.

"Not yet," Guttman told her. "I'm getting some kind of idea, only I don't know what it is yet. Maybe we should think about things first, and on Monday we could sum up."

"We won't be here Monday morning," Mrs. Kaplan reminded him. "We'll be working."

"Okay," Guttman sighed. "So we'll tell you what we found out today, and then everybody will get together maybe Monday afternoon for a summing up things. Miss Brady, maybe it would be better if you told about today," he suggested.

As she began to recount their interviews, Guttman relit his cigar, hardly listening, and tried to find out what it was that was in the back of his mind. But it wouldn't emerge. By the time Miss Brady had finished her narration and answered Mrs. Kaplan's questions, none of which seemed important to Guttman, there were only a few minutes left before it was time for him to go outside and wait for Lois.

"Okay," he said, "so on Monday—"

"Mr. Mishkin!" Mrs. O'Rourke exclaimed.

"You're still here," Mishkin said. "Good." He sat down

heavily in the chair next to Guttman, loosened his tie, and sighed deeply. "I ain't walked around so much for years."

"What happened to you? We came back to the car and you was gone without saying anything—"

"Please, Guttman. Let me rest for a minute," Mishkin said. "Then I'll tell about everything. I practically ran from the bus stop so I should be here before you was gone."

"Would you like a cup of tea?" Mrs. O'Rourke asked.

"I'd love a cup of tea. Only it ain't allowed on my diet."

"Perhaps a glass of water?"

"That would be very nice. Thank you. Oy," Mishkin said, "with the diet they got me on, it's a wonder I don't starve to death."

Guttman relaxed. If Mishkin was able to complain about his diet, he was all right. By the time Mrs. O'Rourke returned, Mishkin had recovered and seemed anxious to begin. Still, he sipped at the water and automatically began fingering the deck of cards that lay on the table, where he had left them that morning.

"Okay," Guttman said. "So tell us, please, whatever it is."

"I'm telling," Mishkin said. "The first thing is, when you was going to talk to the people in the company, in the car this morning, I was thinking how I couldn't help much—"

"You could've helped," Guttman said.

"Please, Guttman. Like I say, I was thinking. And you know how we was wondering about this Vincent's gambling, how much money he owed and like that? Well, if you make bets at the race track or someplace, you got to pay cash. There's no credit. So if he owed people money, it had to be to the bookies, I figured. And I remembered, from before, how once in a while I used to make a bet with somebody, never a lot of money, maybe five dollars. And also, there was some people I knew . . ." Mishkin stopped, as if unsure of himself.

"See, the thing is," he went on, "you know I was a plumber before I retired. But also, I did a little contracting business too. So from that I knew some people, not the nicest people, but if you do contracting, sometimes you got to take care of people, grease some wheels, and anyway, all these people is tied up together, they know each other and all. So I figured I'd see if I could find out something about Vincent."

"You mean you knew the bookies and people like that?" Mrs. O'Rourke asked.

"Not just bookies. The thing is," Mishkin explained, "if you go to a bookie, maybe he gives you some credit, a couple of hundred dollars. But if somebody like Vincent was worrying about money, it had to be more than just a couple of hundred dollars, I figured. So that means maybe the big boys."

"The big boys," Mrs. O'Rourke repeated.

"The ones on the top," Mishkin said. "Not just from the neighborhood."

"The syndicate . . ." Agnes O'Rourke whispered, her eyes wide.

"Syndicate, shmindicate," Mishkin said. "I don't know from that, and I don't want to."

"Mishkin, please, tell us what happened," Guttman pleaded.

"I'm trying, I'm trying. Like I said, I went talking to people—believe me, it wasn't easy finding some of them—seeing if I could find out who Vincent might've owed money to."

"Were you able to find out, Mr. Mishkin?" Mr. Carstairs asked.

"I found out. Nobody's gonna swear in court about it, naturally, but I found out."

"So?"

"So he owed to some of the big shots. The ones who when you don't pay up they break your legs, or something like that."

"You know people like that?" Mrs. O'Rourke asked.

"They're not exactly friends," Mishkin said. "But like I said, when you do some contracting along with the plumbing, you get to meet all kinds of people."

"How much did he owe?" Miss Brady asked.

"About ten thousand, to the ones I was able to find out about. It could be there's more."

"Ten thousand dollars?" Mr. Carstairs asked. "In gambling debts?"

"That's how much they say."

"No wonder he was worried about money," Mrs. Kaplan said.

"This," Guttman said, "this is really something good to know."

"I figured it could help," Mishkin said modestly.

"Help? It's fantastic," Miss Brady said.

Mishkin blushed slightly. "Also," he went on, "Vincent was a big loser for a while. The ten thousand is what he owed now. For a while before that, he kept losing."

"Didn't he ever win?" Mr. Carstairs wanted to know.

"He must've, once in a while. But usually he was losing."

"Did he pay the other times?" Guttman asked.

"He must've, otherwise they wouldn't let him get in so deep this time," Mishkin explained. "I didn't ask too much about that."

"Mr. Mishkin, is it possible that these gangsters killed Vincent because he couldn't pay up?" Mrs. Kaplan asked.

"I don't think so. I didn't exactly ask, but it ain't the way they usually do business."

"Why not?" Mrs. O'Rourke asked.

"Because if they kill someone, they can't ever get their money. So instead they beat somebody up, and then tell him to get the money or they'll do worse. But if they kill somebody, they don't get anything."

"Very sound business practice," Mr. Carstairs said. "Not that I approve."

"So Vincent was probably worried they'd beat him up," Guttman said.

"But he wasn't a poor man," Mrs. O'Rourke commented. "Ten thousand dollars is a lot of money, but couldn't he have paid it?"

"He didn't have that much in the bank," Mr. Carstairs said. "But still, he could have paid some of the debt. And if he sold his securities . . ."

"But then his wife would have found out about it," Miss Brady said.

"So he had to get the money some other way," Mrs. Kaplan said.

"Not just this money," Guttman said. "There was the money he lost before. Mr. Carstairs said Vincent spent most of what he made, and there was no special stuff in the accounts, like he was paying off debts . . ."

"Blackmail," Agnes O'Rourke finally said.

"Blackmail?" Mishkin repeated.

"Later Mrs. O'Rourke could tell you about it," Guttman said. "But Mrs. Kaplan and I got to leave in a minute. And we already been over this before you got here. So now we could sum up, quick," he continued. "If we're looking for somebody what could've killed Vincent, we got a possible motive."

"But we don't know there was blackmail involved," Miss Brady cautioned.

"Still, it's possible. So, Mrs. Kaplan, on Monday you and Mrs. O'Rourke could try to find out about who was at the parties."

"Mr. Guttman, may I make a suggestion?"

"Naturally, Mr. Carstairs."

"It needn't have been blackmail. Vincent might have gotten the money in some other way."

"Like what?"

"Well, perhaps embezzlement."

"Embezzlement?" Guttman repeated. Well, he thought, Carstairs was an accountant. That was the way he thought.

"Monday I'm going to the S.E.C. offices."

"The sec?"

"The Securities and Exchange Commission. I want to do some research on Armstrong Industries," Mr. Carstairs said.

"Good," Guttman told him, without the slightest idea of what it was that Mr. Carstairs was going to research. He looked at his watch. "And on Monday, Miss Brady and me will talk to this Carole Edwards, if we can. Also, I want to talk to Susan's husband, only he don't answer his phone."

"What about me?" Mishkin asked.

"Monday," Guttman told him. "What you done today is more

than anyone else. So Monday you could come with us, maybe, or else we could think of something else. Meanwhile, I think we done pretty good so far, considering."

"Considering what?" Mrs. Kaplan asked.

"Considering we didn't have nothing to start with."

Nine

The weekend dragged for Guttman. In television mysteries there never seemed to be Saturdays or Sundays when nothing happened. On television, detectives always solved cases in one, maybe two days, and they never had to wait to get to see somebody. Of course, the Sherlock Holmes he had read, after Mrs. Kaplan kept referring to them as modern-day Irregulars, sometimes took longer, weeks even. But that was different. And, he thought, with Sherlock Holmes there was always one reason for everything, even if nobody else besides Holmes understood it until the end. But this case was different.

Saturday afternoon, while Lois and Michael played tennis, and the boys were at the movies with their friends, Guttman sat with his granddaughter, Sara, and forced himself to go back to the beginning. First, there was the noise. The neighbor hadn't heard anything except the shot. That meant that whoever killed Vincent wasn't there making a fuss. It meant Vincent didn't surprise a burglar, or something like that.

No, Guttman told himself. That don't have to be true. If it was a burglar, he could've found the gun while he was looking for money, and if Vincent came in, shot him so he wouldn't call the police. So that meant the killer didn't even have to be somebody Vincent knew, Guttman told himself. He got up from his chair in front of the television set, where he was watching the

Mets play the Pirates on the network program, and got a pad and pencil from his room. He'd better take notes.

"1. Ask Lieutenant Weiss if somebody could have broken into the apartment," he wrote. Then he remembered he had been told that Susan Eliot unlocked the door when she arrived. That meant the lock wasn't broken. But still, it could have been picked. But more likely, whoever it was got in with a key.

"2. Who could have a key to the apartment?" Guttman printed. Anybody, he told himself. Anybody what knew Vincent could have taken the keys from him and made one. Also Susan Eliot, and the other girl, Carole Edwards, had keys. So someone could have gotten their key and used it, or made a copy. That made Guttman feel a little better. At this point, the more possibilities he could keep open, the more chance he felt he had of finding a solution.

"3. Did Susan know about the parties? Did she go along with them? Also Carole Edwards?" Just because she's the grand-daughter don't mean she couldn't do something like that, Guttman told himself. Everybody got to be somebody's grand-daughter, and whether it makes sense or not, there's people doing things like that for money. Or for other reasons.

It was a subject about which he knew very little. Guttman knew what he had read in the newspapers, what he had seen on television or occasionally in the movies. He knew that some of the men with whom he had worked, over the years, had visited prostitutes. He had even been invited to join them. But he hadn't been very friendly with those men. If any of his friends had done that, they kept it to themselves. Not that it's any different, he admitted to himself. But it ain't the kind of thing we talked about.

With a sigh, Guttman tore the top sheet from the pad, folded it, and put it in his wallet. All he had was questions. No answers. He'd have to talk to Susan again. And her husband. When the next inning was over he tried the number again. To his surprise, there was an answer.

"Mr. Eliot?" he asked.

"Yes."

"Mr. Eliot, my name is Max Guttman. I'm a friend of Mrs. Stone, Susan's grandmother."

"Oh, yes. What can I do for you?" He sounded young to Guttman.

"Well, I was wondering if I could talk with you."

"What about?"

"About Susan, and this thing what happened."

"What did you say your name was again?"

"Guttman. Max Guttman."

"Well . . . Exactly what did you want to talk to me about?" Eliot asked.

"Mrs. Stone, she asked if I could help. We're trying to get Susan out of jail, Mrs. Stone knows she didn't kill this Vincent, so any help . . ."

"You've lost me. Are you a lawyer?"

"No. I'm . . . I'm doing some detective stuff for Mrs. Stone."

"Detective stuff?"

Guttman could hear the uncertainty in Eliot's voice. "Believe me, Mr. Eliot, this isn't a joke. You could call Mrs. Stone and ask, if you want. Or you could call the lawyer, Paul Taylor."

"I'm sorry. It's just that you don't sound like a detective," Eliot said.

"Sometimes I don't feel like one, either. But the thing is, I'm trying to help."

"Sure . . ." Eliot said. "Well, what can I do for you?"

"Like I said, I was wondering if I could talk with you."

"Go ahead."

"No, I mean in person."

"Uh . . . okay. I guess that would be all right. When do you want to come over?"

"Could it be on Monday? Maybe about ten o'clock, say. Or even in the afternoon. Whatever's okay for you."

"All right. Look, I expect to be here all day. I've got some work that has to get done," Eliot said. "Why don't you just call first?"

"That would be fine, since I also got to see Susan on Monday, and I ain't sure what time that would be. So I'll call first to let you know," Guttman said.

"Uh . . . fine. So I'll see you Monday. Do you have the address?"

"Mrs. Stone gave it to me," Guttman told him. "And thank you."

"It's okay," Eliot said.

Guttman could almost picture him standing with the receiver in his hand, confused. He knew he hadn't sounded like a professional detective. So why should I? A professional, I'm not. But at least, Guttman thought, I got something done for the weekend. After that, Sunday dragged even more slowly than Saturday.

Guttman went straight to Mrs. Stone's cottage when he arrived at the Center Monday morning. The nurse let him in and then left him waiting. He began pacing the floor of the living room. He had chafed all weekend, and now he was anxious to get started. He understood why on television there were no weekends for detectives. It would make everybody nervous.

"Good morning," Mrs. Stone said as the nurse wheeled her into the room.

"Good morning. I came because we're gonna need the car again today. I forgot to tell you on Friday."

"Margaret Brady told me about it," Mrs. Stone said.

"She did?"

"Yes."

"Oh. Well, I didn't know, so I wanted to check first thing," Guttman said lamely. "Also, I got to talk to your granddaughter again. Today, if I could."

"I'll have the attorneys arrange it. And thank you for telling Margaret to give me that report Friday," Mrs. Stone said. "I must say, I'm surprised that you seem to be getting somewhere."

"I don't know how much we're getting," Guttman said. "But we're trying." Miss Brady, he thought, had been busy. "Anyway, I just wanted to check on the car, since you already know the rest."

. . .

He found Miss Brady in the lounge, sitting with Mishkin. Guttman got a cup of coffee and joined them at their table.

"Mr. Carstairs isn't here?"

"He already left to go downtown," Miss Brady said.

"I just talked to Mrs. Stone. She told me you gave her a report."

"I didn't think you'd mind. Since you had to leave, I just . . ."

"Why should I mind?" Guttman asked. "The only thing I mind is I didn't think to ask you myself." He stirred his coffee and took a sip.

"So what's for today?" Mishkin asked.

"That depends."

"Everything depends," Mishkin said. "Depends on what?"

"On who we could see. Mrs. Stone's calling the lawyer to see if we could talk again with Susan. And then there's the girl at the office, what used to be the girl friend of Vincent. We got to see if she's there today. Also, I talked to Susan's husband on the telephone. Him, too, we got to talk to."

"It looks like it's going to be a busy day," Miss Brady said. "Who do we see first?"

"We got to wait to find out about when we could see Susan. Then we'll work the others in around that."

"Would you like me to call about Carole Edwards, find out if she's in today?" she asked. "While you finish your coffee."

"That would be nice. Thank you." Guttman found the slip of paper onto which he'd transferred the phone numbers he thought he'd need, and handed it to her.

"What do you got for me?" Mishkin asked when Miss Brady had left.

"I ain't sure," Guttman admitted. "Unless you want to come along when we talk to these people."

"Three's a crowd," Mishkin said.

"What's that supposed to mean?" Guttman asked warily.

"It means if there's three people asking questions, somebody acts like they're making a speech sometimes. Two people is enough."

"It don't have to be that way."

"But it is."

"Well, if you don't want to go along, there could be something else," Guttman said.

"What?"

"Well, these friends of yours, the ones what Vincent owed money to . . ."

"Friends they're not."

"Okay, so these people you know. It could be good to know when he owed the money from before, and maybe when he paid it back, too."

"You mean like the days and the amounts?"

"Anything like that," Guttman affirmed.

"What for?"

"Well, let's say a person buys a new car that costs a thousand dollars one day, and—"

"A new car's got to cost at least three thousand, maybe four," Mishkin corrected.

"Okay, so three thousand. And the day before he buys, you find out somebody stole three thousand dollars, and it could be the same person was doing the buying and the stealing."

"You got me confused," Mishkin said.

"Okay. So suppose Carstairs finds out what he said, about somebody taking money from the company—embezzling, right?" Guttman had looked the word up over the weekend.

"Okay."

"Well, just because he finds it, that don't prove it was Vincent. But if we find out somebody took a thousand dollars, and the same time Vincent pays the gamblers a thousand dollars, then . . ."

"Then we know Vincent's the crook," Mishkin said.

"Right."

"I don't know if they'll tell me that kind of thing."

"Would it hurt to try?" Guttman asked. "I mean, I don't know if they'd like you asking about it."

"I could try," Mishkin said after a moment. "I don't think they'd get mad if I just ask."

"You're sure?"

"Don't worry," Mishkin said more confidently. "But what you just said, you know, about what day and all. If it turns out Vincent was stealing money from the company, that wouldn't be so good, would it?"

"Why not?"

"Because it don't give a reason for somebody killing him. If somebody steals money from you, you don't kill him. You tell the police to arrest him."

"You know, I didn't even think about that," Guttman admitted.

"So you don't want I should try to find out?"

"No," Guttman said after a moment. "You might as well find out, if you could. The more we know, the better."

"Okay. So when Miss Brady comes back we'll see what you're gonna do, and maybe you could drop me off someplace in the car."

"Paul Taylor says we can see Susan this afternoon about two-thirty," Miss Brady reported. "And Carole Edwards is still out sick, so I called Donald Eliot, his name was on the piece of paper, and he said it would be all right for us to come over any time. I told him we'd be there in an hour."

"That gives us time to drop off Mishkin," Guttman said.

"I'll get my jacket," Mishkin said.

Donald Eliot had an apartment in a four-story building in a middle-class area of the city, not quite suburban but not really commercial either. Guttman was reminded of sections of Brooklyn. They waited in the hallway until Eliot used the speaker, then buzzed to admit them. They climbed two flights of stairs to his apartment, and Guttman found himself short of breath when they reached the second floor. Not enough exercise, he thought. In New York, at least I walked a lot. Around here everybody rides, and I'm not gonna start playing tennis like Lois and Michael for exercise. I better start walking, he told himself. Every day. I'll walk for exercise. Harry Truman was older when he was still walking fast in the mornings, and the reporters couldn't keep up.

There were six apartments on each floor. Donald Eliot stood in his doorway, waiting. He stepped back, and Guttman followed Miss Brady into a medium-sized room, with two windows at one end, bright, clean, but with little furniture. There was a couch, which Guttman decided must open up into a bed, one easy chair, a dining table and a couple of wooden chairs. The table was covered with books and papers. Against the wall opposite the couch was a bookcase, with a record player and some records. If the furniture was older, Guttman thought, and not so clean, it would look poor.

Donald Eliot invited them to sit, offered them coffee, which they refused, and when they sat on the couch, stood across the room from them. He was in his late twenties, Guttman assumed, but he looked younger—the way he sounded on the phone. Eliot's dark-blond hair was a little messy and a bit too long, to Guttman's way of thinking. He wore dungarees and a polo shirt, and his feet were bare in a pair of leather sandals. Donald Eliot was not very impressive, Guttman thought, and he had a difficult time picturing him as half a couple with Susan. She seemed older, more mature. Eliot wasn't particularly handsome, and he was skinny. Also nervous. He looked from Guttman to Miss Brady, then took a chair from the dining table and sat on it, facing them.

"I don't really know what this is all about," he said.

"It's like I told you on the phone—"

"I know. You're trying to help Susan. But I mean . . ."

"It's all right, Mr. Eliot," Miss Brady said. "We're accustomed to it. Mr. Guttman and I realize that we don't look like detectives. And we're not. Not exactly, anyway."

"Then . . ."

"Mrs. Stone asked us to help. And since no one else has been able to do very much, we felt there was no harm in trying. Actually, our incongruity seems to help. People sometimes talk to us when they wouldn't to the police."

"Uh-huh," Eliot said. He was still uncertain.

"Mr. Eliot, this is a little awkward, so you'll forgive if we're blunt," Guttman said. "But when was the last time you saw Susan?"

"I haven't seen her since before she was arrested. I should have, but . . ."

"How much before?"

"The police asked me that too. Maybe a month before, I guess."

"How come?" Guttman asked.

"How come what?"

"How come you happened to see her then?"

"We just . . . got together. There were some details to be worked out, about the divorce."

"You saw her with the lawyers for that, then?" Guttman asked.

"No, just the two of us. We had dinner."

"So it was more a social get-together," Guttman suggested.

"I told you, there were some things to work out."

"Excuse me, Mr. Eliot," Miss Brady said. "I thought usually these things were handled through lawyers."

"Too much hassle that way. Everybody starts arguing . . ."

"I thought the judge set the amount, and everything," Guttman said.

"That's alimony," Eliot told him. "We're working out a settlement."

"Oh. I didn't know."

"You wanted to work things out yourselves, if you could?" Miss Brady said.

"Yeah. There isn't much for us to split up, anyway. And Susan said she didn't want any money. Hell, I don't have any. So we figured, why get into a big legal hassle over who got which books or records, stuff like that."

"Naturally," Miss Brady agreed. "Do you mind if I ask whether you lived here at this address while . . . before you separated?"

"Yeah. Same apartment. She moved out, lived with her grandmother for a while before she got her own place."

One room, Guttman thought. The kitchen, he could see, was tucked into the space behind the front door, and the other door just this side of it, he decided, must be the bathroom. Two people in a room so small could be hard if they wasn't getting along.

"Mr. Eliot, what did you talk about the time you saw Susan?" he asked.

"Nothing much. To tell you the truth, it was awkward. But we agreed she'd just come by and pick up whatever she wanted from this stuff."

"You didn't have an argument or anything, did you?"

"There was nothing left to argue about," Eliot said. He got up to get a pack of cigarettes from the table, lit one, and then sat down again, moving his chair a little closer to the coffee table between them to use the ashtray.

"I don't imagine you was so happy about her and Vincent," Guttman said.

"She was living her own life, I was living mine," Eliot said.

"But you knew about it, didn't you?"

"More or less," Eliot replied.

"I'm sorry, but more or less, what does that mean?"

"It means . . . We had some friends in common, you know, so I heard she was seeing this guy who was married. It was none of my business, really."

"You didn't care?" Guttman asked.

"I didn't say that," Eliot answered. "But . . . look, the whole thing was hard enough without me getting jealous because she was . . . or worrying about how she was screwing up her life. There was nothing I could do."

"I'm sure you cared enough to try to talk to her about it," Miss Brady said.

"Yeah. I said something about it. She didn't appreciate it."

"Did you know this man Vincent?" Guttman asked.

"No. I never met him. And it's probably just as well."

"Would you have been jealous?" Miss Brady asked.

"Probably. Oh, hell. Yeah, I would have been jealous." Eliot managed a wry smile for them. "Let's face it, I was . . . I am still in love with her. The separation and divorce, it was Susan's idea. Not mine."

"You'd want to be back with her?" Guttman asked.

"It might not be very bright of me, but yes," Eliot said. He got up and walked to the windows.

"Mr. Eliot, is there anything you can think of that might help us?" Miss Brady asked.

"Like what?"

"We really don't know."

Donald Eliot turned his head to look at them, the sunlight behind him shadowing his face. "I think I know what you're hinting at, so I might as well say it. The only thing I know is that after what he did to Susan, I might have killed him myself. But I didn't."

"You knew about that?" Guttman asked.

"It was in the papers."

"But that was when you found out? It didn't sound that way when you just said it," Guttman told him.

"I . . . No, I knew about it before. Susan called me. That night. The truth is I was ready to go out looking for the son of a bitch . . . Excuse me," he said to Miss Brady.

"But you didn't?"

"No. Susan talked me out of it."

"Mr. Eliot, I got to ask you something. The only other person we talked with what really knows Susan is her grandmother, and now you. So I got to ask—do you think Susan could've killed Vincent?" Guttman tried to see Eliot's expression as he waited for an answer.

"She didn't kill him."

"But could she've done it?"

"She didn't. I don't know about could have. Look, I just told you, I was ready to go after him myself, but she wouldn't let me. She said she just wanted to forget it. It was over, and that was all there was to it."

"Still, it's not the kind of thing that's easy to forget," Guttman said.

"Look," Eliot said earnestly, moving closer to them, "if Susan

130

was going to kill him, why didn't she do it right then? The night he beat her up? She knew where the gun was, so she could have just gotten it and shot the bastard right then, if she was going to."

"Mr. Eliot, there's another question we must ask," Miss Brady said. "Did you know, that is, did Susan ever talk about . . . what might have gone on at that apartment. Parties, or something like that?"

"No. We never discussed any of it. I mean, it's not exactly the kind of thing we'd have talked about, is it? What kind of parties are you talking about?"

"It's just something we heard," Guttman said quickly. "And we don't know if it's true or not."

"Like what?" Eliot asked.

"Entertaining customers," Margaret Brady said softly. "As a salesman, Vincent seemed to have done some of that, and we were just wondering . . ."

Donald Eliot looked at them for a moment, then shook his head. "No way," he said loudly. "No way. You don't know what you're talking about. Who said she—"

"Mr. Eliot, we wasn't suggesting—"

"The hell you weren't. Look, get out of here, will you? I don't know what you're trying to say about Susan, but I don't want to hear it."

"I'm sorry if we got you mad," Guttman said, rising. "Believe me, we don't—"

"Sure. But just get the hell out of here!"

"In a moment," Margaret Brady said quietly. "Mr. Eliot, if you're as anxious to help Susan as you say, then please calm down." Eliot just stared at her, as did Guttman. "Surely you realize that we have to ask these questions. The fact that we heard something about it makes it necessary. Your belief that Susan wasn't involved in anything like . . . what was mentioned is important to us. Believe me, we'd much rather hear that than another opinion. But we have to ask."

"Who told you about that?" Eliot asked her finally.

"It's a rumor."

"It's a lie."

"That may well be. But we're concerned about saving Susan's life, and we can't afford the luxury of worrying about your feelings or anyone else's. And neither can you, if you really care for her," Miss Brady said calmly.

Guttman looked at her and then sat down on the couch again. After a moment Eliot sank onto his chair.

"Christ, what a mess," he said, hanging his head. Then he looked up at them. "She didn't do it. I know she didn't. Susan couldn't kill anyone."

"Mr. Eliot, this fight, when Vincent beat her up, do you know what it was all about?" Guttman asked.

"No. She wouldn't tell me."

"But there must've been a reason."

"I guess. But I don't know what it was."

"Mr. Eliot, you mentioned that Susan called you the night that she was hurt," Miss Brady said.

"That's right."

"Didn't you go to see her?"

"I haven't seen Susan since . . . that time we had dinner."

"Forgive me," Miss Brady said, "but it doesn't seem reasonable to me that caring for her as you obviously do, you wouldn't have made sure she was all right."

"She told me not to come."

"Then why did she call you?"

"I don't know. I guess she just wanted to talk to someone."

"Mr. Eliot, if you lie to us, you're only going to confuse us. And that won't help Susan at all," Margaret Brady said calmly. "Now, if you want to help her, you'll have to be honest with us."

Eliot looked at her, then nodded his head wearily. "I saw her," he said quietly. "She told me not to say anything about it."

"Where did you see her? Here?" Guttman asked.

"No. At her apartment. She called me, and when she told me what happened, I went over. She didn't want me to, but I did. I had to make sure she was all right."

"Of course you did," Miss Brady said.

"Why didn't you just tell us that?" Guttman asked.

"Because of how it might have looked. I mean, with Vincent dead, if the police knew I saw Susan when I did, well, it would have looked bad for me."

"But Susan didn't say anything to the police about it either, did she?"

"I guess not, otherwise they would have asked me. I guess she thought they'd figure I killed Vincent myself."

"You mean she was covering up for you?" Guttman asked.

"I guess so. But there's nothing to cover up."

"Then why didn't you tell the police about it yourself?" Miss Brady asked.

"There didn't seem to be any point in it, that's all."

"When you went there that night, what happened?" Guttman asked.

"Nothing. I mean, I helped her clean up a little, then I went to the drugstore to get some stuff, an ice bag for the bruises. She wasn't feeling so bad when I got back, so after a while I left," Eliot said, his voice flat.

Guttman looked at Miss Brady, then at the young man sitting dejectedly across from them, arms resting on his thighs, head hanging down. "We wouldn't tell nobody about it," he said, getting to his feet. "Like you, we only want to help Susan, not to make trouble." He and Miss Brady were at the door before Eliot roused himself enough to stand up. "I hope we didn't mess up your working," Guttman said, looking at the papers on the table.

"It's okay."

"Are you a writer?"

"No. I'm a student, I guess. Part time. I do some substitute teaching once in a while. This is a little free-lance work, a thesis I'm editing for someone."

"Well, I'm sorry if we interrupted," Guttman told him.

"It's okay," Eliot said.

As he closed the door, Guttman saw Eliot walk across the room to stand staring out the window at the street.

Ten

They went back to the Center for lunch. Miss Brady stopped off at her cottage for a while, and Guttman sat outside on the back lawn to look through the morning paper. Without realizing it, he checked each page for some mention of Susan Eliot, but the story was old enough now so that no one seemed interested. When the trial starts, Guttman thought, they might have something.

He thought about playing a quick game of bocce before lunch, but the Bowseniors weren't around and he didn't feel like practicing by himself. Besides, he admitted, the game wasn't quite as much fun as he had thought it would be. Maybe one day I'll have to try the croquet. At the moment he would have even welcomed a game of pinochle, but Mishkin hadn't returned from his visit to the city. After a while he decided that he'd have to talk to Mrs. Stone about that. None of them really had very much money, and there were some expenses involved in playing detective. The car was provided, of course, but there were other expenses. Mishkin had taken a bus to the city Friday, and back. And he'd probably had lunch there too. And now today the same thing. And even if Miss Brady had insisted on paying for her own lunch when they had eaten on Friday, it was still a cost to both of them that they wouldn't have had otherwise. Mrs.

Kaplan and Mrs. O'Rourke would get paid for their work at Armstrong Industries, so they wouldn't be losing anything, and he was sure they wouldn't make enough to affect their Social Security. But Mr. Carstairs had done some things too, and he must have had expenses. He'd have to talk to Mrs. Stone about it.

Miss Brady stayed in her cottage for lunch, and Guttman ate alone. Ordinarily he wouldn't have minded. For three years, before moving here to live with Lois and Michael, he had taken most of his meals alone, but it was different when you were in your own home, he thought. In New York, when he went out to eat, it was at the cafeteria, and he could read the newspaper if he didn't run into somebody he knew to say hello to. But he didn't know that many people at the Center, aside from the Irregulars and the Bowseniors. He finished his lunch quickly and went back outside to wait for Miss Brady.

It was just two-thirty when they arrived at the House of Detention. The check-in procedures were different this time. They didn't have the lawyer with them, and they had to talk to the police officers themselves, sign themselves in, go through the search again, but instead of going into the private room where they'd met Susan last time, Guttman and Miss Brady followed several other people to a regular visiting room. There they sat at a long counter, facing a thick glass partition with chicken wire built into it for strength, and waited for Susan to appear.

They saw her come in through the door at the far end of the room and walk slowly toward them, as if she wasn't sure whom she was going to be seeing. Her face showed no emotion as she sat down across from them and took a cigarette from her dress pocket. Guttman thought she didn't look quite as attractive as she had the last time, and he wondered whether she had put on make-up to impress her lawyer. After all, Paul Taylor was an interesting young man.

"Your grandmother sent her regards," Guttman lied. She hadn't really said anything to him about the visit.

"How is she?" Susan asked.

It was an automatic question. Guttman couldn't tell if she was really concerned. "She's okay."

"Good," Susan said. She lit her cigarette and leaned back a little. "How's your investigation going? Paul tells me you've been busy little beavers."

Guttman looked at her for a moment and decided not to let himself get mad. "It's going along. We're talking to people, finding out some things."

"Good for you."

Susan Eliot seemed distant, and Guttman wondered whether it was because she didn't think they could help or because she didn't care about anything. "We talked to your husband," he told her.

"Donald? How is he?"

"He's concerned about you," Miss Brady said.

"Donald was always a worrier."

"And you're not?" Guttman suggested.

The girl shrugged and glanced idly around the room.

"Susan, we want to talk to you about something . . ." He wasn't sure quite how to lead into it, and finally decided he'd have to just say it. "It's about some parties Harry Vincent used to have."

"What parties?"

"Parties where he'd invite customers, and there'd be . . . girls . . ."

"You say that like it's strange," Susan said. "Generally, when someone has a party, there are girls. And men too."

"These girls was different. Susan, did you know about the parties he had where there was . . . party girls?"

"Party girls," she repeated, smiling. "I like that."

"Did you know about it, Susan?" Miss Brady asked.

"Harry didn't tell me everything he did."

"He had the parties at the apartment where the two of you was living," Guttman said.

"We didn't really live there," the girl said. "I had my apartment, and Harry was still living with his wife."

"Susan, you're not answering our question," Miss Brady told her.

"I've forgotten what it was."

"Did you know about the parties?"

"Look, it's really nice of you to try to help Grandmother, but if you don't mind, I'm kind of tired, so much to do around here, so maybe I'll . . ."

"We're not helping your grandmother," Guttman said sharply. "We're trying to help you. You're the one what's in jail for murder."

"I seem to remember something about that."

"Look, Susan," Miss Brady said sternly, "we know about the parties. All we want to find out from you is whether you knew about them. Susan, we need your cooperation."

"Harry used to do some entertaining," she said after a moment. "That's normal for salesmen, you know."

"We wasn't saying it wasn't normal," Guttman said. "We just wanted to know if you knew about the parties with the girls."

"So?"

"So does that mean yes?" he asked. The girl didn't answer. "Susan, your grandmother ain't so healthy. She's worrying about you. Okay, so maybe you think it's a waste of time. Maybe you like it here so much you don't mind spending a couple of months until you get a trial, and you figure they'll send you home after that. Only she don't see it that way. She don't have a guarantee you'll go home afterward. And neither does the lawyer, Mr. Taylor. So what harm could it be to talk to us?"

It took the girl a moment to make up her mind. Then she sighed and nodded her head. "I knew about the parties."

"Did you go to any of them?" Guttman asked gently.

"No."

"Never? I mean, maybe you had dinner out or something, and then went back to the apartment?"

"No. We didn't . . . that is, I didn't go out with the customers."

"How about if Vincent invited them to the apartment. You was never there?"

"Look—"

"Susan," Miss Brady said quickly, "you might as well talk to us. As Mr. Guttman said, it can't hurt and it might help."

"I don't see how."

"Because we're trying, that's how," Miss Brady said. "Susan, if you didn't kill Vincent, and we believe that you didn't, then obviously someone else did. We're trying to learn as much as we can in the hopes that we can get some direction to follow, some lead."

"Once," Susan said.

"What happened?" Guttman asked. "I mean, was there girls there?"

"Two. Harry had a pair of customers in town, and he wanted to entertain them."

"And you was there?"

"Harry said it would be easier if I joined them. Otherwise, he said, it might make them feel uncomfortable, with him just sitting around in the living room, you know. They'd be self-conscious. But if I was there, he said, it wouldn't be as awkward."

"I imagine it was awkward for you, though," Miss Brady said.

"Not as much as you imagine, I suspect," Susan said. "But that's beside the point, isn't it?"

"It is," Guttman agreed. "But it brings a question to my mind. Nobody ever told us why he beat you up that night."

"We had a fight," Susan said.

"That much we could figure out. But what was the fighting about?"

"It doesn't matter."

"It might," Guttman said. "The police think you wanted he should divorce his wife and marry you."

"I'd rather not talk about it."

"Susan, you're going to have to trust us. We want to help you. And believe me, we're not going to talk about this with anyone else," Miss Brady said.

Guttman thought of Mrs. Kaplan, but he kept quiet. Susan looked at them for a moment, then leaned forward to stub her cigarette out on the counter in front of her. "I don't know where you heard about Harry's parties," she said. "The police never asked me about it. Maybe you know what you're doing after all." She lit another cigarette, and they waited as patiently as they could. "Harry had some guy he wanted me to entertain. I said no."

"By entertain, you mean . . ." Guttman asked.

"Sleep with," the girl said. "I told him no."

"And you had a fight."

"Susan, this man Harry wanted you to . . . entertain. Did you know him?" Miss Brady asked.

"No. Why?"

"Well, I was wondering why Harry asked you, that's all. He must have known girls . . . that is, girls who did that regularly."

"You're sharp," Susan Eliot said. "You catch on to things quickly."

"Senility isn't automatic with age," Margaret Brady said. "Some of us manage to hang on to at least a trace of intelligence."

"I didn't mean it that way," the girl apologized.

"Never mind. I'm accustomed to it," Miss Brady said. "But now tell us why Harry suddenly decided to ask you to entertain one of his customers."

"He was there the time I was. The time before. Harry said he'd asked about me, and . . . and he was a good customer."

"And Vincent said he wanted you to go with this man," Guttman said, just to be sure he had it right in his mind.

"Yes."

"And when you said no, he hit you?"

"More or less. Harry said it was important, and I'd have to do it. I told him I didn't have to do anything, and . . . and he told me I'd do it, if I knew what was good for me. I told him to go to hell. And he hit me." The girl told it in a monotone, not looking directly at either of them.

"It must have been . . ." Miss Brady changed her mind about what she was going to say. "Did you love him, Susan?"

"I . . . I thought I did," the girl said. "I thought he loved me

139

too. Shows you how stupid you can be when you try. I deserved what I got."

"Nobody deserves to get beat up like that," Guttman said.

"Well . . . Anyway, that's what happened."

"Did you tell the police any of this?" Guttman asked.

"No. I just said we had a fight. I didn't tell them why."

"Why didn't you?"

"Because by the time they got around to asking, I'd done a little thinking. I figured it would only make things worse if I told them about it, so I just didn't say anything."

"You didn't tell them about your husband, either," Guttman said.

"They never asked me. I figured Donald hadn't mentioned it, so I kept my mouth shut. I didn't want them to start badgering him."

"Why would they do that?" Guttman asked.

"I don't know. I wasn't thinking too clearly, but I figured if they knew that Donald knew, they might think he'd killed Harry. You know, to avenge my honor, or something. And I didn't want them hassling him, not in his condition. How did you know about Donald?" she asked suddenly.

"He told us."

"What about his condition?" Miss Brady asked.

"Well, Donald is . . . nervous. Excitable."

"We talked to him today," Miss Brady said. "I think he's still in love with you."

"I know," Susan said. "The trouble is, I'm not in love with him."

"Is that why you separated?" Guttman asked.

"Mostly. It was just a mistake from the beginning."

"Yet you went out of your way to protect him," Miss Brady said.

"That doesn't mean I'm in love with him. But, well, I just didn't see any reason to get him involved, that's all."

"Still," Guttman said, "you called him up after Vincent beat you up."

"I . . . I was scared. I didn't know how badly I was hurt . . .

and I had to talk to someone. Donald was the only one I could call."

"What happened when he came over?" Guttman asked.

"Nothing, really. Donald helped me clean up—he was in Vietnam, and he knows about first-aid and stuff like that. And then he went out and got some stuff, an ice bag, some iodine. And after a while he left."

"Susan, you said Donald was nervous. What does that mean?" Miss Brady asked.

"Donald was under psychiatric care for a while. When he came out of the army, and after that. But he's all right now. Still, you can see how bad it would have looked."

"Susan," Guttman said after a moment, "could you think of anybody what would've wanted to kill Vincent?"

"No," she said.

"You answered very quickly," Miss Brady said.

"I've thought about it a lot. There were people who didn't like Harry, but that's different. I used to think they didn't understand him . . . I guess they were right."

"Who didn't like him?" Guttman asked.

"Nobody who would have killed him," Susan said.

"How about this David Hiller, at the company where you worked. Didn't Vincent use to go with the girl he's gonna marry?" Guttman asked.

"Carole? That was over a long time ago. Before I started going with Harry."

"But maybe Vincent . . ." Guttman stopped and thought for a moment. "Susan, do you know if maybe this other girl, Carole, ever . . . entertained anybody for Harry?"

"Why?"

"I'm asking, that's all."

"I don't know. What difference does it make?"

"Maybe none. It was just something I was thinking."

"Susan, the girls you mentioned, the ones who entertained Harry's customers. Would you know their names?" Miss Brady asked.

"No."

"Or how to locate them?"

"No. I told you, that was the only time I ever saw them."

"You wouldn't know whether Harry always used the same girls, would you?"

"No . . . except he seemed to know one of them. Debbie, I think. I remember she introduced the other one when they first came into the apartment."

"Do you remember what they looked like?" Guttman asked.

"Dark . . . Debbie, I guess, she was dark. She might have been Italian. Long hair, about my age. Close to my height. I don't remember . . ."

"Was she pretty, did she have anything special about her you could remember?"

"No . . . nothing special. She was okay-looking, not terribly pretty . . . She had a good figure. The other one was a little bigger, blond, not taller but, you know, a little heavier."

"More *zoftig*," Guttman said.

"What does that mean?"

"It means, well, maybe a little bit like . . ." Guttman was at a loss. He couldn't find an equivalent word in English, at least none that he cared to say out loud. "A woman what's *zoftig*," he said finally, "is . . ." He had to resort to describing a shape with his hands.

"Built," Susan Eliot said, smiling at him.

"Mr. Guttman, you're blushing," Margaret Brady said. And she was right.

"You don't know their last names, maybe you could remember?" Guttman asked, trying to change the subject.

"Last names weren't mentioned. I didn't even know the names of the men," Susan said.

"How did Harry call—"

"Did Vincent have an address book?" Guttman asked. He and Miss Brady had thought of the same thing together.

"I guess so. I mean, I assume so. I don't remember seeing it, though . . ."

"We'll find out," Guttman told her. "Meanwhile, if there's anything else you could think of . . ."

"Like what?"

"Like trying to remember the day when you found him. According to the police, there was just a minute between when the shot came and you got there, so . . ."

"I've thought about it. But I didn't see anything and I didn't hear anything."

"Okay," Guttman said. "But if you remember something, you could tell us. Or Mr. Taylor. He'll give us a message, if you ask him."

"All right. I'll try," Susan promised. "Look, I want you to know . . . well, I appreciate what you're trying to do."

"It's okay," Guttman said.

"I just hope we come up with something," Miss Brady told her.

"There's one more thing," Guttman said. "The day Vincent was shot, you called the office in the morning, right?"

"That's right. I told them I was sick. I figured maybe if I stayed out a couple of days, by the time I went back in, the bruises wouldn't show so much."

"Did you talk to anybody else that day?"

"No. No one."

"Are you sure?"

"I'm sure. As a matter of fact, I almost did, but didn't," Susan said.

"What do you mean?"

"Well, before I went over to get my things, and . . . found Harry, I tried to get Donald."

"You called him?" Guttman asked.

"He wasn't there," Susan said.

"But why did you call in the first place?"

"To find out where the car was. He used it when he went to the drugstore. It was late, so he had to drive around until he found one open, and I didn't know where he'd left the car. So I called to find out. But he wasn't home. It didn't matter. He'd left it right out front."

"How come he used your car?"

"He doesn't have one," Susan said simply.

"Oh. Well, I guess that's it," Guttman said.

"Would you tell Grandmother I'm all right?" Susan asked. "And tell her not to try to come here. The trip wouldn't be good for her. Besides, you two will probably have me out of here in no time."

"Stranger things have happened," Margaret Brady said under her breath. "But not much."

"We'll tell her," Guttman said.

Guttman waited until they were outside. "Miss Brady . . ."

"Margaret."

"Miss Brady. Would you mind telling me why it is you said what you did about strange things happening?"

"You weren't supposed to hear that," she said.

"But I heard it anyway."

"I was just kidding, that's all."

"I see," Guttman said stiffly.

"I'm afraid you don't, Mr. Guttman." She looked at him, started to say something, then changed her mind. Finally she did speak. "I have a tendency to make fun of myself, Mr. Guttman. And that's all I was doing. I'm sorry you're so sensitive, but it was just my way of . . . Oh, to hell with it," she said, looking around to see where the limousine was parked.

"I'm sorry," Guttman said after a moment. "And it wouldn't matter so much if you was talking about me. Because I'm not so sure what I'm doing, anyway." They looked at each other for a moment, and then they both smiled. "I get a little sensitive sometimes," Guttman said.

"And I make fun of myself before anyone else has a chance to," she told him. "So now that we have that out of the way, what's next?"

"Well, I was thinking maybe we should have a little talk with the police."

"With the police? Why?"

"Because we want to know about if Vincent had an address book, and who else could we ask?"

"That makes sense. But if they have it, do you think we're going to be able to look at it?"

"It wouldn't hurt to try. Also, there's something else I want to ask about."

Guttman went back to the limousine to tell the driver he might as well wait there, since they were only going to be a block away, unless he wanted to drive to police headquarters and wait there. He and Miss Brady were going to walk. They'd gone only half a block when the car passed them. When they arrived at the old two-story building, the limousine was standing directly in front of the entrance, in an area marked "No Parking." The driver, Guttman thought, must not have to pay for tickets himself.

Guttman asked for Lieutenant Weiss at the desk, and after a moment was sent upstairs. He led Miss Brady up the wide flight of stairs and across the room, with its desks and file cabinets and the wire cage in the corner, to the frosted-glass door. He knocked, then pushed open the door and let Miss Brady go in first.

"Lieutenant Weiss, this is Miss Brady. She's also from the Center, and she's helping me."

"How do you do?" Lieutenant Weiss said, getting up to greet her.

"I remember you very well, Lieutenant. You were in charge of the investigation of Miss Walter's death, weren't you?"

"Uh . . . yeah. That's right," Weiss said. "And you're one of Mr. Guttman's . . . friends."

"That's right."

"Well, what brings you here, Mr. Guttman?"

"It was what you said," Guttman began. "About letting you know how things was going."

"Uh-huh. You've been busy, I hear."

"Somebody was complaining?" Guttman asked.

"No. I talked to Paul Taylor the other day. He wanted to get an okay for you two to visit Susan Eliot."

"I didn't know he had to get permission from you," Guttman said.

"I like to keep track of things when I can," Weiss said. He lit a cigarette and Guttman promptly took a cigar from his leather case. Weiss wrinkled his nose as the smoke reached him.

"Anyway," Guttman said after the cigar was burning properly, "I figured I should stop by, since we was only down the street, and help you keep track."

"I appreciate that. Have you come up with anything interesting?"

"To be perfectly honest, no." Out of the corner of his eye Guttman saw Miss Brady look at him quickly, but he went on. "So far we talked to a couple of people what knew Vincent, but we didn't get anything yet."

"Who have you talked to?"

"We talked to the people at the company. Mr. Armstrong, and the sales manager Mr. Forester. Also to David Hiller," Guttman said.

"What made you pick on them?" Weiss asked.

"Well, they all knew Vincent, and anyway, Mrs. Stone owns some shares in the company, so we figured they'd have to talk with us. You know, it ain't like you, where people have to talk whether they feel like it or not."

"I know," Weiss said, smiling a bit. "It must be quite a handicap for you."

"Not as much as you might think," Miss Brady said.

"Anyway, the thing is, we was wondering about something," Guttman said. "We asked Susan about it, and she didn't know, so I thought maybe you could help us."

"In what way?" Weiss asked cautiously.

"Well, none of the people we talked to was really what you'd call friends with Vincent. They only knew him from the work. So we was wondering, maybe we could find out who some of his friends were."

"And how am I supposed to help you?"

"Well, we was wondering if Vincent had an address book,

with phone numbers for his friends. That way we'd know who to go see."

"An address book," Weiss said. "Yeah, I think we found one . . ." He got up and went to the file cabinet. "It should be on the list." Weiss looked into a folder, extracted a sheet of paper, read it and put it back in its place, closing the drawer. "Yeah," he said, "there was an address book."

"Could we maybe look at it?" Guttman asked.

"You'll have to ask Mrs. Vincent."

"You gave it to her?"

"Sure. We turned over all of his things to her. Except the gun, of course. She had someone pick them up last week, I think," Weiss said.

"You wouldn't have a copy of the book, by any chance, would you?" Miss Brady asked.

"Afraid not. Like I said, we turned it all over. None of it related to the case."

"Well, I guess that's that," Guttman said.

"That's all you came for?"

"What else?"

"I don't know, Mr. Guttman. It just struck me that you made a trip down here, so . . ."

"We was only a block away. We just seen Susan."

"Oh. I was thinking that otherwise you could have just called about the address book," Weiss said.

"We could've. But also, I promised I'd tell you what we was doing, too."

"I appreciate that, Mr. Guttman. Well, if there's nothing else I can do for you . . ."

"Now that you mention it, a question just come to me," Guttman said.

"Yes?"

"Well, I just remembered, I never found out how many bullets was in Vincent. I mean, like did somebody shoot him one time, or what?"

"That's right. One time. Caught him right in the middle of the chest. Got the heart. He died instantly."

"From how far away do you suppose the gun was shot?" Guttman asked.

"Oh, roughly fifteen feet. It's hard to be more precise."

"One shot," Guttman said to himself.

"Does that mean something special to you?"

"No. It's just another fact. And facts is the only thing we got to look for," Guttman explained.

"Uh-huh. Well, if that's it, I'd better get back to work," Lieutenant Weiss said.

"There was one more question."

"Yes?"

"I was just wondering, there was no tampering with the lock on the apartment, was there? I mean, nobody could've broke in, like a burglar?"

"No. No signs of tampering."

"Thank you very much."

When they got outside, Guttman stopped for a moment to try and think. Miss Brady, however, couldn't wait. "That," she said, "was very impressive. You're much sneakier than I thought."

"Sneaky? How?"

"The way you told that policeman absolutely nothing, and still found out what you wanted to know."

"All I really wanted to know was about the address book," Guttman said. "And he didn't have it."

"I know, but the way you let him think we were getting nowhere. You even made him feel smug. That was beautiful."

"He's a nice young man, really," Guttman said. "But like a lot of people, he also figures if you're getting older, you don't think so good. So I didn't try to convince him different, that's all."

"And you didn't mention Donald Eliot, either," Miss Brady reminded him.

"Susan didn't want to make trouble for him, and we promised, also," Guttman said. "But I was trying to think about the one shot."

"What about it?"

"I don't know. But one shot from a gun . . . ." He stepped

back from her until there were about five yards between them. "This isn't so far, I guess," he said, pointing his finger at her.

"What are you getting at?"

"I was just trying to figure if a person had to be a good shot to kill somebody with one bullet from this far," Guttman told her. "I guess if he hit Vincent at all, it could've been in the chest, like Lieutenant Weiss said. If you aim for the middle, I mean."

"If it were a little further, then we could be looking for someone familiar with firearms, is that what you're suggesting?" Miss Brady asked.

"I was wondering about it," Guttman said. "Only from this distance, it could be either way."

They walked back to the car and told the driver to return to the Center. They wouldn't have much time, when they got back, before he would have to leave for home. And he wanted to find out if Mrs. Kaplan and Mrs. O'Rourke had learned anything. Also, Mr. Carstairs and Mishkin might be back. Pretty soon now, he thought, they'd have to come up with something.

"Safety catches," Miss Brady said suddenly.

"I beg your pardon?"

"I said safety catches. Pistols all have safety catches, don't they?"

"I wouldn't know."

"That's the point. I've seen enough weapons, myself, to know. But I've read stories where someone points a gun at the hero and he just takes it away because they forget to release the safety catch."

"So?"

"So, if you had a gun with a safety catch, you'd probably make sure it was always set. So it wouldn't go off by accident."

"I guess that's what they're for," Guttman said.

"And if I didn't know anything about weapons, and I picked up that gun to fire it . . . I wouldn't be able to, because I wouldn't know how to release the safety catch."

"Neither would I," Guttman said, suddenly understanding.

"So if someone who was unfamiliar with firearms picked up the pistol, the chances are they wouldn't be able to use it."

"But if you knew about guns, you'd be able to," Guttman said. "It don't help Susan, but . . ."

"Why not?"

"Because Vincent could've shown her how it worked. But someone else, whoever killed Vincent, they didn't have to be an expert, but at least they had to know a little about guns."

"If Vincent's gun had a safety catch," Miss Brady said.

"We'll call Mr. Taylor and see if he could find out," Guttman said. Then he smiled and sat back against the leather upholstery. One more fact.

Mrs. Kaplan hadn't learned anything. Guttman knew as soon as they entered the lounge and saw her. She was busy with her needlepoint, while Mrs. O'Rourke was reading a movie magazine. If Mrs. Kaplan had any information, she would have been practically pacing the floor waiting for them to return. Mishkin and Mr. Carstairs weren't there. So maybe I'll find out about that tomorrow, Guttman thought.

"Nu, Guttman, you're finally back?" Mrs. Kaplan greeted him.

"We was at the jail," he explained. "We had to see Susan again."

"How are things going with our big investigation?" she asked.

"What does that mean?"

"Well, I was just asking. After all, Agnes and I aren't really doing anything, at least not that we're aware of. We just go to work, that's all, while you're out gallivanting around."

"The girl, Carole Edwards, we heard she was home sick again."

"What difference does it make?" Mrs. Kaplan asked. "You told us we shouldn't talk to her, didn't you?"

"But she wasn't there, anyway."

"She has the flu," Mrs. O'Rourke explained.

"So how about the other stuff?" Guttman asked.

"What other stuff?"

"Vincent's parties. So far that's the most important thing we got, practically," Guttman said. "And we wouldn't've got it if you wasn't there in the office."

"Well . . ." Mrs. Kaplan seemed mollified. "We weren't able to find out anything definite about it."

"What does that mean?"

"It means, so far as we could tell, nobody went to the parties," Mrs. Kaplan explained.

"Who did you check on?" Guttman asked.

"The salespeople, of course. That was what you asked us to do, wasn't it?"

"I know what I asked, but—"

"Mr. Forester never went," Mrs. O'Rourke interrupted.

"You're sure on that?"

"I talked to his secretary, you know, I just asked about it because I said I'd heard from one of the other girls, and she was telling me how one time she heard Mr. Vincent asking Mr. Forester if he wanted to go, and Mr. Forester said as how he wasn't interested. She was proud of him, because she'd heard of the parties too."

"Who was proud of him?" Guttman asked. He'd never before heard Mrs. O'Rourke say so much at one time.

"His secretary. Joanne. She was proud of Mr. Forester for saying no."

"When was this, Mrs. O'Rourke?" Miss Brady asked.

"About a month ago, I think. He and Mr. Vincent didn't get along."

"The secretary told you that too?"

"Not in so many words, but you could tell."

"That's kind of what he told himself," Guttman said.

"Well, is any of this helpful?" Mrs. Kaplan asked.

"Oy. At this time I don't know what helps. Maybe it would've been better if this Forester went to the parties. But facts is facts, and if he didn't, he didn't."

"So where, exactly, do we stand?" Mrs. Kaplan persisted.

"In the middle. We got some things, but not enough yet."

"Well, what's next?"

"Next is to talk to this Carole Edwards," Guttman said. "So tomorrow, if she's there, you could call and tell me, so I'll come talk to her."

"And if she isn't?"

"If she isn't, I guess I'll have to talk to her at home. Maybe you could get the address somehow."

"Naturally."

"And also, I'll have to go talk to Mrs. Vincent. His wife. So I'll do that in the morning."

"You don't seem very happy about it," Mrs. Kaplan observed.

"I ain't, particularly. I don't know what I could say to her about her husband. But maybe by tomorrow I'll think of something. Anyway, if I'm not here when you call about the girl, you could tell Mishkin, and I could talk to him on the phone and find out what's what."

"And that's all you want us to do tomorrow?" Mrs. Kaplan asked.

"It's all I could think of for the minute. Just finding out whatever you could find out, it's a help."

"Some help," Dora Kaplan said, just loudly enough for Guttman to hear.

He decided not to answer. Things were difficult enough without fighting with Mrs. Kaplan.

Eleven

Guttman took the bus to the Center in the morning. If Lois drove him he wouldn't get there until nine, and Mr. Carstairs was usually gone by then. It was eight-thirty when he arrived, and the small lounge was crowded with people having their second cups of coffee, while the breakfast dishes were being cleared in the dining room. It took Guttman a moment to locate Harold Carstairs. He was sitting alone at a small table in the corner, reading the *Wall Street Journal.* It was a newspaper Guttman had never read.

"Ah, Mr. Guttman. You're here early today, aren't you?"

"I wanted to get here before you was gone. I figured maybe you could've learned something, and . . ."

"As a matter of fact, I have. I was going to wait for you, to discuss it, before I went downtown again. There are a few more calls I'd like to make to verify some things, but I think I have enough to give you now."

"That's good to hear," Guttman said, sitting down across the table from him.

"Do you want to wait for the others?" Mr. Carstairs asked.

"I don't know where they is. Mrs. Kaplan and Mrs. O'Rourke is going to their jobs, and Mishkin I didn't see since yesterday morning. Miss Brady might be around, but if you got some more things you want to do, you might as well just tell me whatever now," Guttman said.

Harold Carstairs folded his newspaper, then took his notebook from his inside pocket, opened it, adjusted his glasses, and looked up. "I think I mentioned the possibility of some sort of embezzlement regarding Mr. Vincent."

"I remember."

"Well, I suppose I really used the wrong word, or rather, I was thinking of embezzlement in a generic sense."

Guttman blinked, but he didn't interrupt. If he had to, he'd look the word up later.

"Since Mr. Vincent was in a sales capacity, it was unlikely that he could have actually manipulated the account books. However, that doesn't preclude some sort of unethical activity. Therefore, I decided that a survey of the books of Armstrong Industries might not provide anything germane to our investigation, although based on what I have learned, I would be interested in auditing their books. I suspect that the organization . . ."

"Please, Mr. Carstairs," Guttman said. "I got to admit, already I'm not sure I understand all of this."

"I'm sorry. I'll come right to the point, then," Carstairs said. "I reviewed all of the available records and compiled a list of some of Armstrong Industries' primary customers, since those are the people with whom Mr. Vincent would have had direct contact. Then, as I suspected, I found that some of those companies have done business with my former firm. In fact, in two instances I was personally involved, which made things much easier."

"I'm sure," Guttman said, still not knowing what Mr. Carstairs was talking about.

"It took a number of phone calls, and for a time I feared that the exercise would be fruitless, but finally I found what I was looking for."

"And that was?"

"Do you remember, Mr. Guttman, how concerned Mrs.

Kaplan was some time ago about the overcharges sustained by the Center?"

"I remember."

"Well, there was a similar situation involving Armstrong Industries."

"I think you just lost me completely," Guttman said. "You said you was talking to the customers, not the people they was buying from. If Vincent was paying too much and keeping some of the extra, okay. But he was doing the selling . . ."

"Precisely, Mr. Guttman. Here we were concerned about the dietician. But the merchants she bought from also profited," Mr. Carstairs explained. "It seems that some of the people doing business with Armstrong Industries were to be rewarded rather directly. It's a question of expenses, really. All one has to do is arrange with a customer to cooperate, and since the rewards can be substantial, unfortunately, some are willing."

"Mr. Carstairs, please, I got to go see some people soon. Could you just explain it simple?" Guttman asked.

"I'm trying, Mr. Guttman. What happened, then, was that various expenditures—entertainment, travel, and so forth—were inflated, and these additional funds were turned over, at least in part, to the customers involved. You see, a customer would agree to a purchase from Armstrong Industries, sign a contract. But the contract might be held in abeyance while the purchaser was then ostensibly wined and dined, perhaps even taken on a vacation, until a suitably high level of expenses was reached. Then the buyer in question would receive a share of those spurious expenses."

"So what you're saying is the expenses was padded and then split with the customers. But everybody pads expenses," Guttman said, disappointed.

"It's a matter of degree, though," Mr. Carstairs said. "Thus far I'd say that the amounts involved may be as high as five to ten thousand dollars a year. That is, the split, so to speak. And if you consider that Armstrong Industries has to count those expenditures as part of the cost of doing business, naturally they have to add that expense to their prices. And if they do that, they damage their competitive position. In other words, they may lose other sales. The only ones who profit are the salesmen and the individual at the purchasing organization who is involved."

"Okay," Guttman said. "So it's more than a couple of dollars."

"You seem disappointed, Mr. Guttman."

"To tell the truth, I think I am. I ain't thought it all the way through, but so far, what you're saying don't give nobody a motive to kill Vincent."

"Perhaps if Mr. Vincent found out about what was going on . . ." Mr. Carstairs suggested.

"What do you mean, if Vincent found out? He's the one what was doing it, wasn't he?"

"Did I say that?"

"You didn't say that?"

"Oh, no. It wasn't Mr. Vincent," Mr. Carstairs said.

"Then who?"

"Mr. Forester. The sales manager. He was the one, logically, who would have been able to manage it best, since he had to authorize all of the sales expense accounts."

"It was Forester what was stealing?"

"Stealing may be a strong word, but—"

"So that gives us something," Guttman said happily. "At least it's a possibility. We don't know if Vincent knew, but maybe . . ."

"You think he confronted Forester with what he learned, and as a result . . ."

"I don't know, Mr. Carstairs. But it's something. It's something to try to find out about."

"How?"

"I ain't sure. There's one thing," Guttman said, thinking aloud. "Maybe you could talk to these people, the ones what did the buying, and they could say whether Vincent knew, or not."

"I'll look into it," Harold Carstairs said, putting his notebook away.

156

Guttman decided that it might be a good idea for him to get a notebook like that, too, so he could keep all of his ideas together in one place.

"Good morning," Margaret Brady said.

Guttman hadn't seen her approach. "Good morning," he and Mr. Carstairs replied.

"Well, what's on the agenda today?"

"Talking to Mrs. Vincent, I guess," Guttman said. "But first I want to find Mishkin, if he's here."

"I just saw him outside, reading the paper," Miss Brady said.

"If you'll excuse me," Mr. Carstairs said, "I'll go downtown and look into that matter, Mr. Guttman."

"Certainly," Guttman said. "Oh, listen, I almost forgot. Since we're talking about expenses, maybe you should keep a list of what you spend."

"I always do," Harold Carstairs said.

Guttman and Miss Brady left the lounge with him, and then went to find Mishkin, sitting in the morning sun with a newspaper. He saw them approaching and folded the paper. Miss Brady sat down, leaving Guttman to look around for another lawn chair to bring over and join them.

"So how's it going?" Mishkin asked.

"That's what everybody wants to know," Guttman told him. "I only wish I knew the answer."

"Rome wasn't built in a day," Jacob Mishkin said philosophically.

"We're not building Rome."

"But you shouldn't figure you got to do everything one, two, three. Sometimes it takes four, five, six."

"Thank you very much. So are you telling me you didn't find out anything yesterday?"

"Like I said, Rome wasn't—"

"It's okay," Guttman said. "Now it looks like maybe we wouldn't have to worry too much about those details."

"Which details are those?" Miss Brady asked. "And why not?"

Guttman explained to them what Mr. Carstairs had just told

157

him, and then added, "So even if Mishkin could get the dates when Vincent was owing money and paid off, it wouldn't help if we couldn't get maybe Forester's bank account too. So we'd know if he was paying blackmail."

"Well, even so, now we have something to work on," Miss Brady said.

"So you don't want I should keep trying?" Mishkin asked.

"Today you could do something else," Guttman told him. "Mrs. Kaplan's supposed to call and tell whether this Carole Edwards went to work, and if not, give the address where she lives. Miss Brady and I got to see Mrs. Vincent, so maybe you could wait for her to call, and I could call you later on and find out from you."

"It don't sound very hard," Mishkin said. "I'm sure I could manage it."

"Okay. So I better ask Mrs. Stone if maybe she's got Vincent's address. It might've been in the reports, and then——"

"I took care of it last night," Miss Brady said. "I've got the address, and the car is outside."

Guttman looked at her for a moment, then nodded his head. "Okay, so we might as well get started." As they walked toward the car he wondered why it was that some people seemed to know what he was thinking before he did, sometimes.

Harry Vincent had lived well. The two-story house, dark brick with ivy growing along the walls, was set back some twenty yards from the quiet street. There were tall trees on the front lawn, and from the way the flowers along both sides of the front door and the shrubs along the driveway were tended, Guttman was sure the Vincents had a gardener. The house, he felt, would have looked natural in a movie about England, and he half expected a butler to answer the door. A maid did the honors.

"My name is Guttman," he said. "And this is Miss Brady. I wonder, could we talk to Mrs. Vincent? It's about her husband."

"Is Mrs. Vincent expecting you?" The maid, a middle-aged woman in uniform, didn't look particularly happy.

"No, but maybe she could talk to us for a few minutes . . ."

"I don't think Mrs. Vincent is seeing visitors," the maid said.

"Would you be kind enough to tell her we're here, and that we have some information which may interest her?" Miss Brady asked stiffly. "We'll wait here."

The maid hesitated, then went inside, leaving them standing outside. As if she didn't want to insult them too much, she left the front door open behind her. It was several minutes before she returned.

"Mrs. Vincent will see you," she told them.

They followed her inside, through the foyer and into the living room, where she asked them to wait. The inside of the house didn't look like the outside, to Guttman. Outside, it was English and old; inside, it was white and black and modern. Glass and metal and cushions, tiled floors and modern paintings. Still, it didn't bother him. It wasn't to his taste, but he knew that it was a nice room because nothing clashed. Different things, he thought, could be in good taste, and you don't have to like everything. He didn't like Vivian Vincent as soon as he saw her, although he assumed that she was in good taste too.

She was a small woman, in her late thirties or early forties, Guttman thought, and although she wore a light-blue dressing gown, she was barefoot. Guttman guessed that she had still been in bed when they arrived. Her thick black hair was casually brushed and she had only the slightest hint of make-up on, as if she had hurried but made sure that she looked all right before seeing her unexpected visitors.

"I'm Vivian Vincent," she said. "Can I help you?"

"My name is Max Guttman, this here is Miss Brady. We was wondering if maybe we could talk to you a minute about your husband. And offer our sympathy," he added.

"Thank you."

Obviously she wasn't anxious for their sympathy, Guttman thought, but she hadn't felt it necessary to tell them so. He had the feeling that he might not get very far with her, and he was glad that Miss Brady was with him.

"Mrs. Vincent, this is awkward, naturally, and it's a bit difficult to know quite where to begin," Margaret Brady said, not sounding at all awkward. "Frankly, we're investigating your husband's death."

"Indeed?"

She wants to laugh, Guttman thought, but she's too polite.

"I know, it seems strange," Miss Brady went on. "But it's rather a long story. At any rate, we'd appreciate just a few minutes of your time."

Vivian Vincent looked at them for a moment, then nodded her head. "Won't you sit down?"

Guttman and Miss Brady sat on the couch, and Mrs. Vincent half reclined in a strange-looking easy chair next to them.

"I was under the impression that the police had completed their investigation of my husband's death," Mrs. Vincent said. "Although I realize you are not from the police."

"No. We represent the interests of the girl who is accused of killing your husband," Miss Brady said.

"I assumed as much."

"Why?" Guttman asked.

"Who else would be investigating?" Mrs. Vincent asked simply.

"It was a dumb question," Guttman said. "The thing is, Mrs. Vincent, we don't think it was Susan Eliot what killed your husband."

"Don't you? Then who do you suggest?"

"We don't know. Yet," Guttman said.

The woman looked at them carefully, as if reconsidering her decision to talk to them. "All right," she said. "Why do you think she didn't do it? Not that I'd blame her, you understand."

"You wouldn't blame her?" Guttman asked.

"If Harry had ever laid a hand on me, I might have killed him myself," she said easily. "But you haven't answered my question."

"I don't think we can," Margaret Brady said. "We may just be making the assumption of innocence because it's what we'd like to believe."

"I thought innocence was outdated," Mrs. Vincent said.

"That's a matter of semantics," Miss Brady said.

"Mrs. Vincent, do you know if your husband had money problems before he died?" Guttman asked, anxious to change the subject.

"Everyone has money problems nowadays."

"Naturally. But I mean something special."

"No. He never discussed financial matters with me. We weren't wealthy, but as you can see, we were comfortable. And I know of no reason why he should have been concerned about money."

"How about from gambling?" Guttman asked.

"I don't know what you mean."

"We've been told that Mr. Vincent incurred some fairly large gambling losses," Miss Brady said.

"Who told you that? The girl?"

"We're not in a position to say."

"Then why should I answer?" Mrs. Vincent asked.

"So we could know," Guttman said. "And so we wouldn't have to ask other people about it." He had just made a guess about Harry Vincent's widow, and now he'd find out if he was right.

"I'm not sure I understand."

"Well, if we can't find out this way, I guess we could go to the police and say we heard Mr. Vincent owed money to bookies, and then they'd have to start looking into it, and then maybe the newspapers would write something about it. So instead of that, we're asking you," Guttman explained.

"Harry often gambled," Vivian Vincent said calmly. "I knew that, but if he had any debts, he didn't discuss them with me."

"Not at all?" Guttman asked.

"Not at all."

"But you was his wife, so that's why I ask."

"And I have told you, Harry didn't discuss his financial affairs with me."

"Mrs. Vincent, our information is that Mr. Vincent had been in debt to gamblers before. In the past he was able to make good. Could he have done that without your knowledge?" Miss Brady asked.

"If what you say is true, then he must have. I knew nothing about it."

"Mrs. Vincent, could you think of anybody what might have had something against your husband, maybe enough to kill him?" Guttman asked.

"I can only think of one person."

"Who's that?"

"The girl . . . Susan Eliot."

"Besides her, I meant," Guttman said.

"Mrs. Vincent, may I ask if you think Susan killed your husband?" Miss Brady asked.

"The police seem to think so."

"Yes, but do you?"

"She certainly had a motive. But if you're asking for my evaluation of her personality, I'm afraid I can't help you. I never met the girl."

"Mrs. Vincent, I'm sorry to have to ask this," Miss Brady said, "but regarding your husband's . . . activities. Was this the first time, that is . . ."

"I'm sure that you know it wasn't," Mrs. Vincent said. "However . . ."

"You don't sound like it bothered you," Guttman said.

"That is none of your business," Vivian Vincent answered. "Now if you'll excuse me . . ."

"Some people wouldn't think so."

"I don't care what some people would or wouldn't think." She looked at her watch. "I've given you the few minutes I promised. Unless there's something specific you wish to ask . . ."

"Just one thing," Guttman said. "The police said there was an address book of your husband's that they found. They said they gave it to you with his other stuff. Could we maybe look at it?"

"An address book . . . I don't remember whether I have it or not." She seemed to be thinking, but Guttman suspected that she was stalling. "Why do you want to see it?"

"We're hoping that some of the names might help us," Miss Brady said.

"In what way?"

"We're trying to talk to everyone we can who knew Mr. Vincent. If there are names of friends in the book, well, naturally . . ."

"Of course," Mrs. Vincent said. "Well, I'm really sorry, but I recall that I threw the address book out, with some other things that I had no use for."

"You're sure you threw it out?" Guttman asked.

"Positive."

Guttman looked at Miss Brady sitting beside him, and she made a slight face. There was nothing else to do but thank Mrs. Vincent and leave.

"I don't believe her," Margaret Brady said as they got in the car. "She has that address book."

"I don't think she'll keep it long," Guttman said. "I think she'll probably throw it in the garbage."

"I'm afraid you're right. I sure wish she'd given it to us."

"She didn't want us calling up people and asking questions," Guttman said. "I don't know I could blame her, except Susan's still in jail and it could've helped."

Guttman told the driver to stop at the first phone booth they passed. When he lost his dime in that booth, he suggested they go on until they found someplace to have coffee. In a diner the phone booths were less likely to be out of order, without a sign on them. While Miss Brady ordered coffee for them, he called the Center, and after a long wait, got Mishkin on the phone. Mrs. Kaplan had checked in. Carole Edwards had called in sick again and Mrs. Kaplan had her home address. Guttman copied it down and then read it back to make sure he hadn't made a mistake.

Carole Edwards lived downtown, half an hour's drive from the Vincent home. Guttman felt himself growing more nervous as they drove. If she didn't have something to tell them, he didn't know what they were going to do next. He could turn it all over to Lieutenant Weiss, of course, but that probably wouldn't do much good. The best he could hope for was that

Susan's lawyer would be able to convince a jury she wasn't the only one with a motive to kill Vincent. And Guttman didn't think that, by itself, would be enough to convince them she hadn't done it.

Carole Edwards lived in a new apartment house, and although there was no doorman, the inner door was securely locked and a closed-circuit TV camera protected residents from unwanted guests. Guttman wasn't sure they'd be welcome.

"What do we do now, just ring the bell?" Miss Brady asked.

"I don't know. I mean, if she's really sick, maybe she wouldn't come to answer, and even if she did, maybe she wouldn't want to talk to us."

"That's a point," Miss Brady said, studying the directory. "It's five B. Should we chance it?"

"I guess so. No, wait a minute." Guttman nodded toward the street. A young woman with an armful of packages was coming toward the building.

"You think that's her?" Miss Brady asked, misunderstanding.

"No, but it might be a way to get in." Guttman waited until the woman had shouldered the outside door open and begun trying to get her key from her purse. "Could I help?" he offered, reaching for the packages.

"Thank you." She smiled at him, and a moment later all three of them were in the elevator. The woman took her package from Guttman at the third floor and got out.

"Being old has some advantages," Miss Brady said. "You'll notice that she wasn't worried we'd try to mug her."

"If I was in her place, I wouldn't worry about us neither," Guttman said.

They found the door and he pushed the button. They could hear the chimes. After a moment he rang again, then leaned forward to see if he could hear anything inside. "I think there's somebody moving around," he told Miss Brady, pushing the bell a third time. After a moment they heard the flap on the peephole being pushed aside, and knew they were being studied. Finally the door opened a few inches, held by a chain.

"Miss Edwards?" Guttman asked.

"Yes. Who are you?"

"Miss Edwards, we was wondering if we could talk to you about Harry Vincent," he said.

"What about him?"

"It would only take a couple of minutes," Guttman said. "We got your address from Mr. Armstrong," he added, stretching the truth a little. "And we're sorry to bother you when you're sick, but it's important."

"Mr. Armstrong sent you?" she asked, and when they didn't deny it, she assumed they had agreed. "Oh, you must be the ones David told me about," she said. "Okay, just a minute . . ." She closed the door enough to remove the chain, then pulled it open to let them in.

The apartment carried the odor Guttman always associated with illness, an odor he had lived with for three months before his wife Sara had finally gone to the hospital for the last time. Guttman was willing to assume that Carole Edwards really had been sick.

"Why don't you sit down," the girl suggested, pulling her bathrobe around her. "I don't want to seem unfriendly, but I hope it won't take too long . . ."

"Have you taken your temperature?" Margaret Brady asked.

"Huh? Oh, no. Not today."

"Where's your thermometer?"

"In the bathroom. Look, I don't—"

"I'm a nurse," Miss Brady announced, as if that explained everything. She found the bathroom, and a moment later was back, shaking the thermometer. "You look as if you should be in bed," she told the girl.

"I was," Carole Edwards admitted, sitting down uncertainly as Miss Brady advanced on her, pointing the thermometer at the girl's mouth.

"Don't talk," Miss Brady advised, picking up the girl's wrist in her fingers and looking at her watch.

It all seemed a little strange to Guttman, and he wondered whether Miss Brady was doing this automatically or if she was trying to get the girl's confidence. She took the thermometer from the girl's mouth, read it, then using the thermometer as a tongue depressor, peered down Carole Edwards' throat.

"How long have you had it?" Miss Brady asked.

"I kind of woke up with it Friday."

"Have you been running a fever all along?"

"I think so. On and off. Look, I don't—"

"Did you see a doctor?"

"No."

"Well, it's probably run its course by now, anyway. What have you been taking for it?"

"Just aspirin," the girl said.

"Did you take any today?"

"No . . . not yet. Look, I don't even know your name, for God's sake," Carole Edwards said, starting to get up from her chair.

Miss Brady put a hand on her shoulder to keep her down. "You're running a slight fever," she said. "But I don't think it's serious. May I use your phone?"

"My phone? Look, I wish I knew what the hell was going on here . . ."

"I'm sorry," Miss Brady said, smiling. "I guess I did sort of take over. I was going to call a doctor and have him prescribe something. Then I can run down to a pharmacy and pick it up for you. You'll feel better quicker."

"I appreciate this, I guess, but . . ."

"Miss Edwards, maybe an introduction or two would help," Guttman said. "My name is Max Guttman, and this is Miss Brady. We're friends of Susan Eliot's grandmother and we're trying to help her."

"You're weird. The two of you, you're weird," the girl said, smiling in spite of herself. "Okay, call your doctor."

"What's the name of your pharmacy?" Miss Brady asked.

"Elm, I think. It should be on one of the bottles in the medicine cabinet."

"Thanks."

Miss Brady returned to the bathroom, then emerged with a small vial in her hand and went to the phone. She spoke quietly, but Guttman caught enough to know she was talking to Dr. Aiken at the Center.

"This doctor will prescribe for me without even seeing me?" Carole Edwards asked after Miss Brady hung up.

"I worked with him for, well, it's better than thirty years now. If he can't trust my judgment about a sore throat, well, I don't know. Where is this drugstore of yours?"

The girl told her, and Miss Brady left.

"You might as well sit down," the girl told Guttman.

"Thank you."

"You know, I don't believe any of this. I mean, here I am, lying in bed feeling lousy, the doorbell rings, and it's visiting-nurse time. Weird."

Guttman didn't know quite how to answer her. "Like I said, that's not the real reason we came," he told her. "I guess Miss Brady just can't stop being a nurse, even though she retired." He tried to study the girl without being too obvious. She was in her late twenties, and in the light of the table lamp near her, she looked very pale. Her light hair was fairly long, and without make-up, Guttman thought she was attractive but not pretty. "Maybe while we're waiting I could ask you a couple of questions," Guttman suggested. "Like I told you, we're trying to help Susan Eliot."

"Uh-huh. Well, go ahead. I don't guess I'll be getting a bill for all this, so I figure I owe you."

"Thank you." He tried to decide how to approach the problem. "Did you know Susan very well?" he asked.

"Well enough. We aren't close . . . Under the circumstances, I'm sure you understand. Or do you? Yeah, I guess you do. David said you were at the office, asking questions. You are the ones, aren't you?"

"If you mean David Hiller, then yes, we was the ones," Guttman said.

"Had to be," Carole Edwards said. "There couldn't be two like you. Anyway, then you know about . . . me and Harry. So you know why Susan and I weren't very close. Not that I disliked her, or anything."

"Miss Edwards, forgive me, but we heard the two of you had a fight . . . once," Guttman said.

"Uh . . . yeah. Well, I guess you could call it that. I told Susan some things she didn't want to hear, and she didn't like it."

"About Mr. Vincent?"

"Uh-huh."

"We also heard he started going out with Susan after you two stopped going together," Guttman said.

"You mean like he dumped me for Susan?" she asked. "Yeah, you could look at it that way. But things between me and Harry were over about then, anyway."

"Could I ask—do you think Susan killed him?"

"Why not?"

"I beg your pardon?"

"I mean, why shouldn't I think so? In the first place, I knew Harry, remember? He was a bastard. Charming when he wanted to be, but deep down, a bastard. I wouldn't blame anyone for wanting to kill him. And the police are sure she did it, so why shouldn't I think so?"

"No reason, I suppose," Guttman said. "Except we don't think she done it."

"Well, I've got nothing against Susan. I mean, it's not like I hope she did it, you know?"

"Miss Edwards, there's some questions I got to ask that could be embarrassing," Guttman said after a moment. "I hope you wouldn't take it personal. Whatever I ask, it ain't that I'm suggesting something, it's just that I'm asking."

"Okay, whatever that means."

"Well, the first thing is, we know how Vincent used to have parties sometimes for customers." He waited for a reaction, but the girl just looked at him for a moment. Then she got up and walked out of the room. Guttman was relieved when she came back a moment later with a pack of cigarettes.

"I don't suppose I can ask who told you about . . . No, I don't guess it makes any difference." She lit a cigarette, exhaled smoke, and coughed. "Shit," she said quietly. "Everybody probably knows, anyway."

"Miss Edwards, was you at these parties?"

"Which parties? Harry had two kinds . . . I mean . . ." The girl was upset, and Guttman decided to let her work it out for herself. "I was around once or twice," she said after a moment.

"Just around? I mean . . . when there was customers, he sometimes arranged that there was girls there . . ."

"Just around," she repeated.

"Did Mr. Hiller know about this?" Guttman asked.

"What's David got to do with it?"

"I was just asking. We talked to him a little bit, like you already know. Naturally, he knew you and Mr. Vincent was . . . friends."

"You're really a cute one, aren't you?" Carole Edwards said. "Friends. That's beautiful. And then you talk about David . . ." She shook her head. "What are you looking for, anyway?"

"Facts. Information. If Susan Eliot didn't kill Vincent, then somebody else did."

"Well, it sure as hell wasn't me," Carole Edwards said. "I wouldn't have dirtied my hands on him."

"But you could've had a reason," Guttman prodded. "After all, you was with him from before . . ."

"That was over long ago. Completely."

"But Vincent was the kind of person what could've made trouble. Maybe he was talking to Mr. Hiller about things."

"David knew about me and Harry," the girl said in a soft voice.

"But a person like Vincent, he could've told things, like about the parties, even if they wasn't true . . ."

"I told you, I didn't kill him," she said angrily. "And if you're even hinting that David did it, just forget it!"

"Miss Edwards, I'm not hinting nothing. I'm just trying to find out."

"Well, now you know."

Guttman waited until she seemed calmer. "Did you know anything about Vincent owing money to gamblers?"

"Harry always lost. Story of his life. He was always complaining his wife wouldn't let him touch the money they had. She was smart. I don't know why she stayed with him at all, but she was smart enough to make sure he didn't leave her broke."

"You don't have no idea why she stayed with him?" It was a question that had been bothering Guttman.

"Appearances, I guess. Harry said she was worried about her social status. Came from an old-line family, you know? I guess she could put up with Harry so long as he didn't interfere with her life, didn't become an embarrassment to her. Maybe she figured divorce would have been messy."

"I see," Guttman said. Well, it could be an explanation, he thought.

The bell rang and the girl got up to push the buzzer. "That must be your friend Florence Nightingale."

"Miss Edwards, I got only one more question. These parties Vincent had . . ."

"You're back on that?"

"Please. All I was going to say is I knew there was girls there, and I was wondering do you know any of their names."

"No."

"You answer that very quick."

"Well, I don't know them."

"Not even a first name? You got to remember something," Guttman said.

"Why do I have to?"

"Look, Miss Edwards, believe me, I don't want to make problems. But this could be very important."

"So?"

"So all I'm asking, and I wouldn't tell nobody what you say, is if you know any of these girls, and maybe how to get ahold of them—"

"I told you . . ."

"Miss Edwards, if I find out from you, I wouldn't have to go around asking other people about the parties no more. If I have

170

to, I could get the names of the men what was there, and I could talk to them. I know who some of them are already," he added. It wasn't true, but Mr. Carstairs might be able to help on that score. And, he thought, if Susan Eliot had been asked to entertain a customer, the chances were that this girl had, too.

"So?" the girl said.

"So they could tell me who was there, and maybe who was just like you said, around. And who wasn't just hanging around."

"That's practically blackmail," she said after a moment.

"All I'm asking for is help. A name and an address, or a phone number, if you got it."

"I don't know. Harry used to make the arrangements. There was one girl, Debbie something . . . I don't know her last name."

"The police say they gave Vincent's address book to Mrs. Vincent, and she says she threw it in the garbage. But maybe you got the address, or a phone number . . ."

"I . . . I'm not sure . . ."

"Miss Edwards . . . Carole, I promise I wouldn't tell nobody where I got it. I wouldn't tell nobody nothing about it."

"All right," she said wearily. Then the chimes rang. "You might as well answer the door," she told him, going into the other room.

Guttman let Miss Brady into the apartment and closed the door behind her. "Don't say nothing," he warned.

"About what?"

"I'll tell you outside."

"Here," Carole Edwards said, holding out a slip of paper.

Guttman took a quick look at it, and put it in his pocket. "Thank you."

"Just remember what you promised."

"I wouldn't forget," he assured her.

"Well, if that's all over, here's your medicine," Miss Brady said. "Directions are on the bottle. And stay in bed as much as possible. Drink liquids, lots of liquids."

"Thanks," Carole Edwards said with a trace of sarcasm. "What do I owe you?"

"Three-fifty," Miss Brady said.

"That's cheap. Nowadays drugs cost an arm and a leg."

"Professional discount," Miss Brady told her. "There's enough there to get you through three days," she said as the girl counted out the money. "If you're still not feeling all right after that, you really should see a doctor."

"Okay, okay. Thanks."

Carole Edwards ushered them to the door quickly, and as Guttman stood in the hall with Miss Brady he heard the girl attach the chain and turn the lock behind them. He looked again at the slip of paper she'd given him, and wondered how he'd go about making an appointment with a prostitute.

Twelve

Guttman waited until they were in the car before he told Miss Brady what had happened. The driver, after being told they weren't going anywhere for a few minutes, continued reading his newspaper. As he explained things to Miss Brady, Guttman wondered whether the driver could hear them—or if he cared about what they were talking about.

"I think you did very well," Miss Brady said when he was through. "You got what we really needed, anyway."

"I got it, but now what do we do with it?"

"What's the problem?"

"Well, to be honest, the thing is, I never called up on the telephone before a . . . a prostitute." Why, he wondered, did he feel like he was apologizing?

"Do you have the number?" Guttman handed her the slip of paper.

"I'll be right back," Miss Brady said, getting out of the car.

Guttman watched her walk to the corner and enter a drugstore, the same one, he thought, where she'd gotten the medicine. Miss Brady reappeared only a few minutes later, walked briskly to the car, and got into the back seat next to him.

"It's all set. We'll meet her in half an hour. How much money do you have with you?" Miss Brady asked.

"Money? I got . . ." Guttman had to shift on the seat to get his wallet out. "I got twenty dollars, but . . ."

"It's okay, Max. It's nothing like that," she said, smiling. "But she claimed she had nothing to say until I offered to pay for her time. She's a working girl, after all."

"How much did you tell her we'd pay?"

"Fifteen dollars for fifteen minutes' talk. I've got enough to cover it, but I wanted to make sure we were okay, in case it takes longer. I don't expect that it will, do you?"

"Uh . . . no, I guess it wouldn't," Guttman said, still surprised at how easily Miss Brady had taken care of what had been, to him, a big problem. Of course, he thought, she's a woman. He listened as she gave the driver an address, and because there was nothing else he could think of to do, he sat back and tried to calm himself enough to remember the questions he wanted to ask this girl when they met.

Guttman and Miss Brady sat on one side of the booth in the coffee shop where the meeting had been arranged. They were in a busy commercial section of the city, but the restaurant hadn't yet begun to fill up with the lunchtime crowd. Guttman hoped they could get their interview over before they found themselves surrounded by people. He didn't feel like having anyone listen in.

"How do we know her when she gets here?" he asked Miss Brady.

"I told her what we look like. She'll find us."

Guttman wondered how she had described them, but he didn't ask. Some things, he thought, it's better if you don't know. He chewed on his cigar nervously. He needn't have worried about recognizing the girl. After all, he knew what she did for a living.

Debbie was quite tall, as tall as Miss Brady must have been, he thought, and she had a good figure. She very obviously had a good figure. She was wearing shorts, tight ones, and a blouse that seemed to be transparent. When the girl approached their booth Guttman realized that it was, indeed, transparent. And she wore nothing beneath the blouse. Debbie wore her dark hair long and straight, and she had thick make-up around her eyes. When she reached the table Guttman started to rise, out of habit, but there wasn't enough room in the booth to maneuver.

"Hi. I'm Debbie," she said, sliding into the seat across from them.

"How do you do? My name is Guttman, and this is Miss Brady."

"You the one I spoke to on the phone?"

"Yes," Miss Brady said.

"Okay, listen, I think we should get the money out of the way up front. It's easier that way." She brushed her hair back from her face and smiled.

Her voice, Guttman thought, was surprisingly soft. So why surprisingly? he asked himself. He looked around nervously while Miss Brady reached into her purse and put a five- and a ten-dollar bill on the table.

"It's okay," Debbie said. "They know me here." She slid the bills toward her and stuffed them into her purse. "Okay, now what can I do for you? You said you wanted to talk."

"It's about Harry Vincent," Guttman said.

"Yeah, I read about it," the girl said. "That's rough."

"He was . . . You liked him?" Guttman asked.

"Harry was all right. At least he never gave me any trouble. Oh, once in a while he'd want something for nothing, which he never got, but that's nothing."

"How long did you know him?" Miss Brady asked.

"A couple of years, on and off."

"Miss . . . Debbie, we understand you used to . . . entertain men at his apartment sometimes," Guttman said, not looking directly at her.

"Listen, maybe I better know what this is all about before I say anything, okay? I mean, you said how Carole gave you my number, but . . ."

"We won't cause you any trouble, Debbie," Miss Brady said. "The fact of the matter is that we're investigating Harry Vincent's death."

"They got the chick who killed him, don't they?"

"We don't think she killed him. We're trying to help find out," Guttman told her.

"Oh, heavy, man. The two of you playing cops and robbers, that's heavy." She couldn't keep from laughing.

"Heavy or not, that's the situation," Margaret Brady said.

"Well, okay. I mean, if that's all it is, okay. No offense."

"It's okay," Guttman said. "By now we're used to it."

"Yeah, I can see how you would be. Anyway, what do you want to know?"

"One thing is if Carole Edwards, if she ever also . . . entertained the men when you was at the apartment?" Guttman said.

"What kind of a question is that?"

"It's a question. No special kind."

"You looking to get her into trouble? She's a good kid, and—"

"I think you've already answered it for us," Miss Brady said. "But you can rest assured, we don't want to make trouble for Carole."

"Yeah, I guess I did at that, huh? You two are pretty sharp, you know? I think I underestimated you," Debbie said. She didn't seem upset by it.

"We're used to that already, also," Guttman said, smiling slightly.

"Carole's participation in these parties—was that a normal thing? I mean . . ." Miss Brady stopped in mid-sentence.

"I know what you mean. No, I only remember her there a couple or three times, maybe. I don't think she liked the scene, you know? But you could tell Harry wanted her to go along, so I guess that's why she did."

"Was it the same way with Susan Eliot?" Miss Brady asked.

"Who?"

"Susan Eliot. She's the one who's in jail for killing Vincent," Guttman explained.

"Susan . . . yeah. Hey, is she the one?"

"What do you mean?"

"Well, I just didn't put them together, I guess. She was there once, I can remember. I just forgot her name. No, maybe it was twice. But I didn't realize she was the one zapped Harry."

"She didn't," Guttman said.

"Well, anyway, she wasn't a regular, like I said."

"And did she entertain Harry's friends, that you know of?" Miss Brady asked.

"One time, yeah. I don't think she dug the scene, either. Amateurs," Debbie said.

"Miss Debbie—"

"Debbie's okay."

"Debbie. Do you know the names of any of the men what was at these parties?" Guttman asked.

"The johns? Naw. Just first names, you know."

"Were any of them there more than once?" Miss Brady asked.

"A couple, yeah. Harry's regular customers."

"But you don't know their names?"

"Just first names, like I said. Or nicknames. Usually that's how it is in this business, you know."

The girl probed in her purse for a cigarette, and Guttman tried to digest what he'd just learned. He wasn't surprised that Carole Edwards had lied to them. Neither was he really surprised about Susan Eliot. He couldn't even blame her for lying about things. If you was in her place, he asked himself, would you go around talking about something like that? It's not like with this girl, where it's a job, already.

"Was all of the men customers, do you know?" Guttman asked.

"They were to me," Debbie answered, laughing.

"I mean, was they all customers for Harry, or maybe somebody could've worked with him, you know?"

"No, I don't, man. I mean, they didn't talk about that kind of thing with me."

"How long . . . You said you knew Harry maybe a couple of years, is that right?" Guttman asked.

"Uh-huh."

"And he always called you when he had somebody to entertain?"

"I don't know if he always called me. He might've called other girls, too," Debbie said. "Your time is getting close," she added, looking at her watch.

"Debbie, I'm gonna say something to you, I don't want you should get up and walk out without thinking on it," Guttman said, keeping his voice as calm as he could, hoping it might sound threatening that way. "I'm gonna say I don't think you're telling the whole truth."

"Pops, I don't care what you think, you know? You paid for fifteen minutes, now—"

"I asked you should think before you did anything," Guttman reminded her. "It wasn't so hard for us to find you, and we said we don't want to make no trouble for anybody. But if we could find you so easy, so could the cops."

"What's that supposed to mean?"

"It means, if we tell them all the stuff we learned so far about Vincent, they're gonna have to do some investigating by themselves."

"You want to spell that out for me?" the girl said.

"Like I told you, we don't want no trouble for you or anybody else. Except the person what killed Harry Vincent."

"So?"

"So if you tell us the truth about what really went on, maybe you don't have to worry the police is gonna come around and ask about the same stuff."

"What do you mean, what really went on?"

"We know already how Harry got his money," Guttman said. "He didn't make enough from his job for everything he was spending. Especially the gambling."

"So Harry gambled a little, so what?"

"Harry gambled a lot," Miss Brady said. She wasn't sure what Guttman was up to, but she wanted to help.

"What we want from you," Guttman said, "is the facts on how it was done, how Harry worked it out."

"Your fifteen minutes is up," the girl said. Guttman took a ten-dollar bill from his wallet and put it on the table. "Forget it," she said.

"Debbie, would you believe a promise?" he asked. "A promise that if you tell us the truth, we wouldn't mention your name to the police?"

"Why should I trust you?"

"Because," Margaret Brady said pleasantly, "if you don't, then you can be sure the police will find out about this. And they're not going to sit with you over coffee and pay you to talk to them."

The girl looked at her for a moment, then took the money from the table.

"So now tell us exactly how things worked," Guttman said. He wanted to prompt her more, but he was afraid of saying something that would let her know he was only guessing.

"I think Harry was putting the squeeze on some of these guys," Debbie said after a long moment.

"You only think?" Guttman prompted.

"Well, I don't know for sure," she said defensively. "He said it was a gag, and I acted like I believed it. You know, I don't want none of that grief. If he wanted to say it was a joke, that was all right with me. It could've been. He paid me extra those times, anyway."

"How often was it?" Guttman asked.

"I don't know, maybe six, maybe eight times over the two years," the girl said. She took a fresh cigarette and lit it from the stub of her last one.

"Exactly how was it done?" Miss Brady asked.

"Well, Harry said he had this tape recorder hooked up. That's all I know."

"He said? You don't know?"

"Well, I couldn't very well go looking for it while I was with a john, could I?"

"Of course not," Miss Brady said. "Tell me, Debbie, when was the last time Harry did this?"

"Maybe a month ago. Last time I was there."

"That was about two weeks before he died?"

"About."

"How come he told you about it in the first place?" Guttman

asked. "I mean, if you didn't know to look for the tape recorder . . ."

"You're really sharp, aren't you?" Debbie said. "He tried it one time without telling me. Trouble was he didn't get enough on the tape. After he told me what was coming down, I made sure there were plenty of sound effects. I'd talk to the johns, get them to say a few words for the microphone, you know." Debbie smiled as she remembered.

"And the last time was a month ago?" Guttman asked.

"About, yeah."

"What was the man's name?"

"I don't know."

"Debbie, you just said we was sharp. If you was talking to be sure the tape recorder heard it, you must've called the man by his name, or got him to tell you. Am I right?"

"Wow . . ." Debbie heaved a sigh, and Guttman looked away quickly. For a moment he'd forgotten that her blouse was transparent. "Yeah," she said. "His name was Phil. Phil baby."

"Phil what?"

"I don't know, man. I told you, we didn't use no last names."

"What happened to these tapes?" Miss Brady asked.

"I'm not sure."

"But?"

"But I asked him once, and he said he had them put away someplace."

"Do you remember any of the other names?" Guttman asked.

"No. Look, the last time, before this one I just told you about, was maybe three, four months before. I don't remember any names. It's the truth."

"We believe you," Miss Brady said. "And we appreciate your help."

"Some appreciation. It wasn't like I wanted to tell you about it."

"Debbie, one more thing," Guttman said. "Do you think maybe you could tell us what this last person, this Phil, looked like?"

"I don't remember him, particularly."

"Anything at all would be a help to us," Miss Brady said.

"About fifty-five, maybe," the girl said, trying to remember. "Maybe sixty. A little fat. Bald, partly. Seemed a little nervous, but that's nothing. Lots of them are."

"Nothing else?"

"That's it."

"Thank you very much," Guttman said. "And we meant what we said. We won't tell nobody about this."

"Sure," the girl said, standing up. Again Guttman looked away. "You know, you two are really something else." She shook her head slightly and walked toward the door. A number of people watched her go.

"To quote," Miss Brady said. "Wow. Heavy."

"Very heavy," Guttman agreed.

Before they left the coffee shop Guttman called Armstrong Industries, and after some difficulty, was able to talk to Mrs. Kaplan. She wasn't sure she could get the information he asked for, but she and Mrs. O'Rourke would try.

"Mrs. Kaplan, believe me, I ain't exaggerating when I say the whole case could depend on it," Guttman told her.

"In that case, we'll find out," Dora Kaplan promised. And Guttman knew that if anyone could, she was the one.

They returned to the Golden Valley Senior Citizens' Center in time for a late lunch. Jacob Mishkin, having finished his own meal, sat with them and listened to what had happened. When they were through he was silent for a moment, then shook his head and looked upset.

"What's the matter?" Guttman asked.

"The matter is, next time you ask me to go along talking to people with you, I should go. Around here you don't get to talk to people like that very much."

Mrs. Kaplan and Mrs. O'Rourke arrived at two o'clock. Miss Brady had returned to her cottage, but Guttman and Mishkin were playing pinochle when they got there.

"We got it," Mrs. Kaplan said triumphantly. "So now tell us, already, who done it?"

"I don't know for sure, yet," Guttman said. "But you tell me first. What's the answers to my questions?"

"Okay. Mr. Forester first. The time Vincent was shot, Mr. Forester was supposed to be out seeing customers, only he didn't see nobody."

"How do you know?"

"We saw the sales reports, and he didn't have down that he saw nobody that day. So he's got no alibi."

"Okay," Guttman said. "So now the next one."

"The next one is David Hiller. He wasn't around either," Mrs. Kaplan said. "He said he didn't feel so good and he didn't have no appointments, so he just went home. In plenty of time to kill Vincent," Mrs. Kaplan added.

"And Mr. Armstrong himself was out of town," Mrs. O'Rourke said. "I was talking with his secretary and she told me. He flew back that afternoon, on the plane from San Francisco. But he got back in time to do the killing."

"All three of them," Guttman said.

"You don't sound so happy," Mrs. Kaplan said.

"I'm happy you could find out, but it would be better if only one of them had a chance to do it. Now there's still more work to do."

"Well, how did things go today?" Mrs. Kaplan asked.

"Did you see this Carole Edwards?" Mrs. O'Rourke asked.

"We saw," Guttman said. "It's a long story." And because they wanted to know everything, Guttman told them. From beginning to end.

"And now what?" Mrs. Kaplan asked when he was through.

"And now I'm going to think about things for a while," Guttman said.

"And then?"

"And then tomorrow I'm gonna talk to some people some more."

"And then?"

"And then we'll see. It's enough 'and thens' for now."

"What would you have us do?" Mrs. O'Rourke asked.

"If it isn't asking too much, you could make an appointment for me to talk to Mr. Armstrong, and the others, in the morning. And tell Mrs. Stone I'll need the car. Also, you could tell her that we're doing okay, but I don't want she should know all the details," Guttman added, knowing that part would please Mrs. Kaplan.

"Why don't you want her to know the details? She's the client, isn't she?" Mrs. Kaplan asked.

"She's the client, but I don't know what she's gonna do with what we tell her. I don't want people what ain't really involved to get in trouble. We don't know, she could talk to the lawyer and he could tell the police right away. So where does that leave us?"

"You're right," Mrs. Kaplan said after a moment. "We have to protect our sources."

"At least until we know who the guilty party is," Mrs. O'Rourke agreed.

"Do you want us to go to the office tomorrow?" Mrs. Kaplan asked.

"I don't think it would be necessary for the case. But if you got work to finish there . . ."

"We could finish out the week," Mrs. Kaplan said to Mrs. O'Rourke.

"I think we should," she agreed.

"We'll take care of that other business for you," Mrs. Kaplan said.

"Thank you. I appreciate it. The thing is," Guttman said, "I don't want to talk to them myself now because they'd ask questions and I want to wait until I could see them direct." He didn't want them to think he was using them as secretaries.

Guttman sat alone in the library—playing chess against himself, making a number of blunders—for the rest of the afternoon. He would rather have sat outside in the sun, but at least here in the library he was alone. He didn't mind the mistakes he made on the chessboard. It was only to give himself something to do while he thought. By the time he had to go outside to wait for Lois, he had almost managed to convince himself not to think about the case any more, at least until after he'd paid his calls the next day.

It was after dinner, as usual, before Lois brought it up. Michael was giving the baby her bath, the boys were doing their homework, and the dishes were in the machine.

"Well, Pop, how's the detective business?" she asked lightly, not fooling him at all.

"Complicated," he told her.

"Not getting anywhere, huh?"

"I'm getting too many places."

"What do you mean?"

"I mean I'm finding out a lot of things, only then I got to decide what ones are important and what doesn't matter for the case."

"Oh. I see. You want some more coffee?"

"No, I already had too much coffee today, thank you."

"You look a little tired, Pop," Lois said.

"Dolling, I'm fine. Don't start worrying. And I don't look tired. I might look confused, or upset even. But not tired. One good thing from all this, I sleep good at night."

"Even with all the deciding what's important and what isn't?"

"Even with that. You know, it's something to do. I get out, I'm talking with people, I'm going here and there . . ."

"That's the part that worries me, Pop. All the running around."

"Lois, thank you for worrying. But thank God, I'm in good health. And believe me, I ain't doing nothing hard, unless you call getting in and out of a limousine where the driver opens the door hard."

"A limousine?" Lois asked, and so Guttman had to tell her about the transportation Mrs. Stone had provided. When he was through, Lois seemed to feel better. "I don't know why, but I was imagining you on the bus all the time," she said.

"Nothing like that. And even if not the limousine, Miss Brady has a car of her own, so we could go that way," Guttman added. And then, of course, he had to explain who Miss Brady was. Simply saying that she was "a lady from the Center" wasn't enough for Lois. Guttman was relieved when Michael returned to announce that it was time for everyone to kiss the baby goodnight.

Thirteen

"I just think it would be easier for you to talk to Mr. Armstrong alone, that's all," Margaret Brady said.

"It wasn't easier talking to everybody before," Guttman argued.

"Look, Max, you and I both know what that girl told us yesterday. Now, maybe Armstrong isn't the Phil baby she told us about, but he sure fits the description. And I just think he's more likely to admit it if I'm not around. That's all."

"You really don't want to go?" Guttman asked.

"I'll go," Mishkin volunteered.

"The last time you could've gone," Guttman told him. "Now you'd be a stranger, and he might not talk."

"It was just an offer."

"I tell you what," Miss Brady said. "I'll drive in with you, and then after you talk to Armstrong you can come out and get me, and we'll talk to the others. Okay?"

"Okay," Guttman agreed. "Because the thing is, if I forget something, it could be helpful if you was there also." As they walked to the limousine he wondered why he hadn't just said "I'd feel better if you was there" or maybe just "I like your company." You know why, he told himself. And it ain't that you're afraid you'll forget something, either.

· · ·

Philip Armstrong kept him waiting just long enough for Guttman to begin to fidget on the couch in the outer office. If I didn't have something like this to talk to him about, I probably wouldn't be so nervous, Guttman thought. But if it ain't just that . . . if he's the one what really done it, then it should be a different kind of nervous. I'm confused, Guttman decided, and he began calming himself, going over how he would approach the question with Philip Armstrong. Straight out, he decided. That was the only way.

"I'm sorry I had to keep you waiting, Mr. Guttman," Armstrong said from behind his desk.

He indicated a chair, and Guttman sat down. He still fit the girl Debbie's description. Fifty-five or sixty, a little fat, balding, and if not exactly nervous, then a little uneasy. It's in the eyes, mostly, Guttman thought.

"How's Jessica?" Armstrong asked. "Is she bearing up well?"

"She's okay," Guttman said. "She's still worrying, but she's okay."

"It must be very rough on her. I wish there were more I could do. How is your . . . that is, how are you doing with your efforts?"

"It's a little hard to say," Guttman said. "But maybe we're doing well."

"Really?" Armstrong seemed surprised. "Well, that's good news."

"You might not think so," Guttman told him.

"What do you mean?"

"Mr. Armstrong, I been sitting outside thinking how I could ask you about this, and the only way that makes sense is direct. Yesterday we was talking to a girl named Debbie." Guttman waited for a reaction.

"Debbie?" Armstrong managed to look blank.

"She's a prostitute, Mr. Armstrong. And she knows you."

"Knows me? There must be a mistake, Mr. Guttman. Look, I just don't . . ."

"She met you at Harry Vincent's apartment, not so long ago. About a month."

"Not me. There must be a mistake," Armstrong said, a hint of annoyance in his voice.

"She also told about a tape recording," Guttman went on.

Armstrong didn't speak for a moment. "I see," he said finally. "And now what?"

"Now I got to know what happened after that."

"What do you mean, what happened?"

"Mr. Armstrong, I know how Harry Vincent needed money to pay off gamblers. I also know it wasn't the first time this happened, and it wasn't the first tape recording that was made."

"So?"

"So now you tell me," Guttman suggested.

"What exactly do you want?" Armstrong's voice was cool.

"Like I told you, I want to know what happened. I came here to talk to you direct," he said, "because I don't want to make trouble for nobody if I don't have to."

"I didn't kill Vincent," Armstrong said. "I was out of town that day."

"You also come back in time, on your plane. I checked."

"You . . . I see."

"Did he come to you for blackmail?" Guttman asked.

"Yes."

"Did you pay him?"

"No. I was going to," Armstrong admitted. "I didn't have any choice."

"But you didn't actually give him no money?"

"No. It took me a while to raise it. I'm not really rich, you know," Armstrong said almost apologetically.

"Vincent was asking for a lot of money?"

"Ten thousand dollars. He said I could pay him in installments."

"Mr. Armstrong, you know how this looks, don't you? I mean, like if I went to the police and told them about it . . ." According to Mishkin, Vincent had owed about ten thousand dollars.

"Is this a threat, Mr. Guttman? Because I knuckled under

once. But I'm not going to do it again. I'd rather take my chances."

"Mr. Armstrong, I understand how this could make big problems for you. Not just with your wife, which is natural, but in a business it could be a problem. Suppose one time Vincent came and said instead of money he wanted a different job, or something like that. It could hurt the business, and with the work you done to make it go . . ." Guttman let it hang.

"I told you, I didn't kill him. Look, who else knows about this?"

"That ain't important. I'm just asking if you could see how it could look to the police."

"Of course I can see," Armstrong practically shouted. "Why the hell do you think I've been so damned worried?"

"When you came back on the airplane," Guttman said quietly, "it could be you went to Vincent's apartment, maybe to look around for the tape recording. And when you was looking, you could've found the gun, and maybe Vincent just walked in when you didn't expect him. It could even be he tried to attack you, so it was self-defense," Guttman suggested.

"The tapes weren't at the apartment," Armstrong said.

"You looked?"

"No. Harry told me. When he first came to me with a copy of the damned thing. He warned me not to get cute, that the original was where I couldn't get to it."

"And you believed him?"

"Look, I admit I might have gone there looking for the tape. That is, I might have, if I'd thought about it . . ." Armstrong sighed wearily. "I caved in. I agreed to pay him the money, that's all."

"I read where blackmailers sometimes never stop. They always want a little more money," Guttman said.

"I thought of that. But I figured, Harry worked here, I mean . . . I just wanted to believe him, that's all. He told me he did it as a joke, but he needed the money to pay off some debts, that it was him or me. I wanted to believe him, Mr. Guttman. So I did." Philip Armstrong seemed to shrink in his chair. "Christ, what a mess. Do you realize that I've hardly slept since Vincent was killed? I keep waiting for somebody to find those tapes, wherever they are . . . waiting for a phone call from the police, or someone who wants money . . ."

"Did you stop to think that if Vincent was blackmailing you, maybe he was doing it to others?"

"No. I didn't think about it, one way or another."

"And if he was," Guttman went on, "then maybe somebody else killed him over it?"

"I don't see . . ."

"And if the police knew about that, then maybe they'd be able to know where to look for who really killed him? And Susan Eliot wouldn't have to stay in jail?"

"What do you want me to say? Look, I just assumed that Susan killed him. I mean, from what I heard, what was in the papers, they have an open-and-shut case against her. I just didn't think that someone else did it."

"And now, maybe?"

"I don't know. I told you, I like Susan. I don't want to think she did it, but . . ."

Guttman nodded his head and studied the man across the desk from him.

Armstrong sat back in his chair, tired, staring blankly at the wall. Finally he looked at Guttman. "What are you going to do now?"

"You mean, am I going to the police?"

"I guess so, yes."

"I didn't decide yet," Guttman told him. "There's still a couple of things to find out first."

"I'd like to ask a . . . a favor. I'd like you to tell me when you do decide."

"Why?"

"Because . . . because before you tell them, I want to be able to explain it to my wife. I'd rather she heard it from me than from the police, or read about it in the papers. I'd like to try to explain to her . . ."

"I guess that would be all right," Guttman said slowly. "But you know, even if I don't go to the police, there's still the tape."

"I know," Armstrong said. "I guess I'll have to tell her anyway . . . sometime . . ."

"I could promise you, Mr. Armstrong, if I don't have to tell nobody about this, I wouldn't."

Armstrong nodded his head. He even tried to smile as Guttman got up to leave.

Margaret Brady got out of the car as Guttman appeared at the front entrance to Armstrong Industries, and walked toward him. She listened intently as he reported on his conversation with Philip Armstrong, then lit a cigarette and stared off into the distance.

"You don't think he did it, do you?" she said finally.

"I didn't make up my mind, yet," Guttman said. "But the important thing is, we know he was the one. Now we know for sure he had a motive."

Nick Forester was surprised to see them, but he was polite in an offhand way. "Will this take long?" he asked, and when Guttman told him it shouldn't, he buzzed his secretary and told her to hold his calls for a few minutes. "Now, what's up?" he asked them.

"It's something we found out," Guttman began. "The more people we asked things about Harry Vincent, the more we found out he wasn't a nice person. He was the kind of a person what might use blackmail, even, to get something if he wanted it."

"So Harry wasn't a nice guy. So what's new?"

"So we was thinking," Guttman explained, "about how fast Vincent got promoted here, even though Mr. Hiller should've had the job."

"You're leading up to something, Mr. Guttman. Why don't you just get to the point?"

"The point is about how you do your business, Mr. Forester. And how Harry Vincent knew about it."

"What does that mean?"

"It's a matter of expenses," Miss Brady said. "A question of what is reported and what is actually spent. And how the difference is . . . disbursed."

"I don't know what you're driving at," Forester said.

"We're driving at how you was putting down things on your expenses that you didn't really do, and then when you got the money, you shared it with some of your customers," Guttman said. "And then they gave you contracts for business because you were paying them kickbacks."

"Entertaining customers, providing them with . . . gifts is part of the business world," Forester said evenly.

"But not keeping it yourself," Guttman said. "And also, it's how much. If it's a lot, then the company got to raise the prices to make up for it, and that could mean they lose business someplace else."

"I suppose that makes sense, although I'm not sure what you're talking about," Forester said. "Look, you said this would only take a couple of minutes. I'd appreciate it if you could say what you have to, and leave."

"The point, Mr. Forester, is that you have been stealing from your own company," Miss Brady said. "You keep a lot of that money for yourself. And I'm sure Mr. Armstrong isn't aware of it, either."

"This is all very fascinating. But I have work to do. And it's nonsense, anyway."

"It ain't nonsense," Guttman said. "We already talked to some of the people what got the kickbacks."

"All right," Forester said sharply. "What's the point?"

"The point," Miss Brady said, "is whether one wanted to keep his activities secret. For example, if someone like Harry Vincent found out about it, and threatened to tell Mr. Armstrong, well, you could lose your job, couldn't you?"

"Uh-huh. Now I get the picture. You two are suggesting that Harry was blackmailing me, and I killed him, right?"

"We didn't say that," Miss Brady replied.

"You didn't have to. Look, why don't you just take your theories and get out of here, huh? I know Phil wants to help

Susan because of her grandmother, but this is ridiculous. I'm busy."

"Mr. Forester, if you don't talk to us, we could talk to Mr. Armstrong," Guttman said.

"So talk to him. So what's going to happen? I'll tell you. Sure, maybe Phil will get mad, maybe he'll even tell me to pack up and leave. I doubt it, but he might. So what? Look, you two don't seem to understand that what I've been doing is normal business procedure."

"Including keeping some of the money for yourself?"

"You show me a salesman who doesn't pad his expenses and I'll show you a total idiot," Forester said. "It's part of the salary. Everybody knows it."

"But you made Harry Vincent your assistant, when somebody else should've gotten the job," Guttman said.

"Okay, so I didn't want to make waves. So what? Harry did the job."

"And that's all you have to say on the subject?" Miss Brady asked.

"That's all."

"Then would you mind also telling us, on another subject," Guttman said, "how come on the day Vincent was killed you was supposed to be visiting customers, only you didn't go there?"

"You two are out of your minds," Nick Forester said quietly after a moment. "Do you really think I'd kill Harry to keep him quiet about something like this?"

"It could have cost you your job," Miss Brady suggested.

"So I would have gotten another job. Listen, you don't go around killing people because you're afraid you'll lose your job," Forester said earnestly. "I don't know what you're thinking, I mean . . . I just don't understand. I didn't kill Harry. It's as simple as that. I admit I'm not anxious to have Phil know about this, but killing . . ." He shook his head in amazement.

"Where was you, actually, the day we're talking about?" Guttman asked.

"That's none of your business."

"If we went to the police, they'd ask you the same question."

"You're not the police, though. And I don't have to answer you. Now, I've got work to do, so if there's nothing else . . ."

Reluctantly, they left. They got as far as the secretary's desk before they saw David Hiller coming toward them, a sheaf of papers in his hand. He left the papers on the desk and turned to them.

"I want to talk to you two."

"We was just coming to see you," Guttman said.

"Fine. I'll save you the trouble. You stay away from Carole, do you understand?"

"Look, Mr. Hiller—"

"Look, nothing. Just leave her alone."

"We're not doing this for fun," Guttman said.

"I don't care—" Hiller stopped himself and took a deep breath. "I am sorry, truly sorry, about Susan. But that doesn't give you any right to harass Carole. I want you to leave her alone."

"There was some things we had to find out," Guttman began.

"Not from her. She's not involved in this, for Christ's sake. Just because she was involved with Harry Vincent, once, that doesn't mean she's got anything to do with . . . Oh, forget it," Hiller said.

"There was some things we had to find out," Guttman said again.

"Not from her. Just leave her alone. Do you understand?"

"We understand," Guttman said mildly, ignoring the look of surprise Miss Brady gave him. "And we're sorry we got her upset. But it was important."

"I don't care what it was, just leave her alone," Hiller said angrily.

"What—"

"We said we was sorry," Guttman said, cutting Miss Brady off. "And we're sorry for upsetting you so much, also."

He turned and started for the front door, then had to go back and take the astonished Miss Brady by the arm to lead her out. It was, he realized, practically the first time he had really touched her. As soon as they reached the front entrance he released her arm.

"Max Guttman, what the hell was that all about? That little snip came charging at us and you just tuck your tail between your legs and walk away? I thought we wanted to question him."

"I wasn't tucking my tail," Guttman said. "And when you feel like calming down, maybe you could tell me what we was going to question him on?"

"Why, about the killing, of course."

"What about the killing?" Guttman asked.

"Why . . . well, where he was that afternoon, for example. And . . ." Miss Brady looked at him for a moment, then took a deep breath. "All right," she said. "Please explain."

"All that happened," Guttman said, "is I realized first, in that kind of a mood, he wasn't going to talk with us anyway. And then I thought, if he got a reason to kill Vincent, we don't know it yet. If anybody got a reason, it was the girl friend, Carole."

"The girl?"

"That's right. Don't you remember we found out she helped entertain at the parties, she was with the men? Okay. So suppose Hiller don't know about it, and maybe Vincent said he was going to tell on her . . ."

"You mean he blackmailed her, too?"

"I don't think she got enough money to make it worthwhile," Guttman said. "But he could've done something out of meanness. But let's say he actually threatened. Then the girl would have a reason to kill him, to keep his mouth shut. And if Vincent already told, then Hiller's got a temper, it could be he'd get into a fight with Vincent . . ."

"Suppose Vincent invited Hiller to the apartment, and told him then," Miss Brady said.

"There's two things wrong with that. Number one is the gun. And number two, this Vincent sounds like the kind what would do something like that where there was other people around."

"You're right," Miss Brady said. "He was probably just that mean, too."

"Okay. So with Hiller, all we really know is Vincent got his job. But that was six months ago, already."

"I'm sorry," Margaret Brady said after a moment.

"It's okay."

"I just didn't like the way he talked to us. Made my blood boil."

"I didn't like it especially, either," Guttman told her.

"So now what do we do? Talk to the girl again?"

"Now we go back to the Center, for lunch."

Fourteen

The Golden Valley Irregulars were assembled. Mrs. Kaplan and Mrs. O'Rourke had returned from Armstrong Industries after lunch, and joined Mishkin and Mr. Carstairs in the lounge. Miss Brady, after spending some time in her cottage, was now having a cup of coffee with them. They were all waiting for Guttman.

"Is he still playing that bowling game?" Mrs. Kaplan asked.

"Bocce," Mishkin said. "He's still out there."

"So what do we do?" Mrs. Kaplan asked, looking around the table.

"We wait, I guess," Miss Brady said.

"Wait for what?"

"Wait for Guttman, what else?" Mishkin said.

"But what is Mr. Guttman waiting for?" Mrs. O'Rourke wanted to know.

"That's what we're waiting for him to tell us," Mr. Carstairs explained.

"So we just sit and wait?" Dora Kaplan asked.

No one answered her.

Guttman watched the ball roll down the dirt track, holding to the banked side, watched it slowly lose speed and begin to fall toward the center, curving in to just nudge Mr. Bowsenior's ball and settle in behind it. He'd won the game. For the first time he'd won the game.

"You've been practicing," Mr. Bowsenior accused him from the far end of the court, where he'd watched his defeat close up.

"I was concentrating, that's all," Guttman said, smiling. "But I got to admit, it feels good for a change."

"I'll get even the next one," Mr. Bowsenior said.

"Beat him again," Mrs. Bowsenior said from her chair a few feet away. She had a canvas propped on a small easel and was doing an oil painting of the main house, but she still followed the progress of the game. "He deserves to be taken down a peg or two," she said.

"That's a woman for you," Mr. Bowsenior said, rolling the balls back to the starting position.

"One more game," Guttman said, looking at his watch. "That's all I could manage today."

"It'll be enough for me to win my quarter back," Mr. Bowsenior warned. And he was right.

Guttman hesitated at the door to the lounge, but even if they hadn't seen him, he knew he had to go in. He didn't know what he was going to tell them, but he knew he had to say something. He wasted a few minutes by getting a cup of coffee that he didn't want, and then, after sitting down, took another few minutes to light a fresh cigar.

"So, Guttman?" Mrs. Kaplan finally asked.

"So, what?"

"So are you going to tell us what's what, or are you going to keep it a big secret?"

"Didn't Miss Brady tell you about this morning?"

"She told, but that don't tell us what's what."

"I don't know myself," Guttman admitted. "There's something here I ain't sure of. Only I don't know what it is."

"Perhaps if we reviewed the case, it might help," Mr. Carstairs said.

"It could, but to tell the truth, I ain't even sure enough to review it, actually."

"Why don't we just talk about it, then?" Miss Brady suggested. "And you can just listen. Maybe something will strike you."

"It could," Guttman said. "But maybe the best thing would be for me to just sit and think."

"But you said you didn't know what it is you want to think about," Mrs. Kaplan reminded him. "Why don't we just start, and you can listen."

"So who's gonna be first?" Mishkin asked.

Naturally, Dora Kaplan was.

Guttman listened to them for nearly an hour, trying to keep as much as possible from registering in his mind. I should be able to just get up and tell them I want to think alone. So why don't I? Because they're all trying, and everybody wants to be part of it, and if you walk away to go by yourself, you're leaving them out. You're taking the whole thing for yourself, that way, he told himself. Nu, Guttman, so if you feel it ain't fair, why don't you talk with them? Because I want it for myself, he admitted. And it's there, someplace. Something I already know. Only I can't put a finger on it. He sat with them, feeling a little guilty, until it was time for him to go home.

Guttman didn't have much appetite at dinner, a fact that didn't go unnoticed. However, as was her custom, Lois waited until after the meal to discuss it.

"Do you feel all right, Pop?"

"You do look a little upset," Michael agreed.

"Just something I'm thinking about."

"This detective business, again?" Lois asked.

"What else? Thank God, I ain't got no other problems I know about," Guttman said, managing to smile at his daughter.

"Maybe you should just forget the whole thing, Pop. I mean, if it's going to upset you like this . . ."

"Thinking about something ain't the same thing as being upset," Guttman said.

"Maybe if you talked about it, Pop," Michael suggested.

"Maybe just give us a clue," Lois said.

"There's no clues to give. The only thing is, there's something in my head I can't put a finger on . . ."

"Are you saying that you know who killed this man?" Lois asked nervously.

"I could. I ain't sure if I do or not . . ."

"Well, why not go to the police and tell them about it?" Lois asked.

"I don't want to do that."

"Pop, are you going to pull some sort of crazy stunt, like that last time, because if you are—"

"No stunts, Lois. I promise. But the thing is, if the police start now, they'd have to check everything, and it would make problems for a lot of people."

"So?"

"So these people maybe ain't got nothing to do with this Vincent character being dead, but . . ." Guttman decided to try it another way. "Lois, the one thing I learned with this detective business is when you ask a lot of questions, you find out some things what really ain't your business. They ain't nobody's business."

"Then why ask?" Lois wanted to know.

"Because until you ask, you don't know what you're going to find out. And only later on you know it ain't connected to the crime, or whatever. So then it's none of your business. Now, the police, if they find out, maybe everybody knows. With me, well, maybe because people don't have to talk to me in the first place, it's like they told me a secret, and I don't want to get them in trouble for it."

"In other words, respecting their confidences," Michael said.

"That's it."

"So what are you going to do, Pop?" Lois asked.

"I'm gonna watch the television for a while, there's a ball game on, and then I'm gonna do some more thinking. And tomorrow . . . We'll see."

Guttman watched the ball game. And he did some thinking. And finally he fell asleep. It wasn't until he was having his breakfast the next morning that he found what he was looking for. But, he realized, now he had to figure out what to do about it.

At five past nine they had reassembled in the lounge. Guttman took his place at the head of the table, looked at them one at a time, and announced, "I still don't know what's next. So meanwhile, everybody could do what they want."

"That's all you have to tell us?" Mrs. Kaplan demanded.

"That's everything, for now." He waited for a moment, but they just looked at each other, and no one said anything more to him.

Guttman got up and decided he might as well use the library for his thinking. If he went anywhere else, even if they didn't say anything, they'd be watching. Half an hour later he went out to use the pay phone. Paul Taylor was in his office, and happy to talk to him.

"Hi. Anything we can use yet?" the lawyer asked.

"Not exactly. I called about something else, if you don't mind."

"Sure. What's up?"

"Well, take a person like this Vincent. If he had stuff put away, like in a bank, what happens after he's killed?"

"You mean money in the bank?"

"No, I was thinking like . . . papers."

"A safe deposit box," Taylor said. "Okay. In a case like this, it would depend on whether she was authorized to get into the vault. Sometimes husbands and wives share a vault, sometimes they don't trust each other."

"Let's say they don't trust each other," Guttman said. He didn't think Harry Vincent would keep blackmail tape recordings where his wife could find them.

"Well," Taylor said, "in that case the box would be opened, there'd be a court order, and someone from the bank would be there, the police, the Internal Revenue . . ."

"All those people," Guttman said. "Well, thank you very much."

"What's this all about, Mr. Guttman?"

"Nothing. At least, nothing to do with the case. Again, thank you," Guttman said, hanging up the phone. That was one thing out of the way. Now he could go back to thinking about the main problem.

At eleven forty-five Guttman knocked on the door to Mrs. Stone's cottage, and after being told that Mrs. Stone was "indisposed," asked the nurse if she would tell Mrs. Stone he needed the car at one-thirty. She promised she would, and Guttman left, glad he hadn't had to see the old woman. He joined the others for lunch, expecting a barrage of questions, but was surprised. Mishkin asked how his thinking was going, and Guttman said he wasn't finished yet. And no one said anything else about their case. As soon as lunch was over, Guttman left them and sat in the library, smoking a cigar, until it was time to go outside to the car. He gave the driver the address he wanted and sat back, eyes closed, to think just a little bit more, and to hope. To pray for something like this, he thought, might not be right. But he could hope.

When he heard the voice on the intercom, he announced himself and waited for the buzzer. Then he climbed the two flights of stairs slowly. He didn't want to be out of breath when he arrived. Donald Eliot was waiting for him.

"I tried to call you," Guttman said, "but I got a busy signal. The operator said the line was out of order." That was the first lie.

"Is something wrong?" Eliot asked.

"Could I come in, please?"

"Oh, sure. I'm sorry."

Eliot stepped back and Guttman went inside. The apartment didn't look as neat as it had the last time. The ashtrays hadn't been emptied, there was a sweater on one of the chairs and several newspapers on the coffee table. The papers were still spread out on the dining table.

"Could I sit down? I'm . . . I'm kind of upset," Guttman said.

"Sure. But look, what's the matter? I mean, what's . . . ?"

"I was with Mrs. Stone when she heard," Guttman said. "So

after a while I thought you should know, and that's when I called. But I kept getting a busy, so then I called the operator . . ."

"Mr. Guttman, what is it? What's wrong? You said you were with Mrs. Stone. Is it about Susan?"

"Donald . . . You don't mind I call you that?"

"No, sure. But—"

"Donald, I don't know how to say it . . ."

"Say what?"

"Susan tried to kill herself." Guttman wasn't sure if he'd gotten the tone of voice he wanted, but it didn't seem to matter. Donald Eliot just stared at him, dazed.

"Is . . . is she . . . ?"

"They think she might be all right," Guttman said. "They was getting an ambulance to take Mrs. Stone to see her. The lawyer, Paul Taylor, called."

"My God . . ." Eliot said. "Look, we've got to . . . I've got to see her."

"They wouldn't let you see her," Guttman said quickly. "They told the lawyer nobody could see her except Mrs. Stone. But I thought you should know."

"I have to go . . ." Eliot said.

"I told them, at the Center, where I was. If they find out anything, they'll call here. I don't even know where she is, if she's at the jail or a hospital. The best thing is to wait here." This was almost the most important part, and he tried to sound convincing.

"She . . . What happened? I mean, what did she do?"

"She tried to hang herself."

"Oh . . . my God . . ." Donald Eliot sat down and put his face in his hands. "But why?" he asked finally.

"I guess she got too depressed," Guttman said. "Being in jail like that, afraid you're gonna get convicted of a murder . . . especially when she didn't do it."

"I don't understand. How could something like this happen? Don't they take precautions, for God's sake?"

"I don't know, exactly," Guttman said. "But I guess there's

sheets on a bed, a person could make a rope from them." He'd thought about this, and the answer had the desired effect. Donald Eliot seemed to grow even more pale. "I guess she put it around her neck, and figured to die from strangling," Guttman went on.

"But . . . I thought they were going to get her off. That's the way it seemed, anyway. I mean . . ." He looked at Guttman with just a hint of suspicion.

"Did you ever talk to the lawyer, Mr. Taylor?"

"No. No, I didn't."

"He told me, at the beginning, there was a chance. But only a chance."

"But she was innocent."

"How do you know she's innocent?"

"I know. How do you know?" Eliot asked. "You said you believed she was innocent."

"I believe, yes," Guttman said. It was time to take the next step. "I believe because I know who really killed Vincent. But how about you? Do you think she's innocent for the same reason?"

"You think you know . . ." Eliot studied him carefully. "Then why didn't you go to the police and tell them?"

"I blame myself," Guttman said. "I was thinking there was a better way, and also, I was looking still for details."

"A better way?"

"And I didn't know it was such a rush," Guttman went on. "I didn't know she was so upset she'd try to kill herself."

Donald Eliot stood up and walked to the window for a moment. Then he turned to look at Guttman. "Would you like a drink . . . something? I think I need a drink."

"Maybe some soda, that would be nice," Guttman said. While Eliot was busy in the kitchen, he allowed himself the luxury of several deep breaths, to calm his nerves. So far, so good. He hoped.

"Listen," Eliot said, handing him a glass of ginger ale, "you said something about details. What did you mean?"

"I meant, in a couple of days at the most, I figured I could have the proof, the details."

"You want to explain that?"

"Do you think it's necessary?"

"Yeah. I think so." Eliot took a swallow of his drink and made a face. Then he took a smaller sip.

"Well, there was a couple of things I finally remembered that didn't fit in, exactly, so it finally boiled down to two things, mainly. The first is a key to the apartment where Vincent was killed."

"A key?"

"Nobody forced the door open, so there must've been a key. Whoever killed Vincent used a key to get in, and then found the gun and was waiting for him."

"So what's that got to do with the . . . details you mentioned?" Eliot asked.

There was something in his tone that made Guttman begin to feel uneasy. Still, he had to go on. "The night Susan got beat up, the night before Vincent was killed, you was at her apartment. She called you. And then you had to go out to the drugstore. It was late at night, so you had to drive around to find someplace that was open. Only you used her car."

"I still don't follow you."

"Donald, listen, I didn't come walking in here with the police, did I? You think this is my idea of fun? You think I don't feel bad about Susan? Okay, so what I'm saying, since I got to spell it out, is you made a key for Vincent's apartment from the one Susan had. So now what's left is finding the lock store where you did it. We already know what drugstore you went to, because the name is on the stuff you bought for her. Now we got to find all the lock stores between there and Susan's apartment, and seeing if they remember you. Usually, you know, there's not so much business they wouldn't remember."

"You're telling me I killed Harry Vincent. Is that right?"

"I wasn't gonna tell you anything, to be honest, until Susan did this thing. Up till then, I was gonna go to the police and tell them."

"You can't prove anything. It's crazy."

"I don't know. Maybe," Guttman said. He drank some of his ginger ale. "But it don't matter so much now. Now Susan's trying to kill herself. And it's because of you. You know that, don't you, Donald?"

"Why is it my fault?"

"Why is she in jail? She didn't kill him. I thought you was saying you was in love with her. So you love her so much you let her stay in jail until she tries to kill herself?"

Eliot moved back to the window and looked out.

"Susan knows what happened," Guttman said. "Think about that. Susan knows what happened."

"What do you mean?"

"She must've figured it out by now. Even if she didn't know for sure, she must've been thinking it. Only she didn't say nothing. She sat in the jail and she waited. She figured you wouldn't let her stay there. But she did, until finally she takes the sheets from the bed and puts them around her neck." Guttman held his breath.

"I didn't think she'd . . ." Eliot didn't turn to look at him.

"Of course you didn't think. You didn't think about her at all," Guttman said, with more anger in his voice than he felt.

"I did! How do you think I felt when I saw what he did to her? She left me, and she was with him, and he beat her like that . . ."

"And still you left her in jail, waiting for you to help her," Guttman said. "I think Susan maybe even saw you. That was the other thing I mentioned before. I kept thinking about the time between the shot and when Susan got there. What did you do, Donald? Did you hide in the hallway when she come up the stairs? Or did she see you get into the elevator? You didn't have much time to get away."

Guttman waited, but Eliot just stood by the window, his drink in his hand. He was still wearing jeans and a polo shirt, and Guttman thought he looked terribly young and . . . the word escaped him.

"What's going to happen now, Donald?" he asked.

206

"What do you mean?"

"I mean, what's going to happen with Susan now? You know about these things, these things in the mind. You're educated. You know what it is when somebody tries to kill herself. To me, it's a crazy thing. A person has got to be sick. To do that, you're not thinking good. So now Susan's sick, depressed or whatever. You know about these things, you've gone through some of it yourself. So what happens to her now?" Guttman demanded.

"I don't know. I mean . . ."

"What could happen to her mind if she's got to stay in the jail and have a trial? It could be months. What happens to people after they try to kill themselves? Are they going to take her out of the jail and put her in a crazy house? In a straitjacket, maybe?"

"Shut up!" Eliot yelled.

And Guttman did. He waited, sipping his ginger ale and wondering whether he'd be able to manage the rest of it. "Donald . . . could you explain something to me?" he asked gently. "Could you explain, since you love Susan, how you left her in the jail like that?"

There was no answer for a moment.

"When she needed me . . . she called me," Donald Eliot said, still looking out the window. "She called me. She needed me." Eliot shrugged. "I thought she'd need me now, too. But she didn't ask to see me . . ."

"She does need you, Donald. She needs you to help her now. You're the only one what can."

"How can I help her? What do you expect me to do?"

"You could tell the police what happened."

"They . . . they'd . . . What good would that do? Susan didn't call me, she didn't ask me to help. She doesn't need me."

"Donald, when you love somebody, and you see they need you, it's not the time to wait for an invitation. She didn't call you because she didn't want to make trouble for you. Susan was trying to help you."

"What do you want me to do?" Eliot asked, finally turning to look at him.

"Donald, I know you killed him. And I know why you done it. For Susan. So if you want to help her now, you got to go to the police. You got to tell them what happened."

"What if they don't believe me?" Eliot asked after a moment.

"You could convince them. You could tell the police what happened, and they'd have to believe you. And then they'd know Susan didn't do it."

"But . . ."

"If you don't tell them, Donald, then what could happen to Susan? Not just with the trial and everything, but inside her. In her head. Look what happened already . . ."

Donald Eliot finished his drink, then lit a cigarette, and still standing by the window, smoked it all the way down, letting the ashes fall on the floor. Guttman watched and said nothing. He had nothing left to say.

"Call them," Eliot said very quietly.

"No. No, it would be better if you just went by yourself," Guttman said.

"Why?"

"It's different if you go in by yourself, or if they come to get you. Also . . ."

"Yes?"

"Also it would give more time for the lawyer to get there. This Paul Taylor is a good lawyer. I could call and he'd meet us at the police station."

"It doesn't really make any difference, does it?"

"I don't know. But it couldn't hurt if a lawyer's there."

"Whatever you say."

Eliot finally sat down and watched while Guttman went to the phone and called. Paul Taylor sounded reluctant, but Guttman didn't give him a chance to argue. He didn't want to keep Donald Eliot waiting any longer than he had to.

"There's a car outside," Guttman said. "I could go with you. But you might want to get some things first to take with you."

"Like what?"

"I don't know . . . a toothbrush, maybe," Guttman said, and suddenly Donald Eliot laughed. And then he cried.

• • •

Guttman locked the apartment door behind him, then handed Eliot the keys. Together they went downstairs and outside to the car. Guttman spotted them out of the corner of his eye, but he said nothing. At least he knew what the noise in the hallway had been. He'd talk to them later, of course. He and Eliot sat silently during the twenty-minute ride, and Guttman thought it was perhaps the longest twenty minutes of his life. Each time they stopped for a red light he practically held his breath. When they arrived Eliot just sat there, as he had throughout.

"I think you should go in alone," Guttman said.

"Why? Don't you want to be in at the kill?"

"This ain't something I'm enjoying," Guttman told him. "But it would look better if you went alone. Ask for Lieutenant Weiss. He's the one in charge."

Eliot got out and stood in the sun for a moment, then walked slowly up the wide steps to the police headquarters' entrance. Guttman watched him go inside, and then got out of the car. It was time, now, for another conversation. He walked back toward the car that had stopped behind his limousine. When they saw him approaching, they got out. All five of them.

"It's all over," Guttman said. "Everybody should go back to the Center, and I'll come soon. I'll tell you about it then."

"Go back to the Center?" Mrs. Kaplan said indignantly.

"When did you find out we were following you?" Miss Brady asked.

"As soon as we started out. I saw you in the car behind," Guttman lied. He wasn't going to admit that he hadn't seen them until he left Donald Eliot's apartment.

"I don't believe you," Dora Kaplan said. "And I think we're entitled to know what's happening."

"Donald Eliot, Susan's husband, he's the one what killed Vincent. He just gave himself to the police. So it's over. Except somebody should tell Mrs. Stone about it. Susan will probably be there soon. Her lawyer's here already."

"But how—"

"I'll explain later. The first thing is to tell Mrs. Stone. And I got an errand to do. It ain't connected with this, at least not direct."

The prospect of being able to give the good news to Jessica Stone finally swayed Mrs. Kaplan, and the others followed. Guttman waited in the limousine until they drove off before giving the driver the address he wanted.

Vivian Vincent was surprisingly easy. It took Guttman only a few minutes to explain the situation to her, and to convince her that he didn't believe she had destroyed the tape recordings.

"How did you know I had them?" she asked.

"It was the only logical thing. They wasn't at the apartment, and if it was a safe deposit box, the police would've found them when it was opened. So I figured it must be here, and I also figured when you went through the papers and all, you found them."

"But why did you assume I didn't destroy them?"

"Human nature," Guttman said. "You might not even know who was on the tapes, but it was human nature to keep them."

"And why should I give them to you?"

"Because I'm gonna see they're destroyed, and you don't want nobody knowing your husband was a blackmailer. So if you give them to me, nobody is gonna know."

There were six tapes, in all. Guttman removed all of the penciled labels but one. He handed that one to Philip Armstrong personally. And then Armstrong showed him how the document-shredding machine he used for confidential papers worked. Guttman fed five tape recordings into the machine, while Philip Armstrong had the pleasure of destroying the sixth himself. Guttman kept the labels. Mr. Carstairs might know the names, or be able to trace them. Guttman thought they might just send a letter saying the tapes had been destroyed. They could sign it "A Friend."

It was past five o'clock when he got back to the Center, and he was worried that Lois would be angry at him.

Fifteen

Guttman felt as if he was about to make a speech. Lois had been waiting—not in the car but in Mrs. Stone's cottage. She had finally met the members of the Golden Valley Irregulars, and she'd been told how proud she should be of her father. She'd even met Susan Eliot. Donald had no trouble convincing the police of his guilt, and she was free now. They were all waiting, even Dr. Aiken, who as head of the Center had decided he was entitled to learn, first hand, what had happened. Now they were all seated, except for Mrs. Stone's nurse, and they were looking at Guttman. They'd saved an easy chair for him, the place of honor. And he didn't know where to begin.

"I'm glad they let you out so quick," he told Susan Eliot. "I was a little worried they might not believe Donald right away."

"Paul Taylor took care of that. He said he'd like to talk to you, later on. He's going to defend Donald. Grandmother will pay for it."

She looked different, Guttman thought. She looked a little tired, but dressed in her own clothes, instead of the prison dress, she looked younger. Healthier too, he thought. It was hard for him to match this girl with what Debbie had told him and Miss Brady. So don't worry about it, he told himself. Like you told Lois, whatever you find out what isn't part of the crime is none of your business.

"Mr. Guttman, if you don't mind, maybe you could explain how you figured it out, now?" Mrs. Kaplan asked. "If it isn't too much trouble, that is. Some of us are a little curious, you know."

"Miss Brady and Mrs. Kaplan filled us in on most of it," Dr. Aiken said. "But how did you know who really killed this man?"

"I didn't know, for sure," Guttman said. Then he took his last cigar from the leather case, smiling at Lois as he did, removed the cellophane and lit it. "It was a little bit of guessing," he said through the haze of smoke.

"It had to be more than guessing," Jessica Stone said.

"What else do you want me to call it?" Guttman asked. "I didn't have no proof. I didn't have nothing you could call evidence. But when I thought about it, he was the one most likely."

"But why, Mr. Guttman. We discussed it, but we didn't think of Mr. Eliot," Harold Carstairs said.

"The first thing, of course, is we figured Susan didn't do it." Guttman smiled at her, and got a small smile in return. "And then the second thing was to decide it was somebody we knew about. You got to remember, it could've been somebody else altogether. Except not likely. Because of the key."

"I thought Philip Armstrong had the strongest motive," Mr. Carstairs said.

"He was a good candidate," Guttman agreed. "But since there wasn't no evidence, I had to think about the personalities. Now, first, Armstrong told me he was going to pay off Vincent with the money. I don't know about blackmail, but I figure if you got the money, you probably pay at least one time. Then, if somebody gives you what you're paying for, it's all over."

"But blackmailers are notorious for demanding more money," Mrs. O'Rourke said. "It's in all the stories."

"I heard that too. But you got to remember, Vincent was working for Armstrong. And he wasn't gonna quit his job. So maybe Armstrong decided to pay one time, anyway. That's what I figured. But you got to look at how it actually happened," Guttman said. He paused to puff his cigar. "Most of the people we was talking to didn't have a hurry-up reason to kill Vincent. Maybe they got a reason, but not a right-this-minute reason. Also, they didn't have good alibis. If you're gonna kill somebody, and you got some time, you try to work it out so you got an alibi, right?"

A few heads nodded.

"Also, nobody knew Vincent would be there at that minute. He just walked in, so far as we know. So I figured on somebody what didn't know Vincent so well, didn't know where he'd be, but could just sit and wait."

"And that eliminated Nick Forester, as well as Mr. Armstrong," Miss Brady said.

"Pretty much. Also, the motives for him and for David Hiller wasn't so strong, I thought. And remember, the thing is, I was doing some guessing."

"But why did you settle on Donald?" Mrs. Stone asked.

"First, because the timing was right. The day before, he saw what Vincent done to Susan, and he was mad, very mad about it."

"I never should have called him," Susan said. "It's my fault, in a way."

"Nonsense," Jessica Stone said.

"There was one more thing," Guttman said. "Remember when we started out, the big problem was the time. The police said it was sixty seconds between when the gun was shot and Susan called on the phone."

"That was their case against her," Mrs. Stone said.

"And Mrs. Kaplan and Mrs. O'Rourke and Mr. Carstairs went there and they timed how long it took to go up the stairs, and everything," Guttman said. "And they figured it was possible it happened the way Susan said. But . . ." Guttman paused for effect, beginning to enjoy himself. "But it was very close. It was so close, the more I thought on it, the more I figured the killer didn't get away. I figured Susan probably saw who it was."

"I didn't," the girl said quickly.

"Susan, you was protecting somebody. And all of a sudden it come to me, the only one you would protect was Donald. Because you felt responsible."

"I . . ." The girl just stared at him, while the others looked at her.

"How did you get him to confess?" Miss Brady asked, to change the subject slightly. "We only heard the very end of it."

Guttman chewed on his cigar, sighed, and decided he might as well tell them. They might find out later on, from the lawyer, anyway. Still, he felt ashamed of himself as he explained it.

"Brilliant," Dr. Aiken said quietly when he was through. "Very impressive."

"It wasn't so impressive if you was there," Guttman said. "And it wasn't so nice, either. I didn't like it at all."

Guttman watched the tears finally well up in Susan Eliot's eyes, and more than the rest of them, he felt embarrassed when she began to cry. They left quickly after that.

Lois was standing by the car with Mrs. Kaplan. They were going to give her a lift, since her daughter had been sent home rather than add someone else to the audience in Mrs. Stone's cottage. Guttman suspected, also, that Mrs. Kaplan wanted to be able to tell the whole story to her family by herself. He took a final puff on his cigar and dropped it into an ashtray.

"I'd call it a good day's work," Margaret Brady said behind him.

"I got to admit, I'm a little tired," he said, turning toward her.

"Did Mrs. Vincent agree to destroy the tapes?"

"I done it myself, with Mr. Armstrong . . . How did you know?" he asked.

"The same way you did, I suppose. I guessed."

"Somehow, I should've known you would, Margaret," Guttman said, smiling.

"You know, that's the first time you've called me by my first name without my having to ask," she said.

"I know."

About the Author

ARTHUR D. GOLDSTEIN was born in Brooklyn and attended Stuyvesant High School and Ohio University, and now lives in New York. He has been a public relations executive, a teacher of speed reading, and the editor of a Wall Street publication.

DATE DUE